LEBRON CLETE WYTCH

PRESSURE COOKER

Based on Real-Life Events

Copyright © 2023 **Lebron Wytch Publication**

All rights reserved. No part of this publication may be reproduced, distributed, or transmitted in any form or by any means, including photocopying, recording, or other electronic or mechanical methods, without the prior written permission of the publisher, except in the case of brief quotations embodied in critical reviews and certain other noncommercial uses permitted by copyright law. For permission requests, write to the publisher, addressed "Attention: Book Rights and Permission," at the address below.

Published in the United States of America

ISBN 978-1-960159-36-6 (SC)
ISBN 978-1-960159-35-9 (Ebook)

Lebron Wytch Publication
222 West 6th Street
Suite 400, San Pedro, CA, 90731
lebronwytch@yahoo.com

Order Information and Rights Permission:

Quantity sales. Special discounts might be available on quantity purchases by corporations, associations, and others. For details, contact the publisher at the address above.

For Book Rights Adaptation and other Rights Permission.
Call us at toll-free 1-888-945-8513 or send us an email at
admin@stellarliterary.com.

CONTENTS

PROLOGUE 1

CHAPTER 1   THE BIG GAME 2

CHAPTER 2   ATHLETIC TRAINING CLASS 9

CHAPTER 3   DEON HAS A TALK WITH HIS ROOMMATE, GREG 14

CHAPTER 4   CHRISTMAS BREAK 21

CHAPTER 5   DEON GOES BACK TO CAMPUS AFTER CHRISTMAS 32

CHAPTER 6   DEON GETS A JOB AS A RECRUITER 44

CHAPTER 7   THE WINTER SEMESTER STARTS 52

CHAPTER 8 57

CHAPTER 9 65

CHAPTER 10   DEON GETS ARRESTED 83

CHAPTER 11   DEON GETS FIRED FROM HIS JOB 121

CHAPTER 12 130

CHAPTER 13 178

CHAPTER 14 206

CHAPTER 15 248

Prologue

Deon lay exhausted on his single sized bed looking up at the ceiling in his make shift room from a janitors closet. The sweat and the smell of smoke diffuses though his pores. The horrors of the night rattle in his brain as the sound of firetrucks, police cars and ambulances, breaking glass, explosions, car alarms, gunfire, looting, screaming voices of protesters, the profane sounds of anguish and pain and death, echo through the night. How did this all come to be? How it is that people who would otherwise hug and high five one another after a homerun, a jump shot, or a touchdown could be at each other's throats? How could it be that this demonstrable hate for one another always persisted but hid itself, cloaked in a façade of superficial equality and civility as people appear to go along happily in their great American lives? Could this division be stoked by those who have invested interest, like so many media host and politicians and could it be that this divisiveness lay dormant in the soul of society like a bear in hibernation, but now is awaken and hungry, ready to devour whatever is edible to feed its bigotry and hate. Is it just one incident or a culmination or accumulation and scaffolding of injustices that brings forth such hate and derision? How did we get here thought Deon as he lay in retrospect while continuing to stare at the ceiling. How did I get here…?

Chapter 1
THE BIG GAME

The football stadium was packed with thousands of people, with blue and yellow shirts and banners all over the stadium. The Mid-Union Lions rank number one in the nation. The campus was alive and buzzing. Cars overflowed the parking lot, including vehicles with state license plates from Georgia, North Carolina, and Maryland. The parking lot tailgate party had started hours earlier. Deon sat in the car with his roommate and dorm friends.

"Hell yeah!" they screamed as they chugged beer, one after another. "We're going to kick some West State ass!" they screamed while positioning themselves out the car window. Greg pulled out a bottle of vodka from inside his jeans.

"Yeah, dude!" he yelled with his head out of the window, his blue and yellow shirt splashed with his alcoholic beverage. For a twenty-year-old pre-law student, Greg really was crazy. He could make anybody laugh.

Greg sat back down in the car, and his light brown hippie-length curly hair fell back past his shoulders. Usually, Greg spent most of his time studying during the week, but on the weekends, watch out.

"Y'all don't party like this in the hood!" yelled Andrew, an anthropology major who was sitting in the front seat. Andrew's room was four rooms down from Deon's in the dorms. He played loud metal music until three in the morning. He never got in trouble for it either. Andrew reminded Deon of a young George Carlin, and he could be just as funny. He looked at Deon and said, "Got some crack, Deon?"

Deon knew Andrew was drunk and trying to be funny; still, it was hard for Deon not to feel insulted.

Andrew turned to Deon and added, "I didn't mean to offend you."

"What? You didn't offend me," replied Deon. "Got any meth?"

"You people never can take a frickin' joke," Andrew laughed

Deon experienced a lot of this perspective at school. He'd had to learn to smile and deal with it. Deon looked at Michael, who was in the driver's seat. He screamed "Mid-U!" out of the window at passing cars in the parking lot. Beer gushed from his mouth and sprayed the side panel of the driver door like an elephant spewing water from its trunk. His blue jeans were falling off his behind. Deon looked at Andrew and said, "Say no to crack." Greg poured beer down Michael's butt cleavage.

"*Ahh!*" he yelled as the cold beer ran down in his underwear. "Son of a bitch!" he yelled as he flew back from the window onto the driver's seat. He shook his beer and let it explode in effervescence all over Andrew.

"I'm glad this isn't my car," Deon laughed from the back seat.

"Hey, Bro," said Michael. "Everything okay? You look a little scared."

"No. I'm okay," Deon replied, wondering what was going to happen next.

"Hey, man, let's get the hell out of here and get to our seats," Greg insisted.

All four of them left the car while using excessive profanity.

"You guys need to wash your mouths out with soap," Deon quipped. "Got your key?"

"Yeah, I got it," said Michael.

The four walked into the stadium and stared in awe at the 100,000 people in the coliseum. Deon had attended football games before but nothing like this. The sea of fans waved banners and shirts, towels and signs. The band was playing in the stands, and the cheerleaders were forming pyramids.

Deon and his friends found their seats on the second level near the forty-yard line—good seats. The pregame festivities were winding down, and the excitement was about to boil over.

Greg went into his pants leg and pulled out a flask he had hidden there. "Come on, man," he said. "Don't you want a drink?"

"No, you know I don't like to drink," Deon quipped.

"Suit yourself," Greg responded as he secretly put the flask back in his boot.

The Lions received the kickoff. The kickoff returner ran the ball up the middle for thirty yards. The crowd went wild. "Yeah, baby let's go!" a man screamed from behind Deon.

Everyone was anticipating the play of the star running back, Isaiah Islam. Many wore his number, with his last name stitched on the back of thousands of jerseys. The first play of the game went to Islam, and he ran up the middle for a six-yard gain. The crowd erupted in excitement.

"Run by Islam!" yelled the stadium announcer. Second down and four for the Lions at their thirty-six-yard line.

The next play was a quick pass for twelve yards and out of bounds, with a catch by Laquan Jones.

"First down Lions!" the announcer yelled over the PA.

Islam ran the ball up the middle for fourteen yards. The crowd roared. On the next play, after a give to Islam off the left side, he put his shoulder down and into the oncoming linebackers, bouncing off them. Islam sidestepped and jumped to the inside, outrunning everyone to the end zone for a sixty-yard touchdown. The crowd erupted in celebration and fans cheered "Lions! Lions! Lions!" Many guys took off their shirts and started waving them all over the stands. Girls grabbed their shirts and began swirling them in the air. Cable news stations broadcast from the side of the field.

The crowd continued to go wild. Greg sat down and discretely poured himself another drink in the Coke cup he had purchased earlier. Deon looked at Greg.

"Don't worry about it, bro. I got this," Greg said.

Deon looked and shook his head.

The Lions continued to run the ball all over the West State defense. Islam was thrilling fans with almost impossible runs for first downs, running the ball for 320 yards on some twenty carries. The final score was 28 to 7.

Greg looked like he was going to throw up all over the place. The end of the game found Deon and his friends still sitting in the stands. Everyone was too drunk to make it out of the stadium, using the excuse of waiting until the crowd emptied out before leaving. Thank goodness, they did not have to drive too far from the stadium back to the campus. At least Deon hoped they would be going straight back to school. Deon was concerned about Michael driving because he was totally stoned.

Finally, the four students walked out. When they arrived back at the car, Deon turned to Michael and asked, "You need me to drive?"

"No, I don't need you to drive, nigga," said Michael, making sure he did not accentuate the *R* in the word. He had a smirk on his face.

Deon looked at him sternly in the eye. Michael got in the car. Deon went to the back door and hesitated to get in the back seat.

"Hey, I'm just kidding," Michael, said to Deon as Deon got in the back seat.

"Hey, just be cool," Deon replied, looking at Michael.

Everyone got into the car, and it was quiet for a moment,

"Why you guys get all upset when we say the *N* word? Y'all call each other that all the time!" Michael said while and slurring his words. "You can't even joke around with you guys."

"You have to be politically correct," said Andrew.

Deon looked at Michael. "If I were to call you a Guinea, you would be upset, and you guys call each other Guineas, all the time, right? They do in the movies. I don't dare call you a Guinea, or I might end up with my feet in concrete."

"Oh no, can't say that," said Greg. "That's racist against Italians."

"Yeah, you Greg's moulinyan," quipped Andrew as he pulled out a sandwich bag with little pink pills in it. You know what Deon I have never heard you curse or get mad about anything Andrew said. I just don't feel right using inappropriate language Deon said while looking at the pink pills.

"What's that?" Deon asked.

"Mikey, you want one?" asked Andrew.

"No, thank you."

"You going to take that after drinking?" Deon asked.

"Hell, no. I'm trying to sell this," Andrew said. "I can get ten dollars a hit for these."

The car started to pull off. It was apparent Michael was drunk. Deon worried whether they would make it back to campus in one piece.

"Where the hell are we going?" Andrew asked as they started to leave the parking lot. "Let's go and hang out somewhere. All the girls, or as Deon would say, *hos* are talking about going to Big Peckers bar and grill."

"We all are illegal here," said Deon. "Only Andrew is over twenty-one. We can't get in. I think I'll go back to the campus," Deon insisted. He was feeling increasingly worried about what was going on inside the car, with the open liquor and drugs. Not good.

Suddenly blue lights flashed in the rear window. *Oh, hell no*, everyone thought quietly.

Michael pulled over and rolled down his window. "Yes, Officer?" he muttered.

"Driver's license please," the officer demanded.

Michael jerked abruptly to reach his hands into his back pocket. The officer shined the flashlight in the back of the car and directly in Deon's face.

"Who is that in the back seat?" he asked.

"He's our roommate," Greg and Andrew replied.

The officer seemed taken aback by the immediate response in Deon's defense. Deon was shaking in his tennis shoes.

The officer nodded and kept his eye on Deon as he walked back to the squad car.

"Whew!" Michael said. "We are going to go to jail."

"He ain't going to arrest us," said Andrew confidently.

The officer returned to the car. "You got any ID on you?" he said as he shined the light directly into Deon face again.

"Yes, sir, I have it right here." He went for his back pocket to pull out his wallet.

The officer put his hand on his gun, preparing to pull it. "Let me see your hands!" he yelled at Deon.

Deon's hands went up in the air.

"I told you to give me your identification," the officer shouted again, almost snorting in anger.

"Okay," Deon replied. "It's in my back pocket."

The flashlight shined into the back seat. Deon was shaking as he reached into his back pocket and grabbed his wallet. He handed his ID to Mike, and Mike gave it to the officer. The officer went back to his squad car and got on his radio.

"Aw, damn man, why is he giving you a hard time?" Greg said, turning white with fear.

"You know why," answered Andrew.

Greg went silent, taking it all in.

The officer returned to the car. He handled Deon's license back to Michael.

"You guys coming from the game?" asked the officer.

"Yes, sir," everyone replied in unison.

"I suggest you guys get back to the campus and off the street for tonight."

"Thank you, Officer," replied Andrew and Michael, again in unison. The officer went back to his squad car. Michael started the vehicle and headed back toward the campus. Deon sat in the back seat, stunned. Nobody said a word.

"That was pretty screwed up," said Greg finally. "I feel like I should apologize for the police." "Why?" Deon asked. "You didn't do anything. Why do you have to apologize for someone else?"

"Aw, man, you know what I mean," Greg said.

Andrew shook his head in agreement.

They all went back to Greg and Deon's room and sat watching television.

"Well, I'm going to head out," said Andrew as he checked the pills in the plastic bag he carried.

"You be careful out there with that on you," Michael said as Andrew headed for the door. Then he added, "I think I'm going to get out of here too."

"All right, y'all. Take it easy," Deon said. Deon and Greg sat on their beds opposite each other across the room.

"You going back out?" Deon asked.

"No. I think I need to sleep this off," Greg said as he lay back on his bed.

"Good move," replied Deon. "Me too."

Deon lay back on his bed and thought about home. His brother Sean, his mom and dad, their middle class house in their middle class neighborhood in North City. He thought about his trip home for thanksgiving break, the lavish thanksgiving dinner his mom prepared, with his father at the head of the table. He also thought about what his brother told him about what was going on at home, that mom and dad were having difficulties, and for what appeared so wonderful was actually very uncertain. He thought about calling home, but it was much too late, so Deon nodded off and went to sleep.

Chapter 2
ATHLETIC TRAINING CLASS

Deon sat in his athletic training class, looking over the notes he took on the previous Friday before the game.

Let's see, the articulation of the ball joint in the acetabulum, he said to himself as he continued to turn the pages.

The table was padded and soft for palpating and physical therapy. His seat was a padded stool on rollers, like the ones in a doctor's office. Other students piled in the classroom, which had padded exam tables all over the room. Deon thought about what had occurred over the weekend and tried to put the incident out of his mind.

Other students piled into the classroom. Most were jibber-jabbering about the game. Isaiah Islam's name bounced off the walls. Some of the trainers were already working as interns for the football team.

"What's up, dude?"

It was Reggie, Deon's table partner.

"Nothing," Deon replied.

"I just got back from home a few days ago."

"You went home this weekend?" Deon asked.

"Yeah, it ain't that far a drive, so I went home to check on the fam."

Just then, Dr. Allen, the professor, entered the room wearing his customary long white medical coat. Deon thought he wore it to make himself look like a doctor. He did have a doctoral degree, but he was not a medical doctor.

"All right," said the professor. "I hope everyone has recuperated from this wild weekend." Dr. Allen placed his books at the end of one of the exam tables. "We did have some injuries this weekend, so you guys are going to be busy. For those of you who have not gotten a chance to work with the team, you will get your first shot tomorrow. In fact, I have an arrangement for Wednesday too. You people will have the chance to see how taping goes and injury rehab for some of the players and so forth. Let's all meet at the Sportsplex in about an hour."

Deon and Reggie started the long walk across campus, deciding it was best to make their way there immediately. The walk to the multiplex required walking past the fraternity houses, which were just off campus. The fraternity houses were blasting rock and roll music out of the windows. Skull flags and banners hung from the windows of the some of the fraternity houses. There was a chant coming from the Alpha Sigma house. The path and main walkway toward the stadium sliced across their dormitory yard.

"There will never be a nigger ASE! There will never be a nigger ASE!" The chants from a window got louder and more audible as Deon and Reggie walked past. Deon could see fraternity members with their blue blazers huddled together in the window of the second floor of the dormitory. "There will never be a nigger ASE!" they screamed.

Deon and Reggie looked at each other and stopped. They turned and looked at the window. They could see the members inside jumping up and down with their ties flying up in the air. All were in a circle with arms flailing in an exuberant display of celebration. Deon and Reggie both thought about entering the building and crashing the party. Or maybe tossing a rock through the window.

"I bet they wouldn't chant that around us," Deon said.

"I bet they would," Reggie said. "Niggas ain't going to do nothing but try to kill you and me." Deon agreed with a nauseated expression on his face. "We should report their asses Deon said. But I don't want no trouble and I don't believe in violence."

"Waste of time. They will just tell you to lighten up—literally," Reggie said as they slowly moved away.

They continued to walk the main path to the stadium, which cut across a busy intersection. There were restaurants on the corner and an old-fashioned trolley running down the middle of the street. People from the campus and elsewhere fanned across the boulevard hurrying from one outside café to another, it seemed. Finally, they reached the Sportsplex, located just before the entrance to the university stadium. It was hard to believe nearly a hundred thousand people had been there only two days earlier.

They both walked into the building. The clock on the wall said one-thirty. Trophy cases spanned the room, with numerous trophies displayed inside. As they walked through the hallways, Deon noticed that some of their classmates had already arrived.

Dr. Allen walked into the hall and called out, "Hey, you guys, come on down here."

They all trampled down the hallway, which was adorned with pictures and portraits of athletic all-Americans. The well-buffed wax floors shone down the hallway to almost blinding effect with the fluorescent light reflecting off them.

The students all made the right turn into the training room. It was large and had cushioned tables and whirlpools, sterile white medical cabinets, and an ice-making machine.

"Okay," said Dr. Allen, "we will get started in a few minutes. The experienced interns will be here in a moment and introduce you to the procedures and what they do."

Soon the interns arrived, wearing the blue and white official athletic training shirts they wore when they work the football games.

One of the trainers stepped forward. "Hi, my name is Britney," she said, "and I am the lead trainer here on campus. I will walk you through the facility before the team arrives."

Everyone filed in behind her as she walked through the training room. "These are our tables and where we initially check the injury of the athlete and determine what might need to be x- rayed or MRI," she said. "We also use these tables for rehabilitation purposes, range of motion, and cold heat therapy. Come this way please."

She directed them into another room where there was an MRI machine. An MRI technician stood by as the students walked in.

"This is a typical MRI machine," said Britney. "This one is quite old, and the university is in the process of purchasing another this year. When we get that, I don't know," she added with a laugh, and everyone laughed along with her.

They proceeded to the training room, which had an indoor swimming pool for aquatic rehabilitation. There were rubber resistance bands, weights, and indoor sled training machines. "This is where we use strength and conditioning in the rehabilitation process," Britney explained as everybody looked on. "There are other rooms we would like to show you, but for now, since the players will be coming in from practice, we are going to go to the main training room to tape the players."

Students were led back to the main training room, and the football players began piling in. They sat on the tables, and athletic trainers sprayed down naked feet with adhesive spray. Then pre-rap was put on the players' feet and ankles. The lead trainer demonstrated how an ankle is taped correctly. Deon and Reggie watched closely.

Suddenly, there was a commotion by the door. It was Isaiah Islam. He walked in and smiled at everyone, and people cleared the way for him to go to one of the padded tables. He sat with his bare feet and football pants, Mid-Union T-shirt, and a headband worn around his cornrows.

"What up?" he said to Deon as Deon caught his eye. "Hey, nice to meet you." He waved at Deon to come closer. "You look like a recruit." "No, I wish," Deon laughed.

"You look like you train or work out, though. You sure you don't play this game?" Isaiah smiled and laughed slightly.

"I did in high school," Deon replied. "I didn't get no scholarship, so I decided to go into this."

"Not a bad choice. You know how hard this can be," Isaiah added, gesturing to his teammates and their injuries.

"You make it look easy, Isaiah," said Deon.

Isaiah looked at Deon. "We both know better than that," he replied.

Deon nodded in agreement.

"I'm looking forward to our championship game," Deon said, trying to keep up the conversation.

"Yeah, me too. I want to get it over with," Isaiah said exhaustedly. "Winning takes a lot of responsibly. It gets tiring after a while. I try to keep perspective; you know what I mean? At the end of the day, it is just a game. I have got to think of it that way to keep my sanity around all this." He laughed.

"Hey, I appreciate the talk, Isaiah, man. I want to let the others get over here."

Isaiah put up his fist, and Deon bumped fists with him. "If I see you on the yard, I will holler at you," Isaiah said while gripping and spinning a football around in his hands.

"All right, Mr. Islam. I'm looking forward to that," said Deon.

Chapter 3
DEON HAS A TALK WITH HIS ROOMMATE, GREG

Deon went back to his room and started looking over his notes from this athletic training class. Sitting at his desk with the hard wooden chair, Deon adjusted himself to get more comfortable. "Hey, what up, Deon," Greg said as he came into the room and slammed his book and backpack down. "I can't believe all the crap I was given for this final exam. I got to pull an all-nighter."

Deon turned around in his seat and looked at Greg, who lay back across his bed and signed.

"I might be right up here with you," Deon replied.

"I won't be here. We have group study at Forest Hall," Greg said. "Everyone is expected to work all freaking night."

"I have that sociology and justice class at six," Deon said, standing up to stretch his legs.

"Dr. Dean?" Greg asked as he sat up and took a sip from an earlier opened can of Monster Energy drink. "I had him last year. That freaking class gets rowdy. An open intellectual discussion should be able to take place on a college campus. But it doesn't work out that way."

"Can I tell you something?" asked Deon.

"Yeah, what?"

Deon scooted his desk chair over toward Greg. "Me and my boy Reggie …" he began.

"Yeah, I know Reggie," Greg interrupted.

"Yeah, well, we were walking across the yard to the Sportsplex and had to cut through the Epsilon house, and we heard this chant: 'No niggers in the ASE!' They chanted that over and over—and loudly," Deon recalled.

Greg breathed out hard. "Those guys are such idiots," he said. "They are a bunch of freaking rich guys, and their dads are heavy alums. Just a bunch of spoiled brats. Don't even pay attention to them assholes. The first thing they will tell you is that you're being too damn sensitive—that they have the right to free speech."

Deon looked poignantly at Greg. Greg gave Deon the same look back.

"By the way," said Greg, "could you run this folder up to Michael's room for me? The idiot left it down here, and he will be crying like a baby if he can't get it. All his notes are in here."

"Yeah, I will take it to him," Deon said, accepting the folder from Greg. Deon walked upstairs past two obviously Southern boys, judging by their accent and cowboy boots. They looked at Deon up and down and glared at him as he walked past. Deon looked at them the same way as he walked past them.

Deon got to the second floor and made the turn toward Michael's room. He started to knock on the door when he heard a radio program coming out of the room next door. Deon listened.

"These college campuses are teaching the liberal philosophy to students to enlighten them. To understand their point of view, which is victimization. These so-called liberal intellectual professors are indoctrinating students. They are being exposed to the liberal agenda and hypocrisies on college campuses. They are not there to educate; they are they to indoctrinate, to tell you that our great founding fathers were racist. They hate everything America stands for, and if you don't follow their warped socialist ideology, you are ostracized."

Deon knocked on Michael's door. A beautiful girl opened it.

"Yes?" she said.

"Is Michael here?" Deon asked.

"Yeah," she replied.

"Who is it?" Michael called out from inside the room. When he came to the door, Deon held up the spiral notebook.

"Oh, thanks, Deon."

"No problem, Mike."

Deon turned and walked toward the steps and down the staircase on his way to his sociology class. The talk radio program continued to blast down the hallway.

Deon sat in Rockefeller Hall. The classroom was in a small theater. It appeared to hold a few hundred people, and it was packed. Students had to stand if they did not get there early enough to secure a seat.

As they waited, students chattered back and forth. There seemed to always be cliques. There was the conservative far right, nearly skinhead clique, many of whom wore green camouflage pants, shirts, and red hats. The evangelical right, the blue-jeaned Southerners, and the minority rightists mostly sat together on the right side of the theatre. The leftist progressives sat on the left side of the theater. There was the elite leftist, the middle-class leftist with pro basketball shoes, and a mix of everything else.

Dr. Dean walked in, and everyone started to settle down a bit. He walked over to the whiteboard, picked up a marker, and wrote *Diversity* across the board. He put two large lines underneath the word, and then he turned around.

"What does this mean? What does this word say to you?" the professor asked.

"It means race set-asides!" yelled out one of the rightists, to the applause of his rightist counterparts.

"Diversity is our strength!" shouted the voices on the left.

"Okay, let's keep it cordial, you guys" Dr. Dean said. "We must be able to have a frank discussion appropriately."

"Diversity is just a synonym for affirmative action!" exhorted another student on the right. Professor Dean cut the lights and went to the overhead. On the screen was a fact on a PowerPoint slide:

Gurin (1999) argued that a diverse student body creates a unique learning environment that leads to the incredible probability that students will interact with a peer from different backgrounds. Experience with diversity also appears to be positively associated with retention rates and degree aspirations.

Dr. Dean used the mouse pointer to emphasize each bullet point as he lectured.

One of the conservative students stood up and said, "Diversity to the left only applies to racial, ethnic, and sexual minorities."

"And your righteousness is about exclusion and judgment of others," yelled one of the students on the left.

"If you from the right were so Christian, you should adhere to what Matthew says in chapters 1 verse 1: 'Judge not that ye be not judged'!" another liberal student shouted.

The theatre was starting to get heated, and opinions were being shot into the room like pepper spray. Deon sat and observed all the people who seemed to hate each other, not just the other point of view. Dr. Dean remained calm while officiating the raucous debate.

"This quote-unquote *diversity* program weakens this and other universities, allowing selection of certain students who can't meet the score or standard admission to this university," yelled someone on the right. "That is not fair to hard-working students who are not a 'certain' student or so-called minority and deserve fairness."

"That is not true!" echoed another on the left side of the theater. "There are numerous factors considered for admission to this university."

One of the minority conservatives stood up. "We are not in agreement with diversity in the form of affirmative action either. I don't want to be a part of a set-aside. I want to accomplish things on my own merit."

Another minority student stood up on the left side of the room. "How do you know you were not selected for diversity? I am sure you may have worked really hard to get here and met all academic requirements, however, how do you know you are not here for the same reason?"

"It may be so," he quipped. "But just because that might be the case doesn't make it right."

"So just eliminate the path you were so fortunate to have available to you and deny that for others who are trying to come up?" said one of the students sitting next to Deon.

"Yeah, that is kind of messed up," Deon replied as he continued to listen to what was going on in the theatre.

Dr. Dean spoke up. "Affirmative action was implemented to correct the injustices to women and blacks and other minorities in the effort to equal the playing field," he said.

"That's bullshit!" yelled a rightist student. "None of us were here two hundred years ago. Why should I have to relinquish my rights?"

Dr. Deon looked to the left side of the room.

"Yeah, you have had that white privilege all your life, and y'all continue to have it," a woman from the left sounded off.

"Everyone wants to talk about slavery!" called out another from the right. "We are not responsible for what happened during slavery, and from what I understand, not all slaves had it terrible. Most were given housing, religion, and decent food, something they did not have in Africa. Some were treated damn good compared to living in huts and disease in Africa somewhere."

The conversation really started to heat up.

"How can you so-called minority conservatives just sit there and listen to this and still represent yourself with it?" yelled voices on the left

A minority conservative stood up and said, "We need to be honest about this. First, Africans sold themselves into slavery. Second, some whites were also enslaved. Third, we are not entitled because of slavery!"

Deon looked on in disbelief. Conservatives on the right side of the theater applauded the minority conservatives and stood up yelling, "Whoop! Whoop! Whoop! They are telling the truth! The left can't handle the truth!"

"Wow," Deon said to himself

I hear you, said the brother who was sitting next to Deon, you can always find an shining ass nigger. Why don't you speak up? We should interject because Im ready to kick somebody ass right about now he said. I respect Dr. King, don't believe in violence, Deon replied. "You can only turn the other cheek so many times "the guy said.

Dr. Dean interrupted. "The point here is that dialogue has to be accepted from both sides to meet a compromise. Is there any compromise to be had on any issues involving this topic? I cannot find any. Can anyone here?"

The auditorium was silent.

"Your assignment will be to establish three items from this topic that both sides might be able to agree on," said the professor. "One page. Have a good evening, ladies and gentlemen."

Deon walked warily up the hallway to exit the building. He took a quiet walk across the campus, thinking about what had occurred in class. Deon didn't know whether to be angry or sad or worried or what.

Soon, Deon arrived at his room and went in. Greg was not there. Deon put his books down on the hard chair at the hard desk. *Better call home*, he thought. Deon pulled out his cell phone.

"Hello, Ma?"

"Hello, Deon baby! How is everything going out there?"

"Everything is okay here," said Deon. "What's going on there?"

"Things are okay," his mother replied. "You need to focus on your finals. When are they?"

"Next week, Ma."

"Okay, well, you concentrate on that. When do you plan to come home?"

"Around the eighteenth, Ma."

"Okay, well, you just do what you need to do and concentrate. Mamma loves you. Talk to you later."

Deon knew something was different about the call. It seemed like something just wasn't right. *Maybe it's just my anxiety*, he thought. He knew his mother was right. *I do need to concentrate*, he said to himself. He sat down at his desk and opened his notebook for his anatomy class. Deon was confident that he would do well on his exam. *I just need to get prepared*, he said to himself.

Deon went through that finals week like a breeze. Greg was never in the room because he was off in-group studies, all night in many cases. Tomorrow was his anatomy final. After that, he was homebound.

The next day, Deon sat at his lab table with the test on his desk. The final was a series of anatomy questions and then identifying body parts on cadavers. Deon finished his exam and handed it to Dr. Allen. The professor looked at Deon then at Deon's paper. He checked his key, made three or so marks, and then wrote a number with a red marker on the upper right side: 92! He gave Deon a look and grin.

"Have a great holiday break," he told Deon.

Deon walked out of the room and breathed a sigh of relief. *Now I got to go back to my room and get my stuff together so I can leave out this afternoon*, thought Deon as he scampered to his room. Deon had already packed his bags, and the bus was scheduled to depart the campus at three. It was going to be an exciting ride back home, he thought.

Chapter 4
CHRISTMAS BREAK

Deon boarded the campus bus that took students to the Greyhound bus station and to the airport. He took a seat by the window just as he had on his Thanksgiving ride home. He looked on as he saw the bus driver putting bags at the bottom of the bus. Deon hoped that he wouldn't have a problem retrieving his bags.

Deon looked out the window, still wondering about his mom. Something certainly didn't sound right the last time he called. Deon remembered what his brother had said about what was going on over Thanksgiving break.

The bus backed out from the student union building, made a U-turn in the circular driveway, and started heading away from campus.

The arrival downtown was smooth and relaxing as Deon prepared to transfer by retrieving his bags once they pulled into the terminal. Deon waited while the bags were taken from the bus, one by one, at a molasses pace.

Finally, Deon's two pieces of luggage were taken off, and Deon quickly grabbed his bags and walked past the bus driver who was standing at the bus's front door.

"See you later," Deon said as he walked toward the terminal.

"Yeah, you too. And Merry Christmas!" the bus driver said.

Deon proceeded to the ticket counter and placed his bags on the scale. There was another man with his son in front of Deon. *They must be hunters*, he thought. They both had on camouflage hats, shirts, shoes, and pants, as if they belonged to a militia. Then Deon thought about some of the conservative students who had been so vocal in class. He remembered them wearing camouflage that day too. Deon remembered one student who said not to be fooled—they were preparing for the next Civil War.

The attendant, a short fat man with a pale complexion and stringy brown hair, checked their bags and was very cordial to the man and his son. He praised one of their bags. Deon thought it looked like a rifle case, but he wasn't too sure.

When Deon pulled his bags that were still on the scale closer to the attendant, the attendant looked at him suspiciously. "Your ticket, please?"

Deon gave him the ticket. The attendant continued to stare at Deon as if to identify him as someone doing something wrong. "What do you have in your bag?"

"I beg your pardon?" Deon answered.

"I need to know the contents of your bag."

"Why, is something wrong?" Deon questioned.

"We need to know for security purposes," the attendant responded.

Suddenly armed security personnel came out of the room behind the counter. The attendant examined the bag and looked at Deon with criminal suspicion. "Could you open the bag, please?"

Deon was completely dumbfounded. "Do I really have to display my personal essentials for the entire bus station?"

The security officer glared at Deon. "Yes, you do."

Deon grabbed his first bag and opened it, displaying his underwear, socks, and shorts—items most do not want to display to the public. The attendant put on rubber glove. He ran his hands through Deon's baggage, displacing his socks and underwear, ruffling through the bag haphazardly.

"Are you carrying any illegal drugs?" asked the armed security guard.

"No," Deon responded.

"Okay, what about that one?" the security officer said, pointing.

Deon pulled the bag over to him. "That is basically my carry-on."

"Open it," the officer ordered.

Deon looked over his shoulder to see the smirks on the faces of certain people standing in line behind him. He opened the bag to reveal his toiletries and shaving needs, along with a couple pairs of athletic shorts.

"Is it okay now?" he asked.

The attendant did not respond, just took off his rubber gloves. Deon gathered his bags together, making sure the ticket was still on the bag. He stood up and waited until the attendant stamped his ticket and tore off the receipt, slamming it down. Then the attendant signaled the next passenger.

Deon looked at the armed security guard and saw him smirk and grin.

Deon was perplexed. Why did everyone seem to enjoy watching that? Deon grabbed his carry-on and walked over to the gate.

A man walked up to Deon as he stood looking out the window. "You know they didn't have no right to make you open that bag."

Deon turned around to see an older man with a short black afro that had a gray streak down the middle. "He ain't had no right to do that," the man said again. "He didn't ask that redneck ahead of you to open all his bags. I started to say something, but I didn't want to start no mess, just trying to get where I'm going and I'm sure you are too."

"Thanks, sir. I appreciate that. I don't want no trouble." The man walked away and gave Deon a nod of assurance.

Soon the bus boarded, and Deon took his assigned seat by the window. Deon wanted peace and quiet, a couple of naps, and some self-reflection. Luckily, no one who got on the bus sat next to him. That was a relief.

The bus door closed with the sound of the pressure brakes releasing as the bus backed out of the terminal. This was Deon's favorite part of the trip: the ride through the city, the lights, and the buildings. They would soon be on the highway with scenic views of trees and farms and hills. It was all so beautiful to Deon as they rode through the countryside on his way back home.

When Deon arrived at the bus station in North City, he pulled out his cell phone and started to make the call home. Then he saw his dad driving up in his 1965 Chevy truck. Deon took his foot off his previously retrieved luggage and waved his hand so his dad would see him. His dad pulled up in the pee-yellow truck.

"Hey, Son. That all you got?"

"Yeah, that is it, Daddy. I'm going to load these in the back," said Deon as he glanced at his dad, who had on his sweater, slacks, and Stacy Adams shoes. It looked like he was just off work.

"Is everything all right?" Deon asked.

"Well, Son, things have changed around here," his dad began. Deon remained quiet and continued to look at his dad. "Your mother left, Son," his dad said finally.

"Left? What do you mean?"

"Well, you know what I mean. She's gone. That's it: she's gone. I did all I could, but that's it."

"Okay, Dad. We aren't looking at the movie *Goodfellas*. What happened?"

"I don't know, Son. She says she been unhappy for a long time."

Deon's dad drove down the usual neighborhood route he had taken for years. They came to the corner house, which had been home for so long but now had a Century 21 real estate for-sale sign on the front lawn.

Deon sighed profoundly and looked down at his lap. "How long has it been?"

"We will talk about it in a minute. Get your stuff and come on in the house," his dad ordered.

Deon grabbed his bags and walked in. All the furniture was gone. Only a chair and a card table remained in what was once a quaint but lovely dining room. No pictures graced the walls. No appliances remained except for an old toaster and a microwave oven.

Deon put down his bags and walked down the hallway into the living room. There was no furniture, just and old hi-fi with a nineteen-inch color TV on it. It wasn't hooked up to the cable.

"Where's Sean?" asked Deon.

"Your brother's with your mother right now. He should be back sometime."

"How long has this been going on?" Deon asked again.

"Your mother has been planning this for a while," said his dad, putting his hands in his pockets and walking to the bay window. "I'm sure you see the house is up for sale. I may take early retirement and move back down to the Bam."

"Y'all can't work this out?" asked Deon.

"I doubt it, Son," his dad said as he walked away from the window. "You hungry? We can go down to Harry's barbeque if you want too."

"I done lost my appetite," Deon responded disappointedly.

"Well, Merry Christmas, Son."

"Not funny, Dad."

"Didn't intend for it to be," his dad quipped.

"I think I'm just going to get some sleep," Deon said as he walked into his room—which now had no furniture, only a mattress on the floor.

"You can go on ahead and go to bed," said his dad. "I know you are tired after a long trip."

"I ain't going to be able to sleep," Deon said, sitting down on the mattress and box spring on the floor.

"Go on and get you a shower. I'm going to run down to Harry's and get me some ribs."

"Hey, Dad, you can bring me back a small rib tip."

His father smiled slightly as he left the house. "Okay, Son."

Deon took a hot shower. There were only two ragged towels in the cabinet. He grabbed the crumbled white bath towel and started drying off.

His cell phone rang. It said Mom on the screen.

"Hey, Ma."

"Oh, I see you made it in," she replied. "That's good. How was your bus ride?"

"It's was okay. I'm at home. Things have changed a lot around here."

"Yes, things have changed," his mom replied. "I didn't want to worry you about it while you were working on your exams."

"I suspected something was wrong then," Deon recalled. "Now I know."

"I want you to come to my apartment at about two o'clock tomorrow," his mom said, "and we can have lunch and talk. Okay?"

"Yes, Ma. What about Sean?"

"He is on his way back right now. He should be there soon, but I will see you tomorrow at two o'clock for lunch, and we can really talk, okay?"

Deon agreed.

Deon had finished putting away his clothes when he saw the light from a car pull up in the driveway. It was Sean. Deon watched his brother get out of the car and look around before coming into the house.

"Oh, so you back, huh? You see Mamma gone. I told you things were in trouble around here when you came back for Thanksgiving break."

"Yeah, I remember," replied Deon.

He and Sean went into the house and sat in front of the TV. Sean grabbed himself an apple juice out of the refrigerator. They both remained silent.

"Well, guess I'll go to bed," said Deon.

"Yeah, me too," Sean replied.

The next morning, Deon put his mom's address in the GPS on his phone. It led Deon to a condominium complex. He found his mother's unit and rang the doorbell.

"Who is it? Is that my baby boy behind this door?"

"Yes, Ma, it's me!"

His mother opened the door, and the two of them hugged and exchanged kisses on the cheek. Deon walked in and saw how lovely the apartment was. It looked better than home. Everything was new and sparkling. The pictures and paintings that adorned the walls at home now hung in her condominium. He also noticed the furniture—the same furniture from the house.

"Did you take all the furniture?"

"I'm the one who bought all the furniture in the house in the first place," she said. "I was kind to your dad. I left the TV, the beds, and the hi-fi."

"Mom, that house is like totally empty."

"Yeah. Now you kids know that through all these years, it was me who was furnishing our house. All the stuff that made all you guys comfortable."

"Okay, Ma," Deon replied while attempting to change the subject.

"Well, come on. Let's go eat," she said.

The restaurant was a short drive away, and it was exquisite. The tables were elegantly decorated with expensive table settings.

"This is too much, Ma," said Deon.

"Don't worry about it. I haven't gotten a chance to take you boys out somewhere really luxurious because your father insisted we could not afford anything nice."

"Daddy says he is trying to get the both of us through school," said Deon.

"Aw, shoot! He acts like he is the only one who is sending their kids to college." She shook her head. "I still love your dad. We have had so many years together."

Deon remained silent as the waitress came to the table.

"Are you ready to order?" the pretty waitress, pleasantly startling Deon.

"You should try their blackened catfish. It is delicious," his mother suggested.

"Okay, I will have the blackened catfish."

Deon and his mom began talking about what had been going on while Deon was in college. She told him his daddy was nuts, and she could no longer live with him. *There are always two sides to a story*, Deon thought, *but this is my mom, and I have to understand how she feels*. Deon knew his dad was a bit frugal, and he knew his mom sometimes embellished, but Deon still could not figure out how breaking up was better than working together. He also knew that what went on between parents should stay between parents. Some of the conversations made Deon a bit uncomfortable. *Then again, I was supposed to be an adult now*, he thought.

"So, no chance you and Dad might come back together and give it another chance?" he asked. "Listen, Deon. I wouldn't give myself to a man again, even if it was Jesus Christ himself. At least that what I'm feeling now."

Deon and his mom went through the delicious main course and delicious dessert. As his mom gave the waitress the credit card, Deon stole a glance at the bill and saw that it was over one hundred dollars. Deon sat back and shook his head. *I guess Ma is trying to live a bit*, Deon thought.

Deon returned home to find his dad sitting in the living room alone watching TV. Sean was in his bedroom, going over his homework. Deon went into the living room and took the only other seat in the room.

"How was dinner with your mother?" his dad asked.

"It was okay," Deon replied.

"What did she say?"

"Daddy, I don't know. She was just talking about what she has been doing lately."

"Don't want to tell me, huh? It's okay. You don't have to let me know," his dad said, laughing sarcastically. Deon knew his dad was serious about fishing around to find out what his mother was thinking.

Deon dad suddenly became serious. He took a deep breath. "We need to talk about school," he said.

Deon exhaled loudly and dropped his head.

"Your room and board are close to ten thousand a year," said his dad. "I have your tuition paid through May, but room and board I don't. I'm being up front with you. Because of this divorce, I may not have the finances to continue your education. So, you have a choice. You can return to school, get a part-time job, and find you a room and board, or you can stay here at home until the house is sold. I don't know when that will be. I'm going to wait here until Sean finishes the school year, but if the house gets sold before then, I am going to get a little apartment to myself. After that, I'm going to move back to the Bam. I'm not going to continue to pay a mortgage on a house that's just sitting."

Deon stared at the floor.

"Again," said his dad, "you may be able to return to the university and find you an off-campus apartment or room. Some folks will rent out a place for about three hundred a month, and sometimes they will give you dinner and so forth. Just check around and see. What I will do is provide you with a few hundred dollars, and hopefully you can find a place. Then you can go out and find you a part-time job or something to help you through."

He added, "But for the next school year, you will need to find you another school loan, and hopefully, you will have a job and means to help yourself through. You will be a senior then, and you won't have too far to go before you graduate. *Son, there comes a time when a man must stand up on his own two feet. Now is that time for you.*" Deon looked up in dismay.

"Now what the matter?" his dad asked. "I know you can do this, Son. I didn't raise a fool, and I know you know how to do the right thing. I believe you will make a sound decision." "You think I should get up there right away?" Deon said quietly

"No," his dad replied. "Just wait till after Christmas and make your way back to campus if that is what you are going to do. You are a good guy. You have a good heart. Just take care of business, that's all. Well, Merry Christmas."

"That's not funny, Dad."

"It wasn't intended to be, Son."

Mom called Deon on the phone. "Are you coming to midnight Mass like we always do?" she asked.

Deon looked at Sean. "You going to Mass at midnight?"

"Yeah, I guess so," Sean answered.

When the time came, Deon sat with his brother and his mother in Immaculate Conception Catholic Church for midnight Christmas mass. The cathedral was packed for the traditional Catholic service with the well-known Catholic hymns like "Ave Maria" being sung from the balcony echoed in Latin.

The Mass continued with the theme of the rite of peace. Parishioners would turn to each other and offer the sign of peace by shaking hands. Many times people didn't want to turn around and shake Deon's family's hands. *Bigotry in church*? Maybe not. *You can't blame everything on bigotry and racism*, he thought. Deon always figured that happened to everybody.

Deon looked at his mom. She smiled as she sat with her two boys. Later, they walked down the aisle for Communion. After Mass, the three walked out to their cars.

"You boys be careful driving back home," said their mother.

"Okay, Ma," Deon said.

Sean had a difficult time saying anything. He was very hurt by their parents breaking up.

Deon awoke on Christmas day. He remembered when this was the most festive and magical time. Usually, a ten-foot Christmas tree touched the ceiling. Presents were piled underneath the base of the tree—dozens of them.

This time, the living room was empty. Only a Charlie Brown–style Christmas tree sat atop the old hi-fi. There were no gifts. No one was waking up at five in the morning to open presents. There was no Mom and Dad in their robes with coffee cups in their hands while Deon and Sean frantically passed out gifts to everyone whose name had one. Now, there was nothing.

Chapter 5
DEON GOES BACK TO CAMPUS AFTER CHRISTMAS

Deon waited to board the bus while his dad and brother waved goodbye. "Don't forget now what I told you," said his dad.

"Okay, Daddy. I won't forget."

"Remember, every man has to do what?" Dad said pointedly.

"Stand on his own two feet," Deon answered.

"Okay," his dad said finally.

Deon boarded the bus and took the long walk back to a seat by the window. What a tumultuous time this Christmas had been. There was shocking news all the way around. Deon felt burdened and wondered if he would be able to manage all this on his own—find a place to stay and find a job. It certainly wasn't something he'd envisioned himself doing.

As the bus backed out of the terminal, he waved at his smiling, joking dad. His brother didn't smile, just waved. *Sean is an unhappy person*, thought Deon. *He had to endure living through all of this.*

Deon sat back and adjusted his seat to lean back slightly. He watched the world whiz by him as he traveled out of the town and into the city. First came the country with its big barns and vast farmlands. It made Deon wonder how people came to live in that way. It appeared to be a beautiful life, full of fresh air, water, and animals. Deon dreamed of one day having such a place out and away from everyone.

He arrived back at the campus in the evening. The university was nearly empty. Deon went to his room and opened the door. The room looked just as he had left it. It was clean and smelled good.

Deon wondered if Greg had even come back to the dorm after finals. He noticed a present sitting on his bed. The tag said, "To Deon. Merry Christmas, Bro."

Damn, and I didn't get Greg anything, he thought. He opened the small package and found a headset for his phone. *That's cool*, he thought.

Deon sat on his bed and pondered what his next move would be. Number one, he had to find a place to live. *Okay, today is December 28*, Deon thought as he grabbed his laptop. He went to the campus website and typed *classified* in the search engine. He entered *rooms for rent*, and then he scrolled down. There were several "Rooms for Rent" listings. Many were asking for a monthly rent about the same as Deon's dad had mentioned—three or four hundred per month.

Deon saved a few of the addresses on this phone. He called three of them and spoke in a perfectly correct way. He remembered what he had been taught over the years. One had to bring a degree of professionalism when presenting oneself. There was no room for slang or vernacular. Never give away who or what you are before you arrive, his dad always told him. Deon knew that the next day, he would have to put his nose to the grindstone, remembering what his dad had told him: *"You have to stand on your own two feet."*

Deon woke at eight o'clock the next morning, ready to head out. He walked down the quiet hallway in the dorm and heard the tapping of his own footsteps as he exited through the back door to the bus stop. There was a long wait for the bus, and he shivered in the winter cold as he waited. Finally, he saw the bus with a big 107 in lights across the top. It pulled to a stop.

"Good morning," the bus driver said.

The bus doors closed slowly. There was a sound of the airbrakes releasing, and then the bus started moving. Deon found a seat again by the window. He put on the new headphones that Greg had left him as a present on his bed.

He had found there was a radio on his phone when he'd toyed around with it before. It really was a cheap phone, and it was a prepaid. His dad had given it to him his freshman year. Deon appreciates his dad frugality very much. He heard his dad's voice in his ear a lot. *Why spend extra money when you don't have to, Son?* Or *what you need with another one while that still works?*

Deon found it hard to get the reception he wanted, so he started fidgeting around and found an AM station with talk radio. He scrolled the station until he heard loud radio voices. It sounded like the same radio host he had heard in the hallway in the dorm.

"What you have here people is an attack against true Americans with this multiculturalist fanaticism that is changing the face and ruining this country. When the left advocates who you have to live next to, work with, hire and fire, especially with so-called minority groups, they are infringing upon the rights and the values of hard-working Americas and destroying your individual liberty. This is what the left does. This is their mantra! It is their rallying cry and their ideology, and indifference and political correctness to anyone who thinks differently than them —people who have morals, unlike the left."

Deon listened and remembered the sociology and issues class in the auditorium where all this talk got out of hand. Deon quieted his radio as he heard the street name being called for his stop. The bus driver smiled at Deon as he got off the bus.

"See you later," she said.

"Thank you," Deon replied with a smile in return.

Deon found the first address. It was a lovely two-floor house with beautiful shrubs surrounding it. The basement floor had a small door painted black that let out on the side of the house. Deon looked through the half-opened blinds and noticed a small room with hardwood floors and a bathroom off the living room. He peered over to the corner and saw a small attached area where there were a stove and little refrigerator. Deon walked up the short steps and knocked on the door.

"Yes?" called a woman from the other side of the door.

"Hi. I called concerning the room for rent."

The door opened slightly. A short old woman with white hair matching her skin seemed startled when she laid eyes on who was speaking.

"I'm sorry, but your name is?"

"I'm Deon. I believe I talked to you about the room for rent."

"Oh yes. Well, we got a deposit from another person last night, and the place is now reserved. I'm sorry," she replied

"Yes, ma'am. Well, thank you."

Deon walked down the front step to the sidewalk. He looked on his phone and crossed that address out. Now on to the next.

Deon followed the navigation on his phone to the next address on his list. It was a single- family home with what looked like a security house on the side of it. Deon walked over to it and looked inside. It was indeed one of those tiny houses.

"Can I help you?" called a person behind Deon.

Deon turned around and saw a taller man who looked somewhat shabby. His sandy brown stringy hair flew to the side and all over his head. His tan skin suggested that he probably worked outside a lot, as did his attire of work boots and Duluth pants.

"Hi, sir. My name is Deon. I believe I spoke to someone over the phone about the room. Is this it?"

"We have a list of people we are deciding on renting it to," the man said in a good-old-boy brogue.

Deon was taken aback. "The person I talked to mentioned that the room was still available." "We're just interviewing tenants," the man said. "You can leave your name, and we can give you a call."

Deon looked suspiciously at the man. "Is there an application or anything I need to fill out?" "No. Just leave me you name and your number."

Deon went into his phone and crossed the address out. *On the next one*, he thought.

He looked back at the small house. The man was still standing outside with what seemed to be a suspicious look on his face. Deon felt a sting in the back of his neck.

Deon followed his navigation to the next house, which was about a mile away. It was red brick and appeared to have a basement room. As Deon stood on the sidewalk looking at the home, a police car pulled up the street and slowed down to a crawl behind Deon as Deon walked up the walkway to the house.

Deon knocked on the door. A middle-aged woman who probably looked older than her age opened the door. She was short, pale, and had wrinkles, and she seemed very uneasy.

"Yes, can I help you?" she asked.

Unbeknownst to Deon, the police officer got out of his car.

"Yes, ma'am. I called yesterday about the room."

"I'm sorry. It's already rented." The old woman slowly closed the door.

"Yes, ma'am."

As Deon walked away from the house, the officer approached him with his hand on his holster.

"Excuse me," said the officer. "What are you doing here?"

Deon stopped. "Checking on rooms for rent," he said.

"Let me see some identification, he said, looking at Deon as if he were a criminal.

Deon reached for his wallet.

"Stop! Put your hands where we can see them!"

Another police car arrived, and two other officers exited their vehicles and swarmed at Deon.

"Do you have anything illegal on you?" one of the officers asked.

Deon's heart raced. "No, sir."

"Keep your hands where I can see them," the officer ordered as he started to pat Deon down.

"He asked me for my identification, and I was giving it to him," Deon said defensively.

"Hey, shut up," the officer replied. "No one asked you to talk."

They took Deon's wallet. One of the officers went up to the house and knocked on the door. The same old woman answered.

"Do you know this man?" the officer asked the woman.

"No, I don't," she replied.

"Okay, thank you!" the officer said as he started to reach for his handcuffs.

The other officers grabbed Deon, transported him, and slammed him against the squad car. "Turn around! Don't resist!"

"I'm not resisting," Deon replied.

"Shut up! We don't need to hear your mouth," another officer ordered. Deon could not believe this was happening.

The officer who went to the door and talked to the old woman came back to the car. "Okay, I spoke to the lady. She said she doesn't know who the hell you are."

"I came here to find a place that is listed the paper for rooms for rent. I'm a student."

"Your story isn't making any sense. This lady says she doesn't know who the hell you are. Were you looking to break in? You couldn't be that stupid. But who knows with you people," he said as he pushed Deon's head into the police car. The car door slammed in Deon's face.

Deon saw the old woman come back out the door and peer outside. She stepped out and called the officer over to her. There was some chitter-chatter between them for what seemed like five minutes. Another officer took Deon's identification to his squad car. They met on the walkway to the woman's house and chatted.

Finally, the officers came back to the car. They grabbed Deon by the arm and ordered him out of the vehicle.

"Okay," said one of the officers. "This lady says she doesn't know who you are. She says she does have her basement for rent. How did you know there was a room for rent here?"

"I found it on the blue sheet newspaper on campus."

"Well, we are checking out your story."

Deon remained silent. Eventually, the officers came back to Deon.

"Turn around!" one of the officers ordered Deon. He then took the handcuffs off Deon's wrists. Deon looked at the officer "What, do you have a problem?" the officer quipped.

"I was just looking for a place to live," Deon answered dejectedly.

"I advise you to get where you need to go in a hurry," the officer said. He tossed Deon's belongings back on the trunk of the squad car. Deon slowly grabbed his wallet.

The officers got back in their squad cars. They laughed as they pulled away from the curb. Deon looked at the officer who initially stopped Deon on the sidewalk. That officer smirked as well as he got back in his squad car.

"Have a good day," the officer said with a laugh as he pulled away from the curb.

Deon stood there feeling violated. He took a deep breath and started walking toward the campus. He was not going to try to catch a bus in this neighborhood now.

Deon arrived back on campus and returned to his room. Never had he experienced such demeaning treatment. Were the officers just doing their job? It seemed to be a lot more than that. Tomorrow would be another day to go out and beat the bushes again. For now, Deon just needed to get something to eat.

Deon walked over to what was called the canteen. It was where students could buy food after hours and on the weekends. Fortunately, it was still open. He went to where there was usually a line when school is in session. This time, there was no line. Sandwiches were sitting on a lighted warmer. He did not know how long they had been sitting up there, but the bottoms of the burgers were hard. That meant they had been sitting there for some time.

A cafe worker walked in. She was short with a long black weave in her hair.

"Are you looking for something?" she asked.

"How long have these been sitting up here?" Deon asked.

"I don't know. They were up there when I got here at two," she said.

Deon looked at his watch. It was after four o'clock.

"Anything else here?" he asked. "No, I'm sorry. That's it."

Deon shook his head and grabbed one of the burgers that seemed less hard on the bottom.

"That will be three-fifty," she said.

Deon dug into his pockets for the change. He politely took his sandwich to a table and fixed it up with whatever condiments he could find. Deon began to eat his lunch while watching the news on the corner ceiling TV. He notices the worker walk up.

"So, why aren't you home enjoying this vacation?" she asked.

"Oh, got work to do," Deon replied.

"Couldn't it wait?"

"No. I got to find a place to live for next semester," Deon answered.

"You not staying in the dorms?"

"No. I got to get myself a room or something. Family financial issues."

"Good luck finding a room. No one going to rent an apartment to you around here," she said.

"What, why?"

"Why? Don't you know? You can't be that naive. Please," she replied. "You would need to take one of your different friends with you, and you know what I mean by a *different* friend."

Deon looked at her and inferred her meaning.

"Have you been out there looking already?" she asked.

"Yeah, I just got back. I got doors slammed in my face, and I almost got arrested."

"Uh-huh," she said. "You are going to have to go over to the south side to find something. My church has rooms for rent. Here, let me give you my card."

Deon took her card. It said *South Ave Church of Christ* on it.

"Thank you," said Deon. "I appreciate it. What was your name?"

"I'm Vivian."

"Nice to meet you. I'm Deon."

Deon walked back to his room, looked up a few more addresses, and saved them to his phone as he lay down for the evening and went to sleep.

Deon woke up the next morning to a knock on the door. He found Andrew standing there, eating a bagel.

"Hey, what's up, dude?" said Andrew.

"I'm back early, as you can see," Deon quipped.

"Why are you back?"

"I have to find a place to stay this semester. My family is going through a divorce, and I can't afford the room and board. I'm trying to find an apartment or something."

"Good luck with that," Andrew replied.

"You know, someone else said the same thing," Deon pointed out.

"You can hide out in our room or whatever until you find something," Andrew assured him.

"I appreciate that, dude; I have to find a part-time job tomorrow too."

"Man, you go a lot on your plate. How are you going to handle all this and school too?" "No clue," Deon said exhaustedly. "But it has got to get done."

"Try one of those employment agencies," Andrew suggested. "They can find you a part-time something to get you over. I have to get some other stuff together too. I will see you later on, man. Don't let this get you down."

"Thanks, Andrew," Deon said with a nod.

Deon went to the student union building to look at the bulletin board for possible jobs. He also looked on the school computer, which was available in the student union. He looked up temporary agencies and found the one closest to the campus, although it was still about three miles away. Deon decided to check that place out.

He went to his room and pulled out a pair of gray slacks and a white button-down business shirt. He had to catch the next bus. Three miles was quite a walk, especially since it was cold outside.

When he arrived at the gray ten-story building, Deon proceeded to the elevator. He noticed the name of the agency on the third floor and pushed the number three in the elevator. He arrived at the suite of the American Temporary Services and introduced himself to the very fair-looking woman at the desk. Her brunette hair was tied behind her head with a blue tie on top. Lipstick painted her thin lips red as she sipped on a cup of coffee.

"I'm looking to follow up on an application for a job," Deon said.

"You have to complete one online," she replied.

"I have," Deon answered.

"Okay, well then, they will give you a call. Did you list your number?"

"Yes, they have it. I'm just following up because I really need a job."

Suddenly, a guy walked into the reception office and handed the woman a manila folder. He looked at Deon.

"How do you do, sir," he said, reaching out to shake Deon's hand. He gave him the hood handshake. "I'm Winston Adams, and you are …"

"I'm Deon."

"Okay. Nice to meet you."

The receptionist spoke up. "I just told him we don't accept walk-ins, that he would have to apply online. He completed it already but was following up."

"Yes, I like that," Mr. Adams said. "Let him come on around."

Deon opened the door from the waiting area to the offices that lined the hallway on both sides. A short balding man with glasses, brown pants, and shoes who resembled George on *Seinfeld* said, "Hi, I'm George," as he shook Deon hand.

That's a coincidence, thought Deon as he smiled back and shook the man's hand.

"Go ahead and interview him. I have another client," Winston said to George as he walked to another room in the newly carpeted hallways.

"Follow me," George said to Deon as they went to another office. He sat down at his brown maple-colored desk, and Deon took the seat in front of it.

George went to his computer and looked up Deon's application.

"It says here you have not been convicted of a crime." George gave Deon a conspicuous look.

"No, sir, I haven't," Deon replied.

George looked at Deon as if he was the biggest liar on the planet. "It is good to be up front about anything," he said, "because it can cause termination if found out later."

"Yes," Deon answered.

"Well, we will be placing people soon. Next week, in fact. We have plenty of custodial jobs available and warehouse jobs at an assembly plant."

"Okay, that would be great," replied Deon.

Suddenly, the man who had introduced himself as Winston walked into the office. "Hey, how's it going?" he asked.

"Everything is fine," replied George. "I see you have some experience in sales," he said to Deon.

"Some, yes," Deon answered.

"I also see you attend Mid-Union State."

"Yes, I do," Deon answered.

Winston interrupted. "We will have a position coming up— tomorrow, actually. It is a commission-only position. Would you be interested in working as an employment specialist here? It does involve cold calling to companies, and of course, selling our services. You would also help in screening applicants. Would you be interested in that?"

"Sure," replied Deon.

They all stood up. "Okay, can you start tomorrow? We have an orientation class at nine o'clock," Winston said.

"Yes, thank you, Mr. Adams, sir."

"You're welcome, and please call me Winston. See you tomorrow."

The next day, Deon readied himself to go to this orientation. He was very cautious about starting a job on commission only. However, there was a chance he could make much more than minimum wage, which is what custodial jobs would pay.

Deon arrived at the office building and checked his watch. It was a quarter till nine. One thing his dad always told Deon was never to be late for anything. Be on time. Do not contribute to stereotypes. Deon walked into the waiting room to find a half dozen others waiting for the same orientation.

Chapter 6
DEON GETS A JOB AS A RECRUITER

All the new recruiters sat in a room and waited for the presenter of the recruiter orientation. Finally, he came in. "Hi, everyone," he said. "My name is Winston Adams. I am your presenter for today. I want you all to feel comfortable, and we have refreshments on the table if you missed breakfast this morning. Let me explain how this position operates," said Winston. "You will be assigned a territory, and it will be your job to take the leads we have and call them and set an appointment for our sales counselors to meet with that company. Based on the number of closes that your sales counselor makes from your leads, you will receive a percentage. If the employee works for us, you will earn fifty cents for every hour they work. It is like a residual. If they work eighty hours a week, you will make forty dollars from that one employee. So the more calls you make the better.

"Sometimes you will sign a contract for five employees with one company to last ninety days. Then others are temporary to hire. That is another compensation package; we will get to them later. If you work, you can make some money here. We know working on commission can be rough, so we have daily hourly work in the office that you would punch in for. You can assist in screening applicants for jobs that we have listed for them. Placing applicants in those jobs would pay you seven dollars an hour. We really call that a draw against your commissions. We will take you through two weeks of training on the phones. Any questions?"

No one answered.

"Okay, we will watch a video on our placement services, and our first day of training will be tomorrow."

Deon sat intently and started counting the possibilities. This could not be as good as it sounds, he speculated.

Deon arrived at the office at eight forty-five for the nine o'clock start time the next morning. There was one lady that came earlier. She was short and with blue eyes and bright red hair. She wore a black pantsuit that hugged her midsized shape. She was quite pretty Deon thought at that moment.

"Hi, I'm Allison, and you?" "I'm Deon",

"It's nice to meet you. You want coffee or something?" Deon asked as he headed for the coffee table.

"No thanks," she said with a friendly smile.

Deon poured himself a cup of coffee. "What do you think about this job?"

"I used to work in recruiting before," she said. "I kind of know what to expect."

"How difficult is it?" Deon inquired.

"It hasn't been great thus far. I'm going to give it another try," she answered.

"Wow, that's encouraging," Deon, mused.

"I'm sure you are going to do well," she said.

Other trainees began pouring in. Deon and Allison took seats next to each other as Winston, the presenter, came into the room. Deon looked at the clock. It was nine on the dot.

"Good morning, everybody. Are you guys ready?" asked Winston.

Everyone shyly responded yes.

"That doesn't sound very enthusiastic to me, you guys. I understand, believe me. You will feel much more excited when you start earning big checks. Today we are going to break you off into two groups. The first group will go to the phones and work on scripts. You others, come with me for employee screening."

Deon was selected to the group for employee screening. The group of three walked to a computer room. "Okay," Winston said, "I am going to need you guys to log in under the number on your desk. The username is on the other side of the log-in."

Deon immediately logged in to his system. Winston began to go over aspects of the application request for temporary employees. He went over the entire form on PowerPoint, highlighting and underlining.

Deon raised his hand. "At the very right-hand side at the top, there is an MWF. What is that? Is it a calendar legend?"

"It means Monday, Wednesday, and Friday," Winston responded to a little laughter from the others. He continued explaining the importance of the original form and being sure it was correct as far as what the client needed. Finally, he told them all to work on their own on a website training. Once completed, they could download a certificate of successful completion.

Finally, Winston walked up to Deon. "Can I see you for a moment?" he asked.

Deon got up and followed Winston out the door and into an adjacent empty meeting room.

"I just need to talk to you a second," Winston said. "Have a seat."

Deon sat down.

"How do you feel about a company policy that adheres entirely to the request of its clients?" Winston asked.

"I have no problem with that, sir. The customer is always right," Deon answered.

"Some of our clients have preferences as to who they want working for them. Do you feel they have that right?"

"Sure, I agree with that," Deon responded.

"So, you will see some denotations on some applications with the letters MWF. If asked, it means Monday, Wednesday, and Friday. However, what it really means is what the client prefers. If you see just a 'W' at the top and it's circled, it means Wednesday only on the document. It also means a white male. If you see a WF, it would mean a white female."

"What do they use for a black male?"

"There is nothing for that," Winston answered.

"Isn't that unethical?"

"It's called making money. Getting paid. That is what you want, isn't it?" Winston challenged him.

"Yes, I do," Deon answered.

"It is part of my job to steer employees to you to be vetted. Are you sure you're ready for this? I want to make sure you are committed."

"I'm ready to start, sir."

Winston glared at Deon for a second, then nodded in approval and shook Deon's hand. "Okay, let's get back to work."

Deon finished the training day and thought about the company policy. He thought about Winston advocating such a system, especially being who he was. Deon was starting to have second thoughts about this job. *How can I work for a place that exploits people like this?* he thought. Deon reconciled himself by saying, *Hey, this can't be the only company that has this procedure. You got to roll with the tide. Besides, it's all about getting paid, right?*

The new orientation class met in the same meeting room as the day before. This time, classes were split up in opposites. The group that did the business calls were in Winston's group that had screened applicants. Deon's group went with another trainer; her name was Emily. She took the group to a phone room that had individual cubicles separated by movable walls. Each cubicle had a desk, computer, and phone.

"Okay," Emily said as she turned to the group. "We are going to rehearse scripts. As you read your scripts, we are going to listen to you while you make a practice call. We will grade you on this. Those of you who do not pass this part of the orientation will be let go. We do this because it is an essential part of the job, and we need to see how well you sell over the phone."

Deon remembered the phone sales job he had over the summer a few years back. He had worked for the fraternal order of police, selling tickets to the police officer's ball.

Deon looked over the script as he sat down at his assigned cubicle. Soon the phone rang. Deon followed the script. "Hello, this is Advanced Temporary Services. How can I help you?" Deon answered as the mock caller began to ask questions. Deon answered all questions in the most professional way, using proper pronunciations and etiquette. One could not possibly discern anything about him other than Deon was male and was utterly professional.

After all the trainees completed their calls, they were instructed to wait to be told where to go next. A full-figured woman Deon had not met came to his cubicle.

"Hi, Mr. White?" she asked.

"Yes?" Deon replied as he turned around.

"I need you to meet in the orientation room now."

Deon slowly stood up and proceeded to the orientation room. Minutes later, the room was only half-full. Deon suspected that the others were told they would not be needed—or maybe they were going to tell him that.

Finally, Emily, the presenter, came into the room. "Okay, everyone, you guys will be proceeding to the next step," she said.

Deon was not sure if he was glad or not glad about that.

"We have divided you guys into territories," Emily continued. "Your territory is either in group A, B, C, or D. There are contacts on the tables in those territories under those letters. You are going to take five from the stack and make your calls. You will be monitored."

Deon's assignment was territory D. He went and got his five contacts and went into the cubicle. He looked over the contacts; all were for custodians or parking lot attendants or sanitation workers, except for one for an assistant manager position. Deon stopped for a moment and thought, *I know Winston's territory has all these menial positions. How did this one for a manager get in here?*

Deon picked up the phone and started calling. He spoke to the resource managers of all five contacts. He received five confirmations and appointments from the connections he called. Deon thought about the commission he would get and then the residuals.

The phone rang. "Advance Temporary Services," Deon answered.

"That was an outstanding job, Mr. White. We are excited for you. Great job!" a voice told him. "Thank you," Deon replied.

"Excuse me," said a heavy voice behind Deon.

Deon turned around to see a sales rep, a sandy-haired lanky guy, standing in front of him.

"How did you get that contact?" he asked.

"They gave me a stack of five. Is there something wrong?" Deon replied.

"Yeah, there is something wrong. This contact is not in your territory," he argued.

"This is the stack they gave me." Deon told him.

The man snatched the contact from Deon's desk and walked toward the manager's office. Deon continued to watch to see what was going on.

Suddenly, a Mr. Colby came over to Deon's cubicle. "Can you explain to me how you got that contact?" he asked Deon.

"It was in the stack, sir."

"What stack?"

"The contacts were separated by territories, and we were to take five and make these calls," Deon explained.

Mr. Colby looked at Deon disdainfully and walked away. Deon noticed the sales rep, obviously upset, standing in Mr. Colby's doorway.

Damn, said Deon to himself. *I am in trouble already around this place.*

Winston walked up to Deon's cubicle. "Let's take a walk," he said.

They walked down the hallway and to the elevators.

"You want to get something to eat?" Winston asked as he pushed button on the elevator for the first floor.

"That's fine," Deon responded.

They went to the café that was inside the building. The smell of coffee and good food wafted throughout the cafe. They took a table toward the center of the room. The brown oak tables looked inviting, with lovely napkins on the side.

"Good job today," Winston said as they sat down.

"Thanks," Deon replied. "I'm still trying to get used to what is going on and how things go."

"Yeah, you will get that chance," Winston replied. "I know it may seem that you are selling out. I grapple with that myself all the time. You have to put those feelings aside and look at the big picture. At the very least, you are helping brothers get jobs that otherwise they would not get. You have to work the system to get what you want and need. This is how the system is set up, not just here but everywhere. Trust me."

Deon continued to listen while stirring a cup of coffee. "To be honest, I did have a problem with what I have been shown so far, but I also understand the necessity."

Winston looked at Deon and nodded in agreement. "So, I can count on you to be back tomorrow?"

"Yes, sir. Absolutely," Deon confirmed.

Deon got off work and took the trip back to campus. He remembered what the canteen worker told him about getting a room—how it was going to be nearly impossible for him to rent a place close to campus. He pulled out the card she had given him and decided to give them a call.

"Hello?" said an old woman's voice.

"Hi, my name is Deon, and I am looking for a room. I am a student at Mid-Union State."

"Yes, Vivian told me you might call. You can come by after service on Sunday, because I have to have to get the room ready. Is that okay?"

"Yes, ma'am. Sunday about four, maybe?" Deon asked.

"Four o'clock is fine," she responded.

"Thank you. I will see you then."

Chapter 7
THE WINTER SEMESTER STARTS

The weekend was uneventful, with students slowly starting to stream in from the Christmas holiday. Radios began blasting in the hallways. It sounded like a New Year's celebration, but Deon was not celebrating this year. No reason to, he felt.

Before Deon knew it, it was Sunday—the day he would ride the bus over to the south side of town. Deon put on his headphones. Every station was playing gospel music or a sermon of sorts. He finally arrived at the address.

It was a small brick house with a nicely cut lawn and shrubs in front of it. He rang the doorbell, and an older woman came slowly to the door.

"Hi," she said, panting as if she was out of breath.

"Hi. I'm Deon."

"Nice meeting you. I'm Ida Mae. Come on in."

Deon smelled something like greens cooking in the kitchen.

"I guess you would like to see the room," she said.

Deon followed the old woman down a hallway that led off the back of the house to stairs that led down to a basement. There was a laundry room and different boxes in the corner of the basement. That had a damp molding smell and was gloomy and dimly lit. On the other side of the laundry area was a place that at one point was probably a storage area. Now there was a carpet on the floor, an old bookcase, a bed, a microwave, and a small space for a TV.

"How much? Deon asked.

"Seventy-five dollars a week," she replied.

Yes, Ma'am well I am going to think about it and try to get my money together. Deon returned to his room on campus. So how did it go asked Greg. Not so good answered Deon, it was damp and too small, I will try again tomorrow.

The next morning, Deon took the bus to work while listening to talk radio. The radio blared with callers calling in.

"Affirmative action is a racist program set up to supposedly assist those people who feel like America has wronged them," claimed one of the callers. "They are the victims and lends to this victimization mind-set. We are supposed to understand that when I go looking for a job and I know I am the most qualified for the position, but they give it to this guy because he is a minority and doesn't have the same experience and obviously not the most qualified person for the job. I'm sick of it. Slavery was two hundred years ago, so why should I have to pay for it?"

"Hey, I agree with you," the radio host said. "And we all agree with you. You wouldn't want an unqualified doctor or dentist or someone coming from some minority program at some traditional minority college or university. That's why they are liberal, because the liberals guarantee these affirmative action programs to these people. We need to elect representatives who are going to get rid of these set-aside quota programs for these people and stop facilitating their perceived entitlements and their so-called victimizations."

Deon continued to listen as his stop came into view. He silenced his radio and stood up to ring the bell to let him off at the office building. Deon arrived at work and started in calling contacts in his territory.

Winston came up and asked Deon to meet him in his office. Deon and Winston were going to go out together to sell contracts. They drove to the first business. It was for an industrial center that needed temporary workers as accounts representatives, groundskeepers, and custodians. Winston got onto his computer and looked at applications that Deon had screened. Deon remembered seeing a few janitors in the building that Deon himself could have been identified as. The groundskeepers all seemed to speak Spanish only.

They walked to the business office. The accounts managers were busy on the phones.

There are a lot of Mondays, Wednesdays, and Fridays up in here, Deon thought. Only one or two were not. They both went into a salesroom and sat at the desk.

"I guess this is how I see it's done—Mondays, Wednesdays, and Fridays in the office with the best pay, everyone else janitors or groundskeepers," Deon said.

Winston looked up from his laptop computer and nodded yes.

A man walked in. "All right, do you have the numbers?" he asked. He was about five-ten and looked like he worked out. He pulled up his gray slacks at the thigh before he sat down.

"How are you doing? I'm Todd," he said.

"I'm Deon."

"I talked to you on the phone. Good job," Todd said.

Todd and Winston discussed the numbers as Deon looked on. They agreed with the number of temporary workers they needed and the hourly pay and percentages. Finally, everyone stood and shook hands.

Later, as Deon and Winston were walking back to the car, Winston said, "We have some screenings to do when we get back, and I have something to give to you as well."

Deon wondered what that could be. They walked into the building to find prospective employees. They seemed to be divided. All professional positions—the Mondays, Wednesday, and Fridays—were in one meeting room, and all manual labor applicants were in another. Many in the manual labor room looked like they came from the south side, some with cornrows and others with braided hair.

"I need you to come to my office," Winston whispered in Deon's ear. Before Deon had a chance to sit down, Winston slid Deon an envelope. In it was a commission check for $300. He looked at Deon and said, "This doesn't count toward your residuals per month."

Deon looked up at Winston and said, "Thank you."

"All right," he replied, trying to map out Deon's response. He was concerned that Deon was not feeling this job.

Deon looked at the check once he got back to his room and wondered how long he was going to work at this job. He was having more and more problems stomaching his role at the company. *I may resign from this job tomorrow*, he thought. *I have enough money until I find a decent job.*

Deon counted his money and prepared to go to the bank to make his deposit the next day. Deon was conflicted. *Should I quit a job and not have one to go to? Then again, I am in school*, he thought. *I cannot put full time into this job even if I wanted to, and I must be able to look myself in the mirror.*

The next day, Deon sat in front of Winston at his desk. "I can't do this job. I have thought about it, and I have tried to reason it away, but it's not for me."

Winston looked at Deon. "I understand," he said. "It's not for everybody." Winston was disappointed but still agreeable.

Deon stood up and shook Winston's hand.

"Good luck to you," Winston said as Deon exited his office.

Deon sneaked up to Greg while Greg was laying across his bed listening to music with his headphones on. "You busy?" Deon asked.

"No what's up, want to take a ride"? Greg asked.

Deon nodded, and they both found themselves driving towards McDonalds.

"I quit my job today," said Deon.

"You quit?"

"Yeah, man," Deon said. "It was some bullshit."

"So what are you going to do?" Greg asked.

"I got money saved to last a few months," said Deon.

"I want to stop by and pick something up from my dad's office," said Greg.

Deon and Greg drove downtown and parked in front of the building where his father's office was. They took the elevator to the main floor, where a security guard was sitting at a desk in the lobby.

"That guy is here all night?" Deon inquired.

"Yeah. He's a rent-a-cop. Why do you ask?"

"No reason."

Deon thought about that guard job. He decided to go ask the guard about his career.

"Can I ask you something?" he said.

"Yes, how can I help you?" the guard asked.

"I'm thinking about trying to get a security guard job. How is it? Do you work overnight too?"

"I do," the guard said, "but not here. I just do the second shift."

"If you don't mind me asking, how much do they start you at?"

"Ten dollars an hour," the guard responded.

"They hiring now?" Deon asked.

"They always hiring," the guard responded.

Greg returned to the desk. "Hey, let's get outta here," Greg said, already heading for the elevator.

"Hang on, dude. I'm coming."

Chapter 8

Deon went to the security agency and picked up a pen and application from the window. Finding a seat over in the corner by a lamp, he glanced over the application.

Have you been convicted of a misdemeanor? If so, please explain

Have you been convicted of a felony? If so, please explain.

I'm glad I don't have to answer yes to any of that, Deon thought.

Deon filled out the application and submitted it to the desk. "Thank you," he said.

"Someone will be with you in just a minute," the receptionist said.

Deon sat and noticed that most applicants were minority and poor.

"Deon White," a voice called.

"Yes, sir," Deon said as he stood up.

"This way, please."

Deon followed the man to a desk in the back. "Have you ever worked security before?" the man asked.

"No, sir."

"I see you attend Mid-Union University," the man noted.

"Yes, sir."

"Would attending school interfere with your duties as a security officer?" the man asked. "We need people who are interested in focusing on being security officers."

"No, sir. It would not interfere," Deon answered.

"Okay. Why do you want to work in security?"

"I would like the experience," Deon said. "I may seek a career in law enforcement."

"Okay," the man said. "I have everything here. We have an orientation on Monday. Can you attend?"

"Yes, sir."

"Okay, I will conduct the background check, and I will give you a call."

"Thank you very much, sir. I greatly appreciate the opportunity," Deon answered.

The next day Deon received the call. "We would like to bring you into the orientations on

Monday. We start at nine o'clock," the man on the phone said. "Yes, sir," Deon replied with a sigh of relief.

The next day, Deon went to the orientation. There were a PowerPoint and video of security procedures. It showed the different contracts that the company had and the various positions in which the guards would be working. Then a man came out and stated the starting salary: ten dollars an hour. Deon thought, *Damn, that will do. If I could just get enough for an apartment.*

Deon looked online and found a studio apartment in a decent area. He rode the bus over to the address he'd found online. He went into the rental office, and the rental agent looked over the application. *Have you been convicted of a felony? Have you ever been arrested?* Deon again looked at those questions and gave a sigh of relief that he could answer no.

Deon completed the application and submitted it to the rental agent.

"Have you ever had an apartment before?" the agent asked.

"No, sir. This would be my first."

"Okay," the agent said. "Do you have pay stubs?"

"I just left one job, and now I am working for a security agency," Deon replied.

"When do you get a paycheck from your new job?"

"It won't be for a few weeks." Deon answered, hoping they would make an exception.

"Okay," the agent said, "let's look at what we have available."

Deon walked around the lovely courtyard that had a waterfall in the middle. They walked to the basement apartment, which was a studio. He opened the door and saw a one-room apartment with a sliding door separating the bedroom from the main room. There was a tiny kitchen, and the place was charming and quaint. Deon liked the apartment and decided to walk back with the man to the office.

"How much is that a month?"

"Seven hundred," the man replied.

Deon looked at his calculations. *I could make it on that*, Deon thought.

The man added, "We would also need one-and-a-half months' rent as a security deposit."

Deon calculated that with the money his dad had given him before he left home and the three hundred he got from the temporary agency, he had just enough with a little change left over.

"I will take it," Deon said.

"Okay," said the agent. "I will submit what you have for references and the copy of your pay stub, and if you can get a payroll form from your current job, that should suffice."

"Thank you, sir," Deon said as he happily left the rental office. All he needed to do was get a copy of his payroll. That should be easy enough.

Deon went to the security training. The topic of the first lesson was "Verbal Judo: How to Verbally Disarm an Assailant—Unarmed Security Nonaggressive Procedures. The video began with, "Verbal Judo is a way of using words to maintain mental and emotional safety. This 'conflict management technique' involves using posture and body language, choice of words, and tone of voice as a means for calming a potentially volatile situation before it can turn into physical violence. This often involves techniques such as deflecting the conversation to less argumentative topics or redirecting the conversation to other individuals in the group who are less passionately engaged."

Deon looked on intently, wondering how anyone would physically restrain someone without a weapon. Since most contracts were in a hospital, it was necessary to learn CPR and other procedures. Most of the security personnel worked in the mental ward or emergency rooms at the hospitals. After the training video, all applicants went to the uniform room and were assigned security uniforms. Deon also received his schedule.

The next day, Deon was assigned to the Mason's Memorial Hospital emergency room. The hospital was in an impoverished area in a city division called Upton. There were a few small business and strip areas, and there was a housing project across the street.

Deon headed for the hospital locker room and got dressed in his new uniform. He checked himself in the mirror and shook his head. *Can't believe I am doing this*, he said to himself. Deon looked at his watch. *I'm early by thirty minutes*, he thought, and again he was reminded of what his dad always told him: one can never be too early, but one can always be late. Deon lived to disprove the old stereotype that certain kinds of people are late and lazy.

Deon sat and waited with the wand by his side. His assignment was at check-in, where patients were screened before coming into the waiting room area. Deon asked people to take everything out of their pockets and put the items in a basket to be searched, and then the basket was pushed to the other end of the table. Patients were then searched for metal. Most had no problem with the procedure, but Deon wondered why this was necessary to go into an emergency room. Several people stood outside the emergency room door, smoking cigarettes, Deon went to them and said they had to move. One person looked at Deon as if he could cut Deon's throat. The man cursed under his breath as he walked down the ramp to the sidewalk and proceeded across the street.

Relief came in the form of the security van used to transport guards and to make security rounds. "Hey, I'm here to relieve you, and you have the security rounds," said the guard just arriving.

Deon jumped into the van, happy for anything to break up the monotony of sitting by that emergency room door and treating potential patients like criminals. Nevertheless, a job is a job.

Deon put on his seat belt and fiddled with the radio. It was only an AM radio, so no music to listen to. He fiddled around and found a talk radio program.

"Look, folks, these people want you to feel like you are privileged. That is the mantra of the left. They don't value the hard work that you have done to get what you have; no, they follow the drumbeat of what they call inequality. We believe in self-responsibility. The reason for your condition is that you have because you put yourself into. No one genuinely put a gun to these people's heads. They sold themselves and now I'm privileged? Not here, folks."

As Deon slowly backed out of the driveway and headed toward the hospital parking garage, he continued to listen to the radio.

"The NAACP is a racist organization in America where the whole platform is about race. Just by the name of the organization, it supports this racist idea that if anyone disagrees with them, then they are racist. Is there a national association of white people? And this what you get from the left ..."

Deon turned down the radio entirely and continued to ride the levels of the garage to where the key for the time clock was located. Deon got out and inserted the key to the security clock, which recorded the time they were in the area. Deon fidgeted around for another radio station. He heard Spanish channels up and down the dial until he found a sport stations talking about the upcoming football season. Deon listened to the sports talk radio host lambasting a football team and making jokes about their terrible play.

He drove back to the emergency room and resumed his position at the emergency entrance desk.

Soon a man walked up to the emergency room door and began banging hard on the window, so hard that he could have easily broken it. The man was wearing blue jeans and a dingy white shirt and tennis shoes. His face was wrinkled, and his thinning brown hair made him look to be fifty- something years old.

Deon stood up and grabbed his radio. "I have a 10.66 at the emergency room entrance," he said into the radio. Then he walked out to the ramp where the emergency vehicles would pull up. Deon and his fellow security officers stood back cautiously, as the man had an object in his hand.

"What's he got?" Deon asked another guard, whose name was Keith.

Keith stepped forward and said, "Okay, let's calm down, sir."

"Naw, to hell with all of you sons of bitches. I don't give a damn," the man screamed at the top of his lungs.

"Let's just calm down here," Deon said as Keith walked a step closer.

"Yeah, everything is going to be all right," said Keith. "Just be cool, sir"

"Don't holler at me about no got-damn religion!" the man screamed. Saliva flew from his mouth like the fizz from a cheap can of beer.

Deon stepped closer. "No one cares about religion right now, okay?"

"You would care for Jesus Christ!" the man screamed. The object in his hand was still unidentifiable.

"Come on, sir. Drop what you have in your hand. We are here to help." "I don't need a stick. I don't need a stick," the man yelled repeatedly. "Okay, sir, we are going to have to take you into the hospital," said Keith. "Do we know who he is?" Deon asked

"Yeah. He has been a patient here before," Keith answered.

"What's his name?"

"Mr. Hart." Keith stepped forward again and said, "Mr. Hart, we can just go back in, and take a shower and get some food to take care of you. Just put the stick down."

Keith stepped forward again and grabbed the stick in the man's hand. Mr. Hart then sat down and started crying. "You think I like being this way? You think I want to be this way?" he repeated. "See what happens if this happens to you," he cried as Keith put his hands on Mr. Hart's shoulder to settle the poor man down.

"I'm only doing this to protect you," said Keith. "We are going to get a chair to help you in a minute. Just be still."

A police car drove up the ramp. The officers got out of the car, holding their hands on their Tasers.

"He's okay," Deon said to the one female officer, who carried herself upright and steady although she was petite.

"Okay," she said. "We had a report of a man with an unidentified object in his hand and threatening?"

"He had a stick in his hand," Deon said.

The other officer walked up. "Well it is good you got that stick out of his hand because we don't play that bullshit out in the street," he said.

"He has been here before," Keith told the officer. "I don't understand how he gets out."

The triage nurse came out to the ramp. "The ward only keeps them until they are stable, and then we have to let him out again," she explained. "We will get him upstairs if you two gentlemen can help, please."

Deon and Keith put the man in a wheelchair, wheeled him to the psych ward, and used a special key for the door to open. A psych nurse met them.

"We got him now. Just stand by in case we need you," the nurse said.

Deon stood by as they put on rubber gloves. "Mr. Hart, we have to give you a shot so you can rest," she said.

He nodded okay and took the injection in his hip. They moved him to a room and shower area, where he finally calmed down.

"Is everything going to be okay from here?" Deon asked.

"Yes, we should be okay."

"I will stay back," said Keith. "You still got the front emergency room door. Come on, midnight, damn."

"You got to work tomorrow?" Deon asked Keith.

"I'm off," he replied. "The next two days, I won't have to deal with this."

<hr>

The next morning, Deon got up and got himself ready for work. He had forgotten to get the copy of his payroll for his new apartment. *Gotta be to work at two,* he said to himself as he looked at his cell phone for the time. It was at eleven o'clock. *Might as well make my way there.*

Deon headed out to the bus. The twenty-minute ride brought him back into the neighborhood of Upton. He walked to a neighborhood basketball court next to a Laundromat, not far from the hospital.

Deon found Keith, his coworker who lived in the neighborhood, watching the basketball game while sitting on the courtside bench.

"What up, bruh," Keith said while fist-bumping Deon. Everyone marveled at two competing players who hit one long jump shot after another. One skinny kid took a fast break and made a slam dunk. Onlookers said ooh and gave each other high fives.

"You going to play?' Keith asked.

"Naw, I'm just chilling."

"Yeah, they hoop out here every afternoon no matter how hot. I come out and get myself a good workout sometimes," Keith said.

Deon continued to watch the players play hitting jump shots from thirty feet out. Eventually, he made his way to work.

Chapter 9

Deon assumed his position at the security desk. The evening passed with the usual crowd of people visiting the emergency room, some with severe cuts, serious scrapes, and broken arms, along with the incapacitated drunks, mentally unstable individuals, and homeless people. One would call them derelicts.

He went to the security office to ask about a copy of his payroll information.

"I can get that for you," a lady at the desk said as she turned to her computer. "What's your social?"

Deon gave her his social security number.

"Okay. I will make a copy for you," she said.

Deon took the copy and told the lady thank you. Then he proceeded to his security post in the emergency room.

Suddenly, a police car and ambulance drove up in the driveway. The emergency van had its lights blaring. Medical personnel rushed to the back of the ambulance and flung the door open. Deon stood up to see if they needed any assistance. It was a little boy about nine or ten years old with his shoe off. He lay there with his eyes closed, and the emergency technician was wheeling him in.

Deon helped the emergency technicians and escorted the wheeled bed to the emergency room doors. He opened the door with the steel plate that you had to mash, and the doors swung open to where doctors were waiting. They pulled the wheeled bed into one of the operating rooms. Deon turned back to the security desk. Deon sat down and took a deep breath.

Minutes later, the emergency tech came out. Deon went to meet him to assist in his exit. The technician stopped for a moment and started writing some notes down.

"The kid—he's going to be all right?" asked Deon.

"Oh no, he's dead," answered the technician.

"Dead?" Deon asked, surprised.

"Yeah, he's gone," he said definitively.

Deon's heart fell heavy in his chest. "What happened?"

"He fell backward out of a ten-story window."

"Oh damn," Deon said, feeling a massive lump in his throat.

Soon people started to arrive. A young woman arrived with a man, and they asked about the boy, calling him by name down the hallway. A chaplain came out of the operating room. They looked at him, and the woman screamed, "Oh no, please, no!" He assisted the grieving mother and the man into the emergency room area. Suddenly, Deon heard loud screaming and agonizing crying.

Others showed up. Deon had to stop them one by one and wand them in, but some brushed past Deon, and Deon did not apprehend them. He knew it was because of the little boy who had died. They went through the emergency room door, and shortly after the loudest screams of agony and crying proceeded uncontrollably. Deon stood and stared as screams ricocheted down the sterile hallway.

Soon Channel 7 arrived with its on-the-spot reporter. She and her camera operator stood out on the sidewalk in front of the hospital. A backlight was added, and she brushed herself off a bit. She stood on a small platform to make herself taller as she reported the incident of a child falling ten stories to his death.

Deon arrived at work the next day. "What's going on, Keith?" Deon said as he walked into the emergency room door.

"We got a meeting in room 100 in five minutes. Don't be late," he said.

Deon rushed to put on his uniform and made it to room 100 as other security guards came in and sat down. Captain Suh walked in with security books and set them on the table

"All right," said Captain Suh. He looked like an island dictator with his uniform on. "Yesterday was an eventful day. As you know, they brought in this kid, his name was Jerome. He died here at the hospital, or he was already dead when they brought him in. Either way, it got pretty bad."

Another security officer spoke up. "What happened to that kid?" he asked.

"Well, from the incident report, his mother left him over with her great-grandmother, and she is an old lady, about seventy-nine or so and disabled, but he was playing with other kids and thought it would be a good idea to sit in the windowsill, and he fell, and that's it."

Deon shook his head. The great-grandmother was almost eighty years old; she probably turned her head for a minute.

They all shook their heads in sorrow.

"Anyway," he continued, "the mother was at work, and both her kids were there. They arrested the great grandmother for child endangerment and the optics didn't look good, it's all over social media the captain said."

"Aw, man, you can't arrest an eighty-year-old woman," everybody mumbled.

"So, the problem we faced was with trying to get the relatives and all adequately searched and past the security gate when we have circumstances like that," the captain continued. "I know these people do not want to be searched and made to go through the procedure, especially when someone is dying or dead or whatever. However, we must do this for every person regardless of the incident. I realize that under the circumstances, it was difficult to do, and we probably need to call a code three so all officers can arrive at the location to assist. Last time it was only one guard, and it is hard for just one to handle all that with the public in this kind of situation, so we are going to call on the radio for assistance when an event like this happens."

He concluded, "Lastly, Channel 7 was here and did a report out front of the hospital. Never talk to the press about anything that is occurring at the hospital. Any information has to be gotten from central command where we have a security public liaison officer."

Everyone agreed and signed a memorandum acknowledging that they received this information. Deon still felt disheartened about what had happened to that kid. He went back to his post and started his shift.

Later, Keith drove up to give Deon a break. Deon got in the van and turned on AM radio.

"Can you feel sorry for some people so irresponsible to let a kid fall ten stories? This is the tragedy created by the liberals. These people living in a housing project, on welfare, they don't work, they are given everything from the government, and they take no responsibility for their actions. Where were the parents, or should I say parent, or should I even say that? These communities are crime-infested and drug-infested, and you can blame the left for what goes on in those projects …"

Deon bought a hamburger at McDonald's and drove back to the hospital. He turned the station back to where it was as he parked the vehicle. He handed Keith a Big Mac he had picked up at the restaurant.

"Thanks, Deon," Keith said as he sat back at his position.

Deon had started eating his hamburger and fries when a young woman with her son beside her startled him.

"Excuse me, can you help me?" she asked as she entered the hospital emergency room door.

Damn, Deon said to himself. *I didn't even get a chance to finish this.*

He looked up. She was a cute little brown-skinned girl with soft yet hardened features, possibly due to hardships she had faced. Her hair was pulled back in a short ponytail. Her hands and feet were small but cute.

"My son got a cold," she said. "He is spitting up."

Deon looked at the boy. He had lots of mucous running from his nose.

"Oh yeah, it looks like he got a cold," said Deon. "How old is he?"

"He is five," she answered.

"Let me process you in," Deon said compassionately. He wanded her down, took the possessions that were in her pants pockets, put them in a bowl, and passed them through the detector to the other side of the table.

"You can go ahead," Deon said as she walked through the doors to the emergency room waiting area. Deon noticed her sit down, then sat back down himself and finished his burger.

The emergency room was starting to fill up. Deon completed a security round in the waiting area. The girl with the little boy had him in her arms, and she was trying to get the mucous out his nose.

"You need any more tissues or anything?" Deon asked her.

"Yes, if you don't mind," she replied.

Deon went to the triage area and asked for some tissues. He brought a Kleenex box back to her.

"I don't know what is taking them so long," Deon said while handing her the box of Kleenex.

"I will be here until they see him," she replied while comforting her son.

Deon nodded and went back to his position. Soon he noticed the triage nurse come to get them. They stayed with her for about ten minutes, and then again she waited in the waiting room.

Deon went to talk to the triage nurse. Hi, is everything good? "Yes, just another night she replied". "I am in sports medicine at Mid Union University," Deon said. "That is good she replied, that might be better than nursing." "I thought nursing was great" Deon responded. "It's ok but it depends on where you are, I have had patients who declined my services because they did not want a Black nurse, and the hospital sides with the patient, and they give you the worst assignments." "Really"? Deon said surprisingly. "Oh yes she said. I been spit on, cursed out, and called the N word." Deon shook his head in disbelief as he asked how long it would be before the young woman sitting in the waiting room could be seen. "As soon as they can. It won't be much longer." She replied.

Time passed on. Deon was watching the clock, since he got off at midnight and it was now a little past nine. He decided to make another round in the emergency room. Deon noticed the girl still sat there in her chair with her son asleep in her arms. She had a weary look on her face.

Just then a nurse, came to the waiting area. "Erica Williams!" she called out.

The girl stood up with her son in her arms. "No, that's me. It's my son. He's the one."

"Okay. Well, come right this way," the nurse said, leading them through the metal steel gray doors. They walked in, and the doors shut behind them.

Finally, midnight came, and it was time to go home. Deon caught the bus and gazed out the window past the vacant buildings and ragged businesses, block after block. Sometimes the ten- mile ride would take almost an hour. He finally arrived back at campus and went straight to bed.

The next day Deon called Greg.

"What's up Deon?"

"Hey, man, I got a new apartment."

"Cool, where is it?" Greg asked.

"Not too far from work. I was wondering if you could help me move."

"Yeah, no problem" Greg replied.

Greg met Deon and loaded his car up with Deon's belongings. They drove to the new apartment.

"Hey, this is pretty cool here," Greg said as he looked around the place. "You are gonna need some furniture."

"Yeah, I got to get a bed today."

"Come on. I'll take you," Greg offered.

Greg and Deon rode to a mattress store close to the apartment. Deon purchased an inexpensive mattress, and the two of them fastened it to the top of Greg's car and drove it over to the new apartment.

"Well, that's it," Deon said as he sat down on the mattress he'd just bought.

"In a way, I envy you," said Greg. "Your own spot with no distractions. You need some furnishings, plates and dishes and stuff," he said.

Deon and Greg hit the thrift store. He bought inexpensive ethnic inspirational pictures and graphs, sheets and pillows for his bed, and curtains for the windows. They stopped by a garage sale and picked up large pillows that could be thrown on the floor, a lamp, and a nice small table. In the end, Deon had only spent about seventy dollars.

"Well, this is a start," Greg said as they loaded what they had bought into the car. They arrived back at the apartment and pretended to be interior designers, moving things around like two women who could not make up their minds. Finally, they sat and chilled out, watching the small TV and smoking a bowl.

"Hey, Deon, you gonna let me come stay a while?" asked Greg.

"You gotta ask?" Deon laughed.

"This is all right," said Greg. "I have to get back to the campus now, though. Holler at me, Deon."

"You know I will, Greg. Peace, dude"

Deon slept well in his new apartment. He was proud of what he had accomplished up to this point. *This may work out after all, just like Daddy said.*

He looked at the time. "I'd better get ready for work."

※

Deon walked to the bus stop and noticed someone putting up a sign on the bus stop pole. "Route time changes," the sign read. Deon took a closer look at the new transit schedule. The last bus was running now at 10:00 p.m.

Damn, thought Deon. *Now I won't have a ride home.*

Deon remembered watching the news last night about bus schedule changes because of budget cuts. He remembered them saying how these bus cuts would hurt many in the inner city. *I am going to have to request a different shift now*, he thought. *I can't walk ten miles home every day.*

It was an ordinary evening at work, as he assumed his regular duties at the hospital security desk. *I need to talk to someone about my schedule*, he thought.

Deon waited until his lunch break to ask the captain. He explained to Captain Suh about the change to the bus schedule. "The last bus is at ten instead of midnight," he said. "Any way I can come in earlier and leave a little earlier?"

"I'm sorry, I can't approve that," said the captain. "The shifts are set."

Deon looked at him. "You know the situation with the bus schedule …"

"It's not the security department's responsibility how you get here. Your shift starts at four, and you are off at midnight. That's all there is,"

Deon hated being talked to like an idiot. *That is what you put up with in menial low-paying jobs*, he thought.

"It's not me that makes these decisions," said the captain. "We've had this issue many times before."

"I appreciate it. Thank you anyway," Deon said as the captain gave him an empathetic look.

Deon went to Keith at the security desk. "Man, can you give me a ride home?"

"Yeah, no problem, dude," Keith said,

"I got to figure out how to get myself a car."

"Why? What happened to the bus?" Keith asked.

"They are stopping service at ten," Deon answered. "Yeah, that happens a lot out here in the hood. They make it hard for the people who struggle the most."

"I guess they consider it a government handout," Deon answered.

"How much you got saved?" asked Keith.

"Not much," Deon replied.

"I might can help you out. I got an uncle who is trying to sell his ride. Not too expensive, either. You interested?"

"Yeah, sure," Deon replied.

"Okay. I will holla at him."

The next day, Deon arrived at work to see Keith talking with another man outside of a gray late-model car.

"Hey, Deon," Keith called out while waving Deon over. "Look at this."

Deon looked at the car.

"It's a 2004 PT Cruiser," the man said. "It's in good shape. Just needs minor work."

"I'm sorry I didn't introduce y'all," Keith said. "This is my Uncle Bo."

"How do you do, sir?" Deon said respectfully.

"How are you, son?" the man asked.

"I'm fine. What kind of minor work does it need?"

"You are going to need a tune-up. The brakes are a little low. I can sell it as-is for eight hundred dollars."

Eight hundred, Deon thought. He still had a few bucks left over from the check his dad had given him, although he was sure his dad would not approve of his buying a car.

"You want to take a ride?" Uncle Bo asked.

The three of them got in the Cruiser and drove off. The car ran well, but as Uncle Bo had mentioned, the brakes seemed a little soft.

"You can get a brake job for about two hundred dollars," Bo said. "Tell you what. I will give it to you for seven hundred". Deon drove around a little farther and used his turn signals to make sure they were working. He turned the lights on and off and stopped the car. He looked under the hood and saw he was going to need a battery soon.

"Well, what do you think?" Keith asked.

Deon thought about it. "Can I get you cash or money order?"

"Either way," Uncle Bo said. "I have the title right here. We can go to the currency exchange and transfer the title."

"Okay, let's do it," said Deon.

He worked his shift and drove home in his old new PT Cruiser. Deon listened carefully to the car as it drove. He heard no strange engine noises. The brakes continued to seem soft, so Deon stopped at the mini-mart gas station, bought a bottle of brake fluid, went under the hood, and opened the brake fluid valve. It was close to empty. Deon filled it and closed it, then let the hood down.

He drove further down the road and used his brakes. They were getting harder as he continued to start and stop. *Wow, problem solved*, he thought.

Deon turned on his radio and found a favorite R & B station. *Guess I will ride around a bit before I go home for the night*, he thought.

Deon sat in kinesiology class, observing the professor demonstrate the motion of different body parts—shoulder rotations and arm extension and flexion and scapular movements.

Reggie tapped Deon. "Stay focused my brother."

"I'm tired," Deon replied.

"You got to get your rest, dog."

"Been working man. What can I do? I got myself a car," Deon said.

"What? Where?" Reggie asked.

"It's out in the parking lot. I will show you," Deon replied.

Deon texted Greg and told him to meet them at his room.

"What's up, G!" Deon said as Greg opened his door.

"What's up, bro? How have you been? Come on in. I shouldn't have to tell you to come in."

Greg passed Deon a vape stick.

"I just bought a car," Deon said while holding up his keys.

"What! Where is it at?" Greg said excitedly.

"It's in the lot. Come on, I'll show you."

The three of them went to the parking lot and walked up to a gray PT Cruiser.

"Hey, man, this is cool. Where you get this?" asked Greg

"A coworker introduced me to his uncle, who sold it to me. It's a decent little ride just to get me back and forth."

"The interior is nice. How many miles?" Greg asked.

"A hundred and fifty thousand," Deon replied.

"When are you going to take us on a ride?" asked Reggie

"We can go now," Deon said while hitting the vape pipe.

"You going to that symposium?" Greg asked Deon.

"What symposium?"

"The one with Dr. Carla Thomas, about mass incarceration."

"Aw, man, I forgot all about that!" Deon said, slapping his forehead.

"It's tonight at seven," Greg said.

Reggie spoke up. "You going?"

"I guess I could," said Greg. "I know my Issues professor probably expects us to be there."

"Oh yeah, that issues class," Reggie said. "That class had my head boiling last semester."

"Me too. I don't know if I could handle that this semester," said Deon.

"Problem is, you have to," Greg added.

"I still remember what happened when we walked past that dorm," Reggie said while looking as if he could spit.

"Yeah, I haven't forgotten that either," Deon said.

"Man, I am so sorry you guys got to go through that," Greg said, shaking his head.

"Hey, man, like I always tell you. It ain't you, so you don't have to apologize for others' ignorance."

"Well maybe after that we can go for a ride," Greg said as they started to make their way back to the main campus.

The auditorium was filled with what seemed to be liberal thinkers. There appeared to be a sprinkle of conservative students sitting together up front, all with a sour expression on their faces. One of the humanities professors was addressing the audience and speaking about diversity and the contributions of the minds of Gandhi, Martin Luther King, and Mother Theresa. Then he started the introduction of the symposium guest speaker.

"Ladies and gentlemen, without further ado, I introduce to you Dr. Carla Thomas."

The crowd stood as she approached the podium. She waved at the crowd.

"Good evening, everyone. It is nice to see so many good people here. People who are the future of your city and state and country. Fresh, new, young, and exciting minds, in an exploration of understanding and justice for all human beings, men and women and children. It is their future and our futures, and equality for all people who dare to roll up their sleeves and stand against what is not right for the good of all people."

Deon listened intently and began to jot down notes. Reggie did the same as he gave Deon with a look of seriousness.

"The United States locks up more people than any other nation on this earth. So much so that now there are for-profit prisons. Stop for a moment and think about that. For-profit penal institutions. What would be their financial incentive? To make sure there is always a supply of inmates available. An investment in the incarceration of human beings and what mechanism could be established to make sure the incarceration is profitable.

How is this accomplished? Well, it is a simple formula. Eliminate opportunity and investment in lower socioeconomic areas and watch the pool of potential clients explode. Inundate the community with aggressive policing, like stop and frisk with no probable cause, creating substantial penalties for a minuscule amount of an illegal substance. The same drug that if caught in the suburbs in its original form, carries a fraction of the sentence. Even if you are not in possession, one can be charged, if some are in possession and they are in your house, apartment, or car. More than the desire to lock certain people up, is to get a felony or even misdemeanor drug convictions, because guess what? As soon as the background check is done, when you answer the question on a job application, have you ever been convicted of a crime, your back is immediately against the wall. That is where they want to keep them: chronically unemployed and susceptible to the urge to survive by any way they can. If you are going to change something, then vote! Oh, I am sorry, felons cannot vote for sometimes seven years, often longer, and in some states not at all. However, if you wait for some time or less, you may be able to purchase a gun legally. How ironic is that?"

Deon continued to listen as the audience of supposed intellectuals jotted down notes as well. Most of this Deon already knew from his own reading, but he just wanted to hear if Dr. Thomas would touch on those points. She began to talk about the statistics that certain people who are in a minority percentage cause the majority of crime and how this is used to justify police actions and reactions, and how law enforcement officers say they feared their life and were in danger as they shot at an unarmed civilian. Even something as basic a human right as clean water is sometimes contaminated with lead affecting the health and cognitive development of thousands of children.

After the symposium, Deon and Reggie crept back to Greg's dorm room.

"So, how was the symposium?" Greg asked as he studied at his computer.

"It was what we expected," Reggie said. "A lot of talk, but who is going to do something about the issues discussed? No one."

Deon sat in his old hard chair. "Hey, man, like they say, if you get caught up, you must be guilty of something, right?" Deon added.

"That is the prevailing sentiment," Greg said. "I hate those classes and speeches. I know it needs to be discussed, but ultimately, we will wake up with the same issues from the day before."

"That is if God sees fit to wake any of us up," Reggie added.

"That part," Deon quipped. Y'all still want to go for a ride?"

"Naw, I got work to do," Greg answered. "Maybe tomorrow."

"Yeah, me too," Reggie said. Deon I got a download I want you to listen to. I'm sending it to your phone," He added.

"That's cool. I will see y'all sometime Friday. Got to work tomorrow."

"All right. See you later, Deon."

"Later, y'all." Deon drove home listening to the download Reggie sent to his phone. It was the voice of Malcolm X. *"So I cite these various revolutions, brothers and sisters, to show you that you don't have a peaceful revolution. You don't have a turn-the-other-cheek revolution. There's no such thing as a nonviolent revolution. The only kind of revolution that is nonviolent is the Negro revolution. The only revolution in which the goal is loving your enemy is the Negro revolution. It's the only revolution in which the goal is a desegregated lunch counter, a desegregated theater, a desegregated park, and a desegregated public toilet; you can sit down next to white folks - on the toilet. That's no revolution!!* Deon continued to listen and thought about the steep contrast to his nonviolent beliefs. *"Maybe I'm a Shine"* he thought.

Deon arrived at work to find an issue being addressed as soon as he walked into the door. A guard Deon did not know was addressing a patient who had an object but did not want to part with it.

"Hey, I'm Officer White," he said. "And you?"

"Officer Sullivan."

"What's going on?"

"This guy is like sixteen years old and has a disability. We're just trying to wand him in." *Man, he is a big sixteen-year-old*, Deon thought. *At least six feet and three hundred pounds*. "He is my son," an older woman called out. "He is autistic. You have to give him time to process what is going on."

"Okay," Deon responded. "What is his name?"

"Donald," she replied.

"Donald, hi. I'm Officer White."

"White!" he said loudly, repeating it twice.

The triage nurse came over. "You okay?" she asked.

"Okay!" he repeated.

"It's called echolalia. It's common with autism," the nurse said.

"I'm going to need you to give me what you have in your hand. Okay?" Deon said in a reassuring tone.

"Okay," Donald said twice and put the object in the bin. It was one of those rubber hand grip and wrist strengtheners.

Not a bad idea, thought Deon. *I imagine you could relieve stress and build up your hands and forearms too.*

"Here you go you can have it back," Deon said as he smiled at the big kid.

His mother spoke up. "He was here a few days ago and I lost the prescription they gave him. I just need a copy of it."

"Oh, sure. You are his mom?" the nurse asked?

"Yes, this is my boy."

The nurse found the prescription, made a copy, and gave it to the lady.

"Thank you," she said as they both left the hospital.

"I guess I am your relief," Deon said to Officer Sullivan.

"Yes, it's been a long day."

"Well, now you can take it easy," Deon assured.

"Thanks," Officer Sullivan replied.

A few hours at the security desk passed before Keith pulled up with the white security van. "Time for your break," he said as he came through the automatic doors.

"Cool," Deon answered, jumping up excitedly. He went to the van and drove off. He was hungry and thought about heading for Mickey Dee's. Deon took the side streets through the neighborhoods, which always seemed to be faster than the boulevard. Deon noticed Donald and his mother, who seemed to be pleading with him. Deon pulled over and got out of the van.

"Hey, is everything okay?" he asked. "I see he still has his hand squeezer."

"He is displaying frustration, that's all," said his mother. "We just got to give him time to process and settle down."

Donald calmed down enough to take the walk up the sidewalk toward their side door.

"Everything okay?" Deon asked the mother.

"Yeah. Everything is going to be fine."

"Okay then," Deon replied as he went back to his security van. He had started up the van and pulled off when suddenly a police car came screeching into the small driveway, startling everyone. Deon turned and watched as the police exited the vehicle.

"We were called about a disturbance," one of the police officers said as Deon began to pull off.

"No," said the mother. "It is just my son. We are trying to get him in the house. He just needs to calm down and take his time.

At that moment, Donald turned around.

"Okay, drop it!" the officer yelled at Donald.

"What! Drop it drop it!" Donald yelled in his echolalia. "What drop it!" he repeated again as he stepped toward the officers with the squeeze grip in his hand.

"Wait! He is autistic!" screamed his mother"

Suddenly, two shots rang out, hitting Donald in the chest.

"Oh, Lord have mercy!" yelled the mother as she ran toward Donald, who lay sprawled out on the ground. Blood came from his mouth and chest.

"Oh, Lord, you shot my baby!" she screamed repeatedly.

The officer's radio echoed, "Shots fired, assailant down." Both officers pointed at the mother and demanded she move away from her son. They grabbed her by the arm pulled her away. The squeeze grip fell from Donald's balled up hand, and they turned his bleeding body over on his stomach and handcuffed his hands behind his back. His mother was hysterical as the officers cornered her away from his body and warned her she would be arrested if she did not comply. People from the building circled the incident as additional police cars came rushing to the scene. People were crying and screaming, some saying they saw what happened.

Deon looked on in disbelief while pulling away down the street, looking in the rear-view mirror as the scene got farther away as he headed back to the hospital.

Deon arrived back at the emergency room ramp and got out of the van. Keith met him in the driveway.

Just then, an ambulance drove up the ramp behind the security van. They went into the back of the ambulance and grabbed the bed with the patient. It was Donald. There was no oxygen given to him, and his eyes were closed. A police car parked behind the ambulance. There was a woman in the back seat of the police vehicle screaming and struggling uncontrollably.

"Listen, lady," the officer said to her has he got out of the car. "I need you to settle down. All that screaming isn't going to make things better."

Other police cars followed. Another officer came up to the back seat of the police vehicle.

"Okay, lady, you going to have to quiet all that screaming. You are already being charged with assaulting a police officer. I advise you to calm down."

They brought Donald into the emergency room with the police following close behind, talking to one another. Deon went to the metal emergency room doors and entered the restricted area. A scramble was ensuing as they wheeled

Donald into surgery. Deon went back to the emergency desk. Keith was standing by.

"Do you know if he is going to be okay?" Keith asked.

"I don't know," Deon replied.

Just then, a surgeon spoke to the emergency medical technician, and the technician headed back to his ambulance. Deon stopped him.

"How is he?" Deon asked.

The paramedic looked at Deon and sadly shook his head as he gathered his medical equipment before putting it back into the ambulance. Deon stood in shock.

Later that night, on the way home, Deon listened to talk radio.

"Go ahead, caller, you're on WITE."

"Here we go again," a caller to the program said. "These people don't know how to follow an order. They resist, and this is what happens when you don't follow police commands. Now watch the leftists blame the police officers, and all the rest will hold marches"

"I agree with you," said the radio host. "The report clearly states that he had a weapon in his hand. Now they are trying to say he had a squeeze toy because he had an intellectual disability. Well, guess what. All those people have intellectual disabilities. They are causing the majority of crime, so this is how the police have to respond. One excuse after another you get from the left. This officer had every reason to be concerned about his own safety. The fact of the matter is if he had followed the police orders, been respectful, and pulled up his pants he would probably be alive today."

Deon sat back in his seat, put his head back, and shook his head at the absurdity of it all. It was going to be tough to get any sleep at all tonight.

Chapter 10
DEON GETS ARRESTED

Deon woke up the next morning and glanced at the corner in his room and the piles of clothes spilling over the top of his laundry basket.

I need to go washing, he said to himself as he gathered a huge laundry bag. He filled the bag with his clothes, twisted the top, and threw it over his back. There were a few washers and dryers on the complex, but they were always being used or broken. The Laundromat in Upton up from the hospital was always available.

Deon got into his car and drove to Upton. He could wash his clothes before work, and everything would be cool. He pulled up next to the Laundromat, which was right next to the park where people in the neighborhood would gather. The basketball courts were there too. Dion looked at the guys playing basketball and wondered whether he should go out and play a few games while his clothes were washing.

Deon grabbed his clothes out of the back seat of his car and went to the Laundromat.

"Hi, you need help?"

It was the Laundromat manager. He was a short older man with a bald head and glasses.

"How are you?" he said in his Nigerian accent. "I'm Mr. Thetu."

"Everything is looking good, Mr. Thetu."

"Alriiiight!" the man replied in a humorous manner.

Deon looked and found a double-load washing machine. He loaded his clothes in the machine, added soap, and pushed the cold wash button so the colors wouldn't bleed. He put in his quarters and started the washing machine. He sat down for a moment to make sure it worked properly. Deon scanned the room and saw the usual people in there washing clothes—the old lady, her daughter, another lady with her son, two ladies with tattoos all over, and a fat woman with just one tooth.

Deon decided to go outside and watch them hoop some ball while he got out of the hot Laundromat. He resigned himself to the bench right next to the court and thought to himself, *Man, I wish I had brought my stuff. I would be playing right now.* Some of the guys out there he had seen play before. One of the guys' name was Tony. He ran to the open space at the three- point line and hit the long-range jumper. Deon laughed. It was a perfect shot.

Deon looked around to see who he could see. It was just the regular hood dogs. *What a beautiful warm day it is today*, he thought as he heard the score on the court. "Fourteen to nine," he heard them say.

The game was over as Tony made a shot from forty feet away. Nothing but net. *Daaaaamn*, laughed everybody on the court. The losing team made their sporting expletives.

"Y'all going to run another one?" Deon asked as they came over to the bench to sit down.

"Yeah. Need some water or something," one said.

"You got to play some defense. He was killing you," one of the other players said. "Switch up next time."

"All right," the other guy said. "Let me see you hold that nigga then."

"Don't get mad because you ain't quick enough, I'm just saying," the other player said.

"Yo, man, all he scored was four points. Come on, dude," the guy said.

"That is four too many," the other guy laughed.

"Sup, nigga? How come you ain't running?" one of the players asked Deon.

"I got my clothes over in the Laundromat," Deon answered.

"Oh, all right," he said while nodding okay.

At that moment, driving in from the street and behind the Laundromat, pulled up three detective cars. Police exited the vehicles.

"All right, all of you stay where you are. Don't fucking move!"

Deon's heart raced. What was the hell going on?

Another cop has his gun out and pointed down by his side.

"All right, all of you down, on your knees now!"

Deon's mouth went dry. He moved over and complied, being extremely careful not to make any sudden jerky moves.

The other cop returned from his car. "All you fucking guys are wrong. We know you are selling drugs out here. I swear to God, if I find just one smidge of narc on you, I am going to be cutting it up twelve times and charge all of you."

One by one, the police searched everyone, yelling commands like barking dogs, slapping Deon's foot and demanding he take off his shoes. "I don't have anything, Officer."

"Just shut the fuck up and do what I tell you!" the officer said vehemently.

Deon sat stunned.

"Everybody up!" the officer yelled."

Everyone stood up and turned around hands in the air. Deon felt the officer's hands grabbing and pulling on his clothes.

"Turn your fucking pockets inside out," the officer ordered.

Deon noticed a bicycle parked on the fences some fifty feet away. The officer looked at the bike and pulled something out of the handlebars.

"Whose heroin?" He turned and looked at them with a huge smile on his face.

"That's it," said the other two officers. "Call a wagon. All you fucking guys are going to jail."

Deon's head dropped in exasperation.

"I didn't do anything, sir," Deon explained while one of the police grabbed him by his arms and jammed his hands together behind his back. "I just came out here to watch some basketball. My clothes and stuff are in the Laundromat before I go to work."

"Work? Yeah, right. Well, you won't be going to work now," the officer said sarcastically, again with the look of pleasure and a grin on his face. "You hear this guy talking about he got to go to work?" one officer said as he laughed as well.

Suddenly there was the wagon. Three additional cars pulled up. The officer grabbed Deon by both hands and brought them together forcefully, and he cranked the cuffs on his wrists.

Deon was speechless. How could this happen?' *I didn't do anything wrong*, he said to himself. Undoubtedly, someone would have to listen.

Deon's naivety began to show. He had never been arrested. Never had he been in trouble. He didn't know what was ahead of him.

One by one in a line, the police led all of them in the wagon.

"Whose shit was it?" one guy asked another.

"I don't know. It wasn't mine," one guy answered.

"Was it yours, nigga?" They looked at Deon.

"No, I don't mess with that stuff."

"You don't mess with that stuff? Where the fuck you from, nigga? You probably one the city finest," one of them said.

"Me? Why me?" Deon asked.

"You look like it."

"Come on, dude, he had nothing to do with this. He has been out there hooping with us before," Tony said.

"So, what that mean?" the other said. "You vouch for this nigga?"

"Damn, nigga, y'all always gotta start up some shit. Ain't none of us know we was gonna git rolled up on today," said Tony.

Deon looked at him in and replied, "Not me."

Deon remained quiet as the wagon banged every pothole there was to hit, throwing people toward the top of the van. On the sharp turns, they all slammed against one another and the steel walls of the police van. Another hard hit on a pothole threw people to the ceiling of the van; another sharp right turn, and everyone slammed against one another. Two guys landed on their backs on the metal floor and were clearly hurt.

"Damn," one said. "My neck," he complained.

The police van arrived at the police station, and Deon was offloaded in single file. He almost tripped from the high level of the back of the police van to the ground. Deon's heart raced as they entered.

"Yo, man, don't act too green up in here. Talk to nobody and answer no questions," one of the guys told Deon.

Deon looked ahead and was led into an area the size of a basketball gym. It was sectioned off for different areas. To the right of Deon were numerous large holding cells. Each had fifty people or more in them. Other areas had suspects with their arms behind their backs sitting at tables talking to police. There were a male nurse and his assistant at one station, and he was barking out orders to an inmate to follow his instructions. Deon also noted that nearly everyone was like himself, and some were from south of the border. There were some others arrested, and you could count them on one hand.

Deon walked down a hallway in line and entered the holding cell. Deon refused to look at anybody and just stared straight ahead, looking at the tile on the floor at a distance. This one inmate was philosophizing all over the cell, and everyone was listening to his renditions. First, he preached about Jesus, then he made statements about righteousness and what the system was doing to people. He sounded like someone who had been in and out of jail numerous times.

Suddenly, police officers came to the cell and ordered everyone out. Deon was marched across the yard and into what looked like a dormitory. With the others, he walked up a small flight of steps and into a lobby with two doors open in the hallway. Deon kept his head down and breathed in the little air he had around himself. He looked around and saw that all inmates were chained together and lined up against the wall.

"Okay, when I tell you, you are going to drop your pants to the floor," the corrections officer ordered. All the inmates dropped their pants. The corrections officers walked between the inmates, jamming their nightsticks between the legs of those who they thought were hiding something.

"Okay, now you are going to drop your shorts. Look at the damn wall. Don't turn your ass around," the officers yelled. "Now grab your butt cheeks and flap them back and forth. Open your ass wide!"

Deon could not believe this.

"Uh oh, looks like we got some heroine in little bags over here," said one of the corrections officers.

"Oh yeah," said the sergeant. "Pull him out the line." To the rest of the inmates, he said, "Pick up your clothes and single file to the showers."

All the inmates were put into the showers, chained to one another.

"Put some soap in your nasty ass," said the sergeant as each inmate pushed the soap dispenser on the wall in front of him. After the shower, the inmates were marched single file and handed underwear, a pair of socks, elastic tennis shoes, and an orange jumpsuit. All the men stood chained together two feet apart from one another putting on their clothes.

This is so demeaning, Deon said to himself.

"All right, you guys, you are in block A," the corrections officer said as they walked into the block.

There were about twenty metal beds with no mattresses on them, five on each wall. In the middle were about another five. In a small space area at the front was a TV attached to the ceiling, with the showers and bathroom right behind it. Bars were up at the windows, and the floor was concrete.

"All right. To the right of you is the mattress for your bed," a corrections officer pointed out.

Deon looked at the mattresses. They were covered with a material to withstand stains. Deon picked the first one he came to and held it in his hand.

"Okay, the other inmates here will assign you from here," said the officer.

One of the inmates seemed to speak for everyone else in the room. "All right listen up. This is our house. Right now, this is where we at. No nasty-type shit is going up in here."

He was a tall dude and kind of big. There was a big ten-point star as on his right bicep. He looked like a defensive lineman off some football team. It was easy to see why he would be the one who was running the block.

"We shower at least every two days," he continued. "If you got a problem with that, you need to solve it. We ain't having no stinking mothers in here. In the bathroom, do not spit in the sink. We must wash our face in that sink. If you get some money from the commissary, you need to get you some shower shoes. All nations on the left, all brothers on the right, all y'all unattached, just find a spot."

Deon knew not where to go. He knew some brothers he had met in the street but had no allegiance. Deon walked toward the back of the block and found a bunk on the brothers' side. "Is this spot here, all right?" Deon said in a hard kind of way.

"Yeah, go ahead," one of the inmates said. Deon looked at him and saw the ten-point star on his arm.

Deon laid his mattress down on his bunk. There was a dresser drawer underneath the bed. *I guess that is where you keep all your toothbrush and all that*, he thought. It could hold a couple of pairs of shoes and snacks if you had it.

"Us, my brother," a dude said as he set down his mattress on his bed next to Deion. "Well, here we is."

"Yeah, we here," Deon replied. "Now what?"

"Wait on the court for a bail hearing. I ain't looking forward to this shit. I just want to get the hell out of here," he said.

Deon was very unsure about everyone he met. In his mind, there might be an incident where he would have to fight. *You got to show you can handle yourself,* he thought. So, Deon continued to have this hard look. He could change characters like a chameleon.

"All right, brothers, over here," yelled one of the inmates. About ten brothers got up and went to the corner of the room. They all dropped their head in prayer as they joined hands in the ritual. Then they broke, and the guy next to Deon came back to his bunk.

"I see you're part of the organization."

He just looked a Deon and started grinning.

"Oh yeah, I should mind my own damn business then, right?" Deon quipped. They both laughed.

"Yeah, you right about that one—around here anyway," the inmate said. "I usually don't ask what a nigga in here for, but I done found that the only niggas who don't want to tell nobody if they some kind of child molester or rapist or something."

"That shore the hell ain't me," said Deon.

"So, what you in here for? Oh, wait just a moment. Ain't none of my mother's business, right?"

They both cracked up laughing.

"Yo, man, I'm Deon."

"Juju, brother," he said as he took Deon's hand to shake it.

"Much respect," they both said.

Deon watched the TV while Juju appeared to be sleeping. The other guy on the left of Deon was reading a book with his drawers on and his legs flexed while he lay on his back. *Little bit too comfortable*, Deon thought.

The guy noticed Deon and said, "Hey, man, I'm Henry. If we gonna be bunked up here next to each other together, we should introduce ourselves."

"Deon."

"All right. Nice to meet you. What you in here for?"

"I don't know yet," said Deon.

"What the hell you mean you don't know yet?"

"I got to see on my bail hearing to see what the hell is going on."

"Were you dealing?" asked Henry.

Deon just looked at him and did not say a word.

"Dude, I ain't your attorney," said Henry. "They gonna try to get you to plead guilty, but hey, that is a Class X felony. You don't want no shit like that on your record. Trust a nigga like me on that."

"What you here for then?" asked Deon.

"I got caught with thirty-five thousand dollars' worth of burglary tools," Henry told him.

"Damn," said Deon. "Is it against the laws to have burglary tools?"

"Yeah, when you get caught. But I hadn't stolen nothing yet."

"How long have you been here?"

"Thirty-three days," Henry replied. "I come up for court next week sometime. They probably give me time served, since they got to me before I could do shit."

Deon had never met a for-real burglar. *Who would have thought? Burglary tools?* Deon laid back on his bunk.

"You don't say no prayer for you sleep?" Henry asked.

"I do," said Deon.

"That's good. Prayers are suitable to send forth from this place."

Deon woke to the sound of men standing in line at the bathroom. It must have been early in the morning, because the sun was not yet out.

"Come on, nigga," Juju said to Deon.

"What's up?"

"We got to go to court," Juju explained.

Deon got up and stood in line. As one inmate after another finished in the bathroom and trickled out, Deon finally has his turn. Some inmates were in there taking a movement out in the open, as there were no walls or stalls.

Deon contorted his tight face, always looking ahead and speaking to nobody. With no toothbrush or paste yet, Deon filled his mouth with water and spat it in the toilet, remembering the house rule not to spit in the sink.

All inmates gathered at the big metal door and were marched downstairs to the cafeteria for breakfast.

"Yo, I'm cutting in front of you, right?" said an inmate.

Deon looked him in the eye with contempt. *You can't show yourself to be no punk*, he told himself. Deon knew this guy was in one of the organizations. *What should I do?* he thought. *If I let him cut in front of me, then I am labeled as a punk up in here.* Deon looked at the guy and didn't say a word.

"So, what's up?" the guy said.

"Whatever," Deon replied, staring him down like a Doberman.

"Naw, it ain't no whatever," he said to Deon as he shoved his way in front.

Another member of the organization turned and looked at Deon, as if to say, *yeah what the hell you gonna do?* Deon continued with his stare and then looked straight ahead.

"All right, move the line," the corrections officer said as Deon walked toward the counter where the food was being served. Everyone was given a beige plastic tray like the kind in a hospital. Deon sat down and tried not to look at anyone.

"What up, nigga! You look like you nervous or somethin'" said this other inmate across the table.

"I ain't nervous."

The inmate looked at Deon and laughed.

Another came up to Deon holding his tray. "Yo, nigga, this is my spot."

"What?" Deon said as he turned around. The guy looked as if he was expecting Deon to get up and leave the table.

Deon looked at him and replied, "Look, I ain't trying to start up nothing, right? I am trying to sit here and eat this food."

"Yo, man, you can't be dissing Brothers up in here," said the guy across the table.

"I ain't disrespecting nobody," Deon answered. He spread his hands beside his tray to indicate he had no intention of moving.

The guy sat down by Deon. "Yo, nigga, you are taking a big chance up in here, man. I'm letting you know that you ain't going to have the officers to protect you all the time."

Deon looked up but not to look at anyone, just stared straight ahead. He opened the tray, and there was his breakfast: Sugar Pops puffed cereal—about a handful, that was it; a hard-boiled egg; dry toast; and warm milk. Deon opened the milk and poured it over the handful of Sugar Pops. He took his spoon and tried to mix things together. Deon thought about how awful this was. He tried eating his toast, but it was half-toasted and soggy, and Deon was not sure from what. He left it. The hard-boiled egg he cracked and peeled. It smelled like the egg was boiled weeks ago.

"Looks like this be the first time you ever been locked up," an inmate across the table said.

Deon didn't reply. He just looked up from his tray and nodded his head slightly up and down,

to indicate *maybe* and *why you give a damn*.

Breakfast remained quiet for Deon, as he said nothing to anyone while others kept talking.

"Three minutes," the corrections officer said.

The inmates were lined back up and taken back to the dormitory room. Deon sat on his bed next to Juju.

"I heard you had a little issue earlier," Juju said.

"I ain't trying to start no mess, man," Deon said as he looked at him with exasperation, "but I can't just let someone bogart me in here."

"Hey, man, you may have done the right thing, but there's probably some repercussions."

Deon noticed others in the room looking at him and nodding their heads up and down.

I know how to fight, Deon said to himself. *I will be damned if any one of these guys has their way with me without a fight*, he thought to himself.

Suddenly, a corrections officer came to the open door. He called out inmate names: Davis, Johnson, Williams, and White.

Deon looked up. "What's this?" he said to Juju.

"You got to go to court," he responded.

"Oh, shit," Deon said.

Deon walked up and stood in line. He was marched with the others to a waiting room area and handcuffed again, then put in a waiting cell.

Deon sat next to a man he had not met before—an older man who looked to be in his fifties.

"How you doing, sir?" Deon said to him,

"How you doing," the man replied.

"I'm Deon."

"Curtis," the man replied. They were quiet for a moment.

"What you in here for, young brother?"

"I was swooped up in a raid or something like that," Deon replied. "I ain't do nothing."

"Let's see if they believe that," he replied.

"How about you?"

"Armed violence. I shot at my wife."

"Damn" Deon said to himself.

Soon, another jail guard walked up with a large ring of keys. He opened the cell and said, "Okay, single file, let's go."

Deon followed the line of inmates to a gray bus sitting out in the parking lot. The bus had fences up to the windows. Deon walked on, took his seat toward the back of the bus, sat down, and stared forward as other inmates piled onto the bus.

A guy sat across from Deon who he had noticed before.

"What ups, nigga?" the guy said to Deon. "We on the grey goose."

"Where we going?" Deon asked.

"Dearborn," he said. "The court's downtown."

The bus left the facility and took the main streets to the downtown area. The L train roared overhead while the bus was at a stoplight. Deon noticed the businesses looking more profitable and pleasant as they moved closer to downtown. Swank condominiums rose from the street and restaurants that one day, he hoped to be able to afford.

The bus went over the bridge across the river to the downtown area. After several lefts and rights, the bus came to the Dearborn center. It was of the tallest buildings in the city. The district courts were there along with lawyers' offices. The bus rolled into the covered garage area and came to a slow stop.

Deon was marched single file down the white tile hallways, through double steel doors, and finally to a room behind glass.

There was a white clock on the wall that Deon could pass the time by looking at. An hour went by, and Deon's feet and legs were starting to cramp up. He kicked his legs a bit to get the circulation of blood back into them.

After thirty more minutes, the line had not moved at all. One hour later, Deon and everyone else was getting restless. Everyone in line was trying to move his legs a bit, some squatting down and standing up.

"Can't, we sit down somewhere?" asked one of the inmates.

"Hell no, nigger. Ain't nobody gives a damn about you sitting down," replied one of the corrections officers.

"Yo, man, you unprofessional," the inmate replied, "talking to me all crazy and shit."

"Hey, you want to shut the fuck up?" the guard said as he put his hand on his club. "You got something to say?"

"Naw, man," the inmate said. "You dogging us though, man. We can't sit nowhere."

The guard looked at him and walked away. After one hour and fifteen minutes of standing, the line finally start to move a bit forward.

After one hour and thirty-five minutes, Deon was second from the front. Two inmates got up and walked out in single file with an officer escort. Deon took the farthest empty seat. Soon a short man with glasses came and sat down on the other side of the glass partition.

"All right. What is your name?"

"Deon White."

"Okay, right here," he said. "Drug conspiracy and gang involvement?"

"I have no idea what they are talking about," Deon said as he shook his head no.

"I'm Mr. Walsh, public defender. Tell me what occurred."

"I was sitting watching the guys play on the court while my clothes were being washed in the washateria," Deon explained, "and then the police came and lined us all up. Some guy had some drugs on him, and suddenly, we all were arrested."

"Gang affiliation?" Mr. Walsh asked.

"No, I ain't in no gang."

The public defended nodded his head as if to say, *yeah, I have heard that nonsense before.*

"Okay, so you are not in a gang, but you are arrested with all these gang members?"

"I don't have anything to do with that."

"Yeah, okay," he said. "So how long have you been in the gang and selling drugs?"

Deon looked stunned. "I am telling you, I am not in the organizations, and I wasn't selling any drugs."

The public defender spoke up. "This judge, he does not play games with you people. I advise you to go in and plead guilty and admit to the validity of the arrest, and since they didn't find any drugs on you personally, they may give you a time served plus two years."

"Two years!" Deon cried out. "Look, I have nothing to do with this. I have a job. I can't get a Class X felony, especially since I never did do anything."

"Listen if you want me to help you, and I am trying to help you," said the public defender. "If you don't need my help that is fine."

Deon watched the man stand up and walk out. Deon's mouth was open in astonishment.

"All right, that's it," said the corrections officer. "Let's go."

Deon walked out under escort to a waiting cell. There he saw Curtis again.

"How you do young man," Curtis said solemnly.

"What's wrong?"

"A hundred-thousand-dollar bond."

Deon stared at him. He remained silent, and so did Deon.

"Deon White!" an officer called.

Deon stood up. "Yes, sir."

Deon walked toward the courtroom. To the right of him was the district attorney, and to the left of him was the public defender. The judge sat at the large bench and witness stand. Behind him was the US flag, and on the other side, the state flag. The judge was fat and had balding white hair on the sides. He looked to be in his seventies. He regarded Deon with disdain.

"All right, how do you plead?" "Innocent," Don replied.

"Innocent," the judge chuckled.

The public defender spoke up. "I tried to council this inmate, Your Honor. He insists on this plea," he said, shaking his head.

"Do you understand what you are doing?" the judge asked Deon.

Deon was perplexed. "I believe I do, Your Honor," Deon replied.

"Gang affiliation, drug conspiracy to deliver, and I am supposed to believe you are innocent?"

"Yes, Your Honor, sir," Deon nodded.

The public defender smirked and laughed.

"Bail set at fifty thousand dollars."

Deon breathed heavily. Where was he going to get $50,000? He hadn't even gotten a chance to call his job to let them know what happened. He hadn't even been given the right to make one phone call. He thought, *I have to call my dad or someone. I gotta get out of here.*

The ride back on the grey goose was quiet. After the bond hearing, everyone was faced with what it would take to get out of jail and what they were charged with.

"Did you get an attorney?"

Deon turned to Curtis, who was speaking to him.

"No," Deon replied. "They had me talk to a public defender, and he tried to get me to take a plea."

"Yeah, that's what they do," said Curtis. "They told you the courts were going to throw the book at you if you don't, right?"

"Yeah," replied Deon.

"You gonna need a lawyer."

"I ain't got no lawyer money," Deon told him.

"What kind of case you got?"

"Conspiracy to sell drugs and gang affiliation."

"What kind of drugs, cocaine?" Curtis asked.

"I guess I heard something about heroin," said Deon.

"Class X felony. You don't want that."

Deon stared out the window. He never knew he could get into so much trouble.

Deon was marched back in single file to another holding area. After returning to jail, they all sat on a concrete floor in a large room that looked to be an old courtyard fenced in. Another officer came in with brown paper bags.

"Lunch is served, fools," he said as he handed the box of food to the other guard. The guard passed the bags out. One by one, inmates were taken out of their cuffs and made to sit back on the floor.

"In your bag, you will find a fried baloney sandwich on toast, warm milk, and a tootsie roll pop with the stem cut off," said the officer.

I guess they thought the stem could be used as a weapon, Deon thought.

Deon returned to the same room and sat on his bed. Later, Juju and the other inmates returned from where they were.

"What was your bail?" Juju asked.

"Fifty thousand," Deon replied.

"Yeah, that is pretty much the standard. You are lucky it is only fifty thousand. You only have to come up with ten percent to get out."

Deon looked around the room. "Yeah, well, I need to make a phone call to let people know I am in here."

"You will get that chance," Juju said.

Deon again looked away in exasperation.

"Can you come up with five grand?" asked Juju.

"Hell, naw," Deon replied

"Well, if you can't raise that, then after like a week, they might drop it if you don't have no priors."

"Drop it? What you mean?"

"They will lower it," Juju explained. "Court supervision until your court date. They gotta make room for other niggas."

Deon certainly hoped so.

⚜

Eventually, the corrections officer came to line everyone up for recreation time. They all were marched to an exercise room where there was a bench press, a boxing ring, and assorted sit-up benches. A short guy with twenty-inch arms protruding out the sleeves of his jumpsuit took the top part of the jumpsuit off and lay on the bench. The weight bar had some 250 pounds on it. He lifted the weight for five or six repetitions and put it down.

He looked at Deon and said, "Come on, get some of these."

Deon didn't want to, but he felt like he had to follow this guy's invitation.

"Want me to take some of this off?" the guy said.

"No, I'm good," Deon replied.

The muscular guy gave Deon a lift off the bench rack. Deon repped it six times and locked it out. He set the weight down.

"All right, my man," the muscular inmate said. "I could tell you do some kind working out, know what I'm saying?"

"A little bit," Deon answered.

"Hell naw, nigga strong as fuck," the inmate said. He held his hand out to shake. "I'm Ed."

"Deon."

"I'm going to break it down to do some more reps," Ed suggested.

"All right. I will hit another set."

Deon reps 225 pounds eight times—just as many but not more than Ed. He didn't want to show him up. Other inmates looked on wide-eyed and surprised. No one could have guessed Deon was that strong. Deon went back and sat down with the other inmates.

Suddenly, it seemed Deon had gained his props from the other inmates in the room. When they returned to the block, Deon was offered to hang out with the so-called top brass of the room. The short, strong man asked Deon if he wanted some Kool-Aid to go into a cup of water; another asked if Deon wanted some cookies. Deon was wary of saying yes and accepting something from anyone, because it could be a trick of some sort, but he also didn't want to seem unfriendly and rude for not receiving something, Deon thought. "Thanks. I will have one of those cookies."

Another brother from one of the gang organizations came by Deon's bunk and said, "Hey brother, I want you to come to join us next time we have a meeting."

Deon looked at him and nodded. "Okay," Deon replied cautiously.

Juju later told Deon, "Hey, they want you in the Brothers nation."

Oh, shit, Deon thought. *I may be in some real kind of trouble now.* They already had Deon as conspiring and having gang involvement. The last thing he needed was to have to join a gang up in the jail.

"Deon White!" a voice called from the cell dorm door. The officer stood there looking sternly at Deon. Deon got up and walked to the door.

"Yes, sir."

"You must see the chaplain."

Deon walked into an empty room that had a desk with nothing on it at all. Only a picture of Jesus graced the wall and nothing else. Then the chaplain came in and sat down at the desk.

"Okay," he said. "Let's see here. You are Mr. White."

"Yes, sir," Deon replied.

The chaplain looked at Deon and shook his head. "I understand you are here for drug conspiracy and gang affiliation?"

"Yes, sir, but it's not me. I didn't do anything."

The chaplain shook his head in a nod. "Yeah, I get that a lot from all you guys."

"I'm telling you the truth."

"Okay, well, I have no reason to personally not believe you, but you do understand that every inmate I see says his is innocent right?

"Yes, sir, I know that," Deon replied.

"If you are innocent, why were you hanging out with these guys?"

"I work a decent job. I am from North City. I was attending college, but circumstances with my family required me to drop out and work for a while."

"Where do you work?" the chaplain asked.

"I am a security guard at the Masonic Hospital."

"Well, this is going to go very well with your bosses, I'm sure," the chaplain quipped.

"It's the neighborhood park," Deon replied. "You can't go to the park?"

"Not in that area," the chaplain said. "You have to know where you should and should not be."

"But it's the neighborhood park, I put my clothes in the washateria and came outside for a minute while my clothes were washing. Everybody hangs out. What is the harm in that?"

"You are an intelligent young man. It is a high crime area. Some things you should or should not do."

"No wonder when a brother makes it out of the neighborhood, he doesn't come back," Deon added.

"Some consider that a wise decision," said the chaplain.

"But how is the hood ever going to get any better if people are afraid to come back and contribute? This is crazy."

The chaplain sat and just looked at Deon. "You are developing hate and rage in your heart. Jesus taught love not hate. Look at your circumstances and determine what it is that you should have done differently."

Deon sat, looking exhausted and confused.

"Have you contacted your job?" asked the chaplain.

"No, sir."

"Just one call," the chaplain said. "The rest will have to be at the payphone."

Deon thought about who he should call first: his job or his family. At this point, Deon felt it was better to try to save his job.

"I'd better calls my captain at work," Deon replied. He picked up the phone and dialed the numbers to the hospital.

"Hospital security," said the captain as he answered the phone.

"Captain Suh, this is Deon."

"Hey Deon, what's going on"?

"I have somehow gotten into trouble. I had nothing to do with it."

"I have heard what happened already. Are you okay?"

"I'm okay. I just need to get out of here."

"What are you charged with?" the captain asked.

"Conspiracy to distribute and gang affiliation."

"Yeah, that is what happens when you get caught up in a sweep," the captain said.

"What about my job?" Deon asked.

"Well, I will have to pass this by the department. Everyone knows you are a hard worker.

You've never had a problem here. Can't make any promises. I will see what I can do. How long do you think you will be?"

"They really have a high bond for me. I can't raise that kind of money."

"That's why you need a bail bondsman."

"Yes, sir. Well, now I know."

"Get back with me when you get out of there. In the meantime, I need to shuffle the schedule to cover you."

"Yes, sir," Deon replied. He hung up the phone.

"Does that do it for you?" asked the chaplain.

"One more," Deon replied. *I got to call Greg*, he thought

Deon called Greg, but the call went straight to voicemail.

"Greg, this is Deon. I'm locked up down on Sacramento Street. I have to make bail. Holler at me when you can."

Deon hung the phone up.

The chaplain nodded his head. "Go on back. If you have no priors, they take that into consideration and lower your bail."

"How long would that be?" Dion asked.

A couple of days," the chaplain answered. "Look, if you are telling me the truth, I will see what I can do. No promises though. Keep your nose clean around here." Deon went back to his bunk and thought about what the Chaplain said, and he thought about that Malcolm X speech Reggie gave him. "When the police put their Billy clubs on your head, to keep you from fighting back, he gets these religious uncle toms who tell us to suffer peacefully.

Blood running down you jaw, because someone has taught you to suffer peacefully, don't stop suffering, just suffer peacefully, let your blood flow in the streets."

The guy who was busted for burglary tools was sitting up reading a book.

"What did they tell you?" he asked.

"I don't know. Looks like I am going to be here for a while."

Deon laid back on his bunk and looked across the room to the barred windows and noticed that darkness had fallen over the city. *It's a metaphor of some sort*, thought Deon, *some allegory with contains some kind of truth.*

Juju walked up to Deon with another inmate. They were looking around at the door, making sure no one was looking.

"Come over here," they said. They went to a corner of the room with about eight other inmates. "You taking prayer with us."

An inmate named Ben Ami put out his hand, and Ed the strong man came up. "We know what you here for. Just want you to know you with us. Don't want to cause you no problems getting out of here, right?"

"Yeah," replied Deon.

"Right hands here," Ben Ami said.

Everyone put out his hand and joined in. The short muscular inmate looked at Deon and put his hand on his shoulder. "Bow heads," he said. "In the word of our father the almighty father of the world and all that is Zion. In the words of the Hebrew Israelites: *Yahawashi Barakathah Yahawah Barakathah*."

Another member said, "Now repeat after me with the translation: Bless you, Yahawah. Bless you, Yahawashi."

Ben Ami chanted, "Kal Il Mawatha Gadal Wa Mashapatyam Wa Haragyam Wa Inashyam Wa Rayam Shalach."

Everyone else responded, "Send evil, and punishments, and killings, and judgment, and great death upon all Edomites, and nations, and our enemies."

Ben Ami continued, "Yahawah coming in the name of Yahawashi. Send upon to me the spirit of Yahawashi of the word of truth in the holy books and more faith to me, and more strength to me, and more love to me, and more healing to me, and more forgiveness to me, and deliver me from all evil, please, please, please. Yahawah coming in the name of Yahawashi, thank you, amen."

Ben Ami took the group through more prayers as Deon followed their rituals. Members all shook Deon hand and patted Deon on the back. The others guarding the door looked to say it was okay.

"Congratulations, brother," they all said to him.

Deon didn't know what had just happened. *Damn did I just join a gang?* he thought. *This is not good.*

Juju came back and sat across from Deon on his bed. "Don't worry about it, brother," he said. "You all good. They don't ask you to kill nobody. It ain't about that. It's about our place in this life and our children's. When you get back out there, do all you can for the Brothers, that's all that is required."

Deon took a deep breath and nodded in approval. He had to survive in this environment in some way. He looked at the TV in the corner of the ceiling. It was playing the news, and everyone has gathered around to watch it.

There was a breaking news flash. "An unarmed teen shot by police on the south side today. We will have that story when we come back."

Juju looked over at the TV. "Damn," he said.

Others in the room started to gather around the TV. The news program returned. "Today a reported assailant being apprehended by police for theft was shot on 113th Street. Witnesses say the man was unarmed and had given himself up to for the police when he was shot multiple times. John Roberts has the story."

The reporter said, "A nineteen-year-old, Eric Adams, was walking down this street when witnesses said that police apprehended the suspect for a reported theft at a convenience store. The suspect was said to be wearing a headset at the time and ignored warnings by police to stop. The police reportedly shot the suspect when he stepped toward the police aggressively after being told to stop. However, witnesses have another story. Sir, can you tell me what happened?"

A man in his early twenties with cornrows in his hair spoke to the reporter.

"Yo, man, dude had his hands in the air. He didn't even know why they were stopping him, so he put his hands up because they surprised him. It all happened so fast. He was looking around, and he threw his hands up when they told him to stop and lay down, you know what I'm saying? They didn't even give him no chance to get down. He was taking his headphones off, and they shot him."

Deon listened closely as the chief of police made a statement.

"We have collected the evidence in this matter, but at this time we don't see any issue with the response of the police. They reacted adequately in this situation. However, this investigation is ongoing concerning the criminal activity of the suspect."

Wow, Deon said to himself.

Two weeks went by. Deon tried not to worry about how long he was going to be locked up.

"Deon White!" called the corrections officer. "Bring your mattress."

Deon looked at the other inmates. They nodded in approval.

Deon looked back at Juju. "Hey, Ju, I got all y'all phone numbers. I am going to holler at you. When I get some money, I try to send something on your books."

"Peace be with you, brother," they all said as Deon gathered his mattress and went with the officer.

The chaplain looked at Deon and nodded.

Deon looked back. "Where am I going?"

"They lowered your bail to five thousand dollars. We are moving you to another room until you bond out."

"I don't have five hundred dollars," Deon replied.

"Yeah, well, someone posted your bail."

"How did all this come about?"

"Don't worry about it. Just make sure you don't end up in this place for good," the chaplain said.

Deon quieted himself. They walked to another dorm room with only two beds in it—one on one side of the room and one on the other. Deon put his belongings down and sat on the makeshift bed. He lay down and tried to sleep a bit.

The corrections officer came back to the room. "Come on, let's go. You getting processed out."

Deon followed the guard to the shower area, where again he was stripped and searched. He was made to take a shower and was given his clothes back. Deon put on his clothes and waited.

"Come on," the officer said as they left the room. They came to a desk, and the police officer pulled out a manila envelope.

"Here are three bus tokens so you can get where you are going."

Deon took the bus tokens.

"This is the bag with your possessions, your wallet and keys. Make sure it is there."

Deon looked in his wallet.

"I want you to know there was a hole in this plastic, and I don't know how it got there," said the officer.

Deon looked for his money. He knew he'd had forty dollars or so in his wallet. It was all gone except for two single dollars. "I had forty dollars here," Deon said.

"It doesn't show that here. It says you came in with two dollars and thirty cents. So I don't know what happened to the thirty cents. There was a hole in the bag."

Deon rubbed his forehead in disbelief. *My cash is gone*, he said to himself. *Who would think that the police would be thieves?*

The officer looked at Deon and grinned, giving Deon a look as to say, "What the hell you gonna do?"

Deon shook his head as he was escorted to the release area. Finally, Deon walked out of the corrections facility.

Deon waited for the bus to take him back to his side of town. He watched cars pass him by and started to wonder what had happened to his car. Other people and released inmates stood silently waiting for the bus. The bus soon arrived, and Deon sat in the back. The bus filled with all kinds of people. Most riders seemed like so many stray dogs.

Deon arrived on his street, and he was thankful that it wasn't too late. He got off the bus and walked toward the Laundromat. His car was gone, and Deon bent over in exasperation. "Where is the hell my car?"

Deon went into the laundry and saw the manager, Mr. Thetu.

"Hey, Mr. Thetu," he said. "I'm sorry, but a few weeks ago I came in to wash my clothes and ended up getting arrested on the court next door."

"Yes, I saw it. Damn shame."

"Are my clothes still here?" Deon asked.

"Yeah, they're here," said Mr. Thetu. "I have them in this Hefty bag."

"Thank you, Mr. Thetu. But could you hold them here a little while longer, because I can't find my car. Can I use your cell?"

Deon called 911. "Yes, my car was stolen. My name is Deon White. I'm at 1141 South Cotton Street."

Deon walked to the place where his car used to be. One police car rolled past, looked Deon up and down, slowed down, and kept moving. Another police car later, going the other direction, slowed down and looking at Deon. The officer had a sarcastic smile on his face as the police car pulled up right next to the curb. Deon backed up to the sidewalk.

The officer got out his car with his hand on his holster. "Is there a problem?" the officer said as he robustly walked toward Deon.

"My car was here. Someone stole it," Deon said.

The other officer got out of his side of the vehicle and walked up to the right of Deon. Deon felt closed in and frightened.

"You have any identification?"

"It's in my wallet, sir," said Deon.

"Do you have anything illegal on you?"

"No, sir." Deon handed the officer his license.

"Where are you coming from?"

"I just got off the bus," Deon told him.

"What is that?"

"It's my school ID."

"School, huh," the officer said with a smirk. "Is that where they give you your liberal education?"

Deon knew right away it may have been a bad idea to call the police. Obviously, the officer was one who listened to those AM radio programs. But he had to find his car.

The other officer went to his car computer.

"Do you have any warrants?" he asked.

"No, sir," Deon replied.

"Are you in connection with those people over there?" the officer asked.

Deon turned and looked, and he noticed other people being questioned against the wall some fifty yards away.

"No, sir."

The other officer came back from his onboard computer. "Yeah, this guy just got out of jail," he said.

Deon remained quiet and felt his eyes start to water.

"Was it your car," the officer asked, "or did you steal it for distributing?"

"No, I just bought the car. I'm trying to find out if it was stolen."

"The car was impounded," the officer said. "Good luck trying to get it back," he added with a smirk. Both officers got back into their car and drove off. Deon felt his blood pressure boiling.

Deon went back to the Laundromat. "Mr. Thetu, may I use your phone one more time?"

"No problem," he answered.

"Hello? Greg, this is Deon."

"Deon what's up man!" said Greg. "I got your message. We had to wait to see if they would lower your bail, and when they did, we all pitched in and paid your bond."

"Oh my God. Thank all you guys."

"No problem. Deon, just get this straightened out. You were gone almost a month."

"Right now," Deon said, "I am trying to find my car. It was impounded."

"Well, call me back when you get the chance," said Greg. "We all want to see you."

Deon boarded the bus to take him to the police pound to pick up his car. The police pound was an underground facility downtown, with overpasses all above it. The office literally was a double-wide trailer that sat in front of a large fenced-in area.

Deon walked in and noticed the paneling inside and a long wooden counter. Behind the counter were two old police officers, one short and white-haired, the other a fat woman. Deon looked around to see where he needed to stand to be next in line. Deon pulled the number 20 on the number dispenser and waited about thirty minutes before they called his number.

"Number 20," called the lady behind the counter.

Deon walked up. "My car was brought here," he said.

She looked at Deon and nodded. "Your driver's license," she said, putting out her hand.

Deon gave her the driver's license. She entered the information in the computer.

"Yes, the car is here on the lot, but you can't get it."

"Why?" Deon asked, getting upset.

"Was your vehicle involved in a drug arrest?"

Deon looked stunned.

"Hello? Was it?" she said.

"I thought they impounded your vehicle if you are riding in it with open liquor or drugs and you're arrested. I didn't have any drugs on nothing on me, and my car was parked," he said.

"Yeah, well, if they believe the car was used in transporting illegal substances, they can impound it," said the officer. They determine the amount of drugs involved then make a determination for release. "How long does that take?" Deon asked. "It can take a few days to a few weeks; you would have to call us to see if the city released your car".

Deon left the facility in a daze. Again, he felt his pressure boiling over. How was he ever going to get to work? Deon could not believe any of this and only knew that as time went on, it would get worse. He thought about his arrest being degraded by police for something he didn't do and how that eroded in his utopic belief in America.

Deon sat in the office of his captain the next day, concerned about the status of his job and pondering how he was going to get home after work.

Captain Suh walked in. "How are you doing, Deon?" he asked.

"It's been some trying times," Deon answered.

"Well, you currently have your job, so stay optimistic," replied Captain Suh.

"I was wondering if I could switch my shift to an overnight," Deon asked.

"I am sure the other officers would not have a problem with that," Captain Suh responded, nodding his head in agreement.

"Thank you," Deon said with a smile on his face.

"Talk to any of the overnights and see if they will switch with you, and I will approve it," the captain said.

Deon blew another sigh of relief. He went to his post. He was determined to do the best job. It definitely was a necessity now.

A pregnant woman arrived at the emergency room; Deon rushed to get a chair. He helped with wheeling the lady to the emergency room doors while her husband went to park the car.

After he delivered the woman to the emergency room area, Deon walked back out to his post. The police arrived with what looked like a half-drunk man, his mouth pouring with blood.

The man cried, "I can't believe y'all hit me in my mouth like this. I ain't do nothing. I want someone to take a picture of my mouth. This man hit me in my mouth. You done knocked mine teeth out! I want a picture. Don't do nothing till someone takes a picture of my mouth!" he screamed.

"Listen—just shut up and sit there," the officer said to him as blood poured from the man's mouth.

A nurse came to his assistance. The man was still crying. "I ain't did nothing for this here. I ain't didn't do nothing for this here," he repeated.

The nurse intervened. "Sir, we cannot help you unless you quiet down."

"I want a picture of my mouth!" he cried.

"You are not going to get a picture of your mouth, you understand?" said the officer.

"Sir, I am sorry, but I can't help you until you are settled down," the nurse said forcefully.

"This police hit me in the mouth. I want a picture!"

"Is he drunk?" she asked the officer.

"Yeah, he's a damn alcoholic, doesn't know how to follow instructions. Resisting arrest and battery," he said.

"I didn't do nothin' to cause you to bust my mouth up!" the man yelled.

"Hey, just sit back and shut up!" the officer ordered.

"Should he be restrained?" the nurse asked

"If you need to control him, we can have him controlled," the officer said.

As Deon looked on, the police officer yelled, "Listen—if you don't sit down and shut up, they are going to put your ass in a straitjacket, you hear me?"

Deon grabbed his radio just in case he had to make a call.

"Naw. I just want someone to take a picture of my mouth. I didn't do nothin' to deserve this here."

"Maybe had you kept your damn mouth shut in the first place, you wouldn't be here now," the officer said full of sarcasm.

"Please, just help me. I'm bleeding all over."

Deon went back out into the emergency room. He stepped out into the driveway area to get some fresh air.

Deon continued at his post all night, fighting sleep with many cups of coffee. The news blared on the TV set with the story of the young kid from Upton shot and killed by police, who supposedly had his hands up. Each news report showed the chief of police doing a press conference, saying the officer felt his life was in danger as the suspect took three steps forward toward him when he was told to stop. The chief of police defended the actions of the officers. Behind him were two officers who looked stern in their position backing the police chief.

"It is reported that there is cell phone video of the incident," a reporter said. "However, that is being examined for authenticity. After that is resolved, we will show the footage as soon as it is available."

Deon watched and continued to do his security rounds in the hospital.

When morning came, Deon, eyes heavy, took the bus, arrived home, and threw his keys on the table. Deon looked at the calendar. It was August 5. He realized the rent was due on the first. However, since being locked up for nearly three weeks, he had missed the payment.

Deon looked at the clock on the wall. It was nine o'clock, and that's when the office opened. He ran right over. A young lady he had not seen before was there.

"Hi, can I help you?" she said.

"Yeah, um, I need to talk to someone about my rent."

"Give me a minute," the renting agent said. She went and got the manager, a young guy who Deon again had not seen before.

"Yes, come on in," the guy said.

"What happened to all the others who were here when I first moved in?" Deon said.

"Oh, they come and go," he replied.

"I am late on this rent this month," said Deon.

"Okay, well, you know there is a late fee of two hundred dollars.

Deon exhaled loudly out of exasperation. "Okay," said Deon, "I can go get it by this evening." He left the rent office and went back to his apartment. He had to get some rest. He reminded himself he needed to leave a bit early before the currency exchange closed.

Deon tried to sleep through the day but was awakened by dogs barking and loud music. It was something he would have to get used to while working the third shift.

Deon awoke to the clock alarm at nine that night. The currency exchange closed at eleven. He got up and got himself dressed, then headed for the bus.

The bus stopped a block from the corner of the hospital where there was an ATM machine at the bank. Around the corner from the bank was the currency exchange. As he had done numerous times before, Deon put in his card and looked at the reflection where he could see a little of who was behind him. He noticed a police car circle the corner and drive slowly past him. Deon turned to the ATM and entered his information. First, he checked his account: he had $820 available, pretty much his entire check for those two weeks and the money left over from what his dad had given him. Deon took the money out of his bank account and counted the twenties quietly to himself. He slipped the money in his pocket and proceeded to walk toward the currency exchange.

"Hey, where are you going?"

Deon looked up, and there was a police officer, startling him. "Excuse me?" Deon replied. He was surprised to be suddenly confronted.

"Where are you going? What do you have there?"

"Nothing, Officer," Deon responded.

"What did you just put in your pocket?"

"What? My wallet," Deon said with surprise.

"Yeah, turn around," the officer said.

Deon complied. He put his hands up and turned around.

"What did I do?" Deon asked as the officer patted him down. The officer reached in his pants pockets.

"You got anything illegal on you?" he said.

"No," Deon replied.

The officer went in his front pocket and grabbed the wad of money.

"Oh, what is this for? Are you doing business?"

Deon turned around.

"Turn back around" he said as he slammed Deon's chest against the wall.

"You have any identification?"

"Yes, sir, in my wallet."

Another police car pulled up—a mixed team. One of the officers grabbed Deon's wallet and looked in it. He looked at Deon's license and other assorted bankcards and grocery cards. He turned Deon around. Another officer took Deon's driver's license and checked his computer. He came back and whispered in the ear of the officer who apprehended Deon.

"I am confiscating your money," he said. "I suspect this money going to be used in a criminal matter."

"No! Listen—that is my rent money. I am going to the currency exchange to get a money order," Deon emphatically explained.

"Yeah, well, you can tell that to the judge."

"No, wait, Officer. That's all I had in my account. I have to pay my rent. Please. I am not here doing anything," Deon pleaded.

"Like I said, tell it to the judge," he said while tearing off a ticket from a ticket book and giving it to Deon. "There's the number you can set a date for a hearing."

Deon felt faint and dizzy as he wobbled back and forth. He felt blackness overcome him.

"Officer, wait, please. You can check—I work right down the street. I work at the hospital."

"Hey, if there is no problem, you'll get your money back. Have a good night." The officers laughed as they got back into their squad car and drove off.

Deon began to hyperventilate. All his money was gone. He would have to obtain a court date to get his money back.

Deon paced the sidewalk. *I have got to get that money back*, he thought. Deon went on to work and somehow made it through the night. He felt the pressure continuing to build inside himself. He started to fear police.

The next morning after work, Deon arrived at the police station. He spoke to the police officer behind the desk.

"Ma'am," he said, "an officer took my rent money on the street yesterday, and I need to find out how I get my money back."

She looked at Deon as if she were about to laugh. "Get your money back, really?" she responded. "You know you can't get your money back."

"Wait, what do you mean?"

"The department does not confiscate money from civilians unless the officer has a strong determination that the money was gained or being used for illegal activity."

Deon pulled the ticket from his wallet the officer had given him the night before and showed it to the woman.

"Okay, I can set up a court date for you, and you can petition the court to return your money," she said.

"How long will that take?" Deon asked.

"The next date I have available for forfeiture issues is in November."

Deon fell back against the wall. "Officer, that's three months away. This was my rent money, utility money, and money to get back and forth to work."

"Well, I can set this date for you. That is all I can do," she answered with a smile on her face.

Deon began to feel the water well up in his eyes. The woman looked at Deon with patronizing dismay. "I'm sorry," she said with a Cheshire cat smile on her face.

The way of the world was starting to take its toll on Deon. He boarded the city bus, looked out the window, and noticed the payday loan store he had passed numerous times. If there was a time he needed a loan, it was now. The pressure continued to mount.

Deon arrived back at home and went to his computer. He looked up the cash store, examining the requirements to get a short-term loan. It said he needed a copy of two paystubs, references, and a working cell phone.

Deon went to the hospital website. He looked under employees and entered his employee number. Deon looked at this payment information and found a copy of his pay stub. He printed two copies and put them on the table along with other forms to complete that he printed from the loan store site. He finished them and left them on the table. Then went to bed, but he was not able to sleep.

Deon took the bus to the payday loan store as he listened to that talk radio program again.

"This past liberal president has put regulations over everything. They put these regulations on businesses, penalizing banks and loan companies for doing business. Big government is intrusive in our lives. Dictating how banks do their business, stifling growth, it's a part of socialism that is ramped up on the left. They want to control everything, every aspect of your life. They want to dismantle legitimate business. People who have worked hard to get what they have, and the left wants to take that away from you through regulation, which is just another form of penalizing success, and to control the market. We are for free markets and capitalism, where everyone has the same opportunity for freedom from the tyrannical government."

"Let's go to Andy on line 1, you are on WITE." "Yes, Mike. I hear a lot of complaining about how banks and loan stores are exploiting these people. It is their personal responsibility to know what they are doing. If you sign for a loan with a thousand percent interest rate, then that is your responsibility. It's not the bank's fault. They are there to make money."

"You are right, Andy. These people don't want to take responsibility for their own actions. If you are uneducated, to where you would sign a loan for a thousand percent interest rate, then that is your responsibility, not the bank's. If you cannot afford the loan, then don't sign for it. It is the same for that mortgage default issue. These people don't know how to pay a loan, and they sign a mortgage they can't afford."

Deon quieted his radio as he pulled up to the stop by the payday store.

There was a line with an old lady at a bulletproof window. "I need to make a payment on this loan," the lady said as she went down into her purse. "How much again?" she asked as she wiped the sweat from her brow.

"If you want just to pay the interest, you can only pay the sixty dollars for now," the teller responded. "That will roll it over to next two weeks."

"How many times have I done that?" she asked the teller.

"You have had to renew just once, so you're okay. And that loan amount again is three hundred," the teller answered with a concerned and caring demeanor.

"Lord," the old lady said. "All I got is sixty dollars."

Deon calculated in his head that the old lady had paid $120 dollars on a $300 dollar loan. *Damn*, Deon thought. The lady completed her transactions, and Deon was next at the window. He thought about what had occurred with the old woman.

"I need a loan for nine hundred dollars," Deon requested.

"Okay. Fill this form out, please."

"No, ma'am, I completed it all online already."

"Your name?" she asked

"Deon White."

The teller entered the name in the computer, and Deon's file came up.

"I have the forms already signed," he said.

The teller looked at Deon and began to verify the information. "It will be just a minute," she said. She went over to another phone and made contact calls. Then she came over and asked Deon to enter his cell phone number in a keypad. She dialed, and Deon's phone rang.

"Okay, your application is approved, and for the amount on the screen".

Deon looked at the screen. It said one thousand dollars. Deon pushed the green button for approval of the loan for nine hundred dollars.

"Okay," she said as she pulled up dozens of sheets of legal papers from the copy machine under the counter. Deon calculated that was 20 percent on loan for two weeks—$160. *Damn*, he thought again.

"You can pay the interest if you cannot pay the full amount," she stated.

"And then what?" asked Deon.

"It will roll over," she responded.

"And I would pay another one hundred sixty dollars? So if I can't pay this by the end of the month, I will have to pay three hundred twenty dollars in interest?"

"Yes, that is correct," she answered.

What can I do? he thought. *I need the money. I just have to pay that back as soon as my next check rolls around.*

Deon flipped through the numerous legal forms and signed all that she instructed him to sign.

"Do you want that in cash?" she asked.

Deon thought for a moment. After what had happened with his money being confiscated before, no way would he take cash.

"Can you put it directly in my bank account?"

"Yes, we can do that for you."

Deon blew a sigh of relief.

Chapter 11
DEON GETS FIRED FROM HIS JOB

Deon arrived at the hospital and proceeded to the locker room. Another security officer passed Deon as he walked in.

"The captain wants to see you."

Deon immediately went to Captain Suh's office, his heart beating a thousand miles an hour. Deon sat at his desk and waited for the captain to come in. He sat down and looked at Deon sternly but sorrowfully.

"Unfortunately," he said, "we are going to have to let you go."

Deon remained silent.

"I'm sorry," he said, "but with the incident where you had to be replaced for the past eighteen days and the circumstances surrounding that, we cannot keep you on."

"But captain, I haven't been convicted of anything."

"I know that," Captain Suh replied, "and to be honest with you, I think it's lousy. But until this situation is resolved, we can't keep you on."

Deon's heart started beating so fast he almost passed out.

"Oh my god," he said aloud.

Captain Suh looked at Deon and then looked down at his paperwork.

Deon stood up and, wobbly, went for the exit door. He walked as if in a trance down the hallway toward the emergency door entrance. He saw Keith.

"Man, I just got fired," he said.

"I know. I heard that was going to happen," Keith acknowledged. "How you getting to the crib?"

"The bus," Deon replied.

Deon waited for the bus to arrive and thought about what he was going to do next. The bus screeched as it pulled up to the stop. Deon boarded the bus and had a seat to himself.

A lady came in with her two children; all other rows were taken. Deon got up out of his seat and said, "Have a seat, ma'am."

Deon held on to the upper rail until his stop. He exited the back door of the bus and waited until the bus pulled off to walk across the street to his complex. It was a long walk this time, and Deon felt like he was in the twilight zone. Certainly now he felt the pressure of his circumstances as he had never felt before.

He arrived at his apartment door. Deon entered, threw his keys on the table, and sat down hard on his bed. *What in the hell do I do now?* he wondered. He thought about calling his parents but thought better of it, remembering what his dad had told him about standing on his own two feet. He certainly didn't want to worry his mother. Deon put his face in his hands and tried not to cry.

Deon took the bus back to campus and was sitting in the canteen talking to Greg.

"Man, how come you didn't call and let me know what the hell was going on?"

"Don't know, man. Things were happening so fast," Deon explained.

Michael came and sat down at the table.

"What's going on, guys?" he said as he slapped Deon five. Michael noticed that there was something wrong.

"I thought it was going to be okay," said Deon, "but I lost my job, and my car is in the pound."

Greg and Michael looked at each other.

"Man, how you let this happen?" asked Greg. "You know you can't be just hanging out down there."

"What? I don't I have the right to sit in the park and watch a basketball game?"

"Down there, no," said Michael.

"That's bogus. We were dirty as hell coming back from that football game. All kind of stuff going on up here, and the police never harass anybody. They pass right by here and right into the hood."

"Yeah, but not you. Remember what that cop did. He shined his flashlight in your face in front of all of us," said Greg.

"So now what?" asked Michael.

"I got to find a job, and in a hurry. I have got to pay you guys back for getting me out"

"Good luck with that too," said Michael. "Your arrest is on your background check."

"What?" Deon said, surprised. "I thought it was after a conviction."

"The law is different in different states," Greg said as he looked up a site for background checks he had saved on his laptop. He put in Deon's name.

"What is your social?" He passed the laptop over to Deon. Deon entered his social security number. Up came the arrest information.

"Oh, damn," Deon said as he sat back in his seat. "I haven't even gone to court yet. I thought I was innocent until proven guilty."

Greg and Michael looked at each other.

"Theoretically," they both said at the same time.

"Hey, man, if you need a place to chill, we are here for you."

"Hey, what's up, guys?" It was Reggie. "Missing you in class," he said to Deon. "What's going on?"

"Hey, we are going to get out of here and let you two catch up," Michael said. "Call us if you need us."

"Thanks y'all," Deon replied as they both got up. He added, "Oh, they told me I'm going to need a lawyer, not a public defender either."

Michael nodded. "I don't know about that. Some public defenders may be able to help you out.

We will talk. Don't do anything drastic. We will see you later."

Reggie looked at Deon. "Okay, what happened?" he asked.

As Deon and Reggie walked over to the Sportsplex, Deon explained the situation.

"Man, that is huge," said Reggie. "What are you going to do?"

"I got to get a job, and as soon as possible."

He gave Deon the handshake. "I'm here if you need me, bro."

"Reggie, I appreciate that, man."

Deon sat in the Sportsplex at the table he had not been to in over a month. Dr. Allen came into the class and looked at Deon, He sat down in what appeared to be deep thought. Then he came over to Deon. "We need to talk," he said.

They both went into Dr. Allen's office.

"There is no way you are going to pass this class this semester," said Dr. Allen. "You have missed eleven classes,"

"I know," replied Deon. "I have run into some unforeseen circumstances."

Dr. Allen sat back in his chair. "Okay, I'm listening."

Deon explained the situation in its entirety.

"Well, what are you going to do?" asked Dr. Allen.

"I'm going to try to make it the best way I can."

Reggie walked into the room. He looked at Dr. Allen and Deon talking and quietly went to the palpations table.

Deon eventually joined Reggie.

"Have you figured out what you are going to do yet?" Reggie asked.

"No, not yet," Deon replied.

Deon sat in his apartment looking over his notes for class. He thought about his current situation.

At least there is a check coming from the hospital, he said to himself. *My last check. It should be enough to cover my rent and maybe get my car out of the pound.* He would know more the next day, as his direct deposit should hit on the fifteenth, along with everything else—utilities, school fees, phone bill. He really needed this check, and he had to be very careful about how he managed it.

The next morning, Deon awoke and went directly to his computer. He opened his account to find that the utility bill had hit, and the gas bill hit. Three music tunes hit his bank account, as well as separate charges for school fees. His bank account was overdrawn by $400!

Deon screamed as he jumped out of his bed. "Oh, damn, where is my check from work?" The direct deposit was not there. "Oh God."

Deon got on the phone and called human resources at the hospital.

"Hello, this is Masonic Hospital, can I help you?"

"Yes, I didn't receive my check in direct deposit," Deon frantically explained.

"Just a moment," she replied. "May I put you on hold?"

Deon was literary out of breath. "Okay," he said.

After five minutes of very annoying music, she suddenly came back to the phone.

"Okay, I'm sorry, what is your name?" she asked.

"Deon White," he replied.

"Okay, I see you were terminated."

"Yes, ma'am."

"Okay, well, your last paycheck is mailed to you."

"I didn't have a forwarding address because I moved," he said frantically.

"Let me see if it is still here," she said, putting Deon on hold.

She returned to the phone. "We have the last check here for you, but it must be mailed."

"Ma'am, please," begged Deon. "I have bills that hit my account, and if I don't cover them, they could exceed what I have on my check-in overdrafts. Please, let me come down and pick it up."

"I'm sorry," she said, "but that is not the procedure. We put the paycheck in the mail, and you should receive it between five and seven business days."

"No, please, I can't wait until then. I didn't know they mailed the last check. If I have to wait a week, it will consume my whole pay with penalties."

"Well, I am sorry, but that is the procedure. I wish I could do more."

"Please let me speak to Captain Suh. This is an emergency," said Deon.

"Just a minute," she said, almost jovially.

It may be my imagination, but it sure seems everyone is getting a massive kick out of my dismay, he thought.

Captain Suh answered the phone. "Hello."

"Hey, Captain Suh, this is Deon. I'm in a terrible predicament. I didn't know they mail out your last check when quitting or terminated, and I have bills that hit my account. If I don't cover them, it is going to cost me the entire paycheck in penalties. I have no job right now. You know my situation. Could you please help me?"

"I will see what I can do," said the captain. "I will call you back."

Damn, thought Deon. *Now I have to sit here and wait.*

Ten, eleven, twelve, one … finally at two o'clock, his phone rang.

"Yes," Deon answered.

"I can get the check for you," said Captain Suh, "but you will have to pick it up at the end of my shift at seven."

Captain Suh said. Deon breathed a sigh of relief. "Thank you, Captain Suh. I really appreciate it."

Deon eagerly anticipated getting on the bus at six o'clock and making it to the hospital. He stopped by security, and there was a new guard there.

"I'm here to see Captain Suh," said Deon.

"Your name?" the guard asked.

"Deon White."

The guard called on the phone. Then he asked Deon for identification. He wrote Deon's name on a sticker and gave it to Deon.

Deon rushed to Captain Suh's office. He sat and waited for the captain to come into the room.

Finally, he arrived. "How is everything going, Deon?" he asked as he sat down at his desk.

"It's tough, man. Just trying to make it," Deon said. "I really appreciate you letting me get my last check."

"I really had to plead a case to get this for you. Here you go."

Deon looked at the paycheck. It had his regular time and his overtime pay. Deon was grateful.

"Thank you," he said.

"It's all good," said the captain. "Let me know how things are going, okay?"

"Yes, sir," Deon replied.

"It's all going to be okay. You must pray, you understand?"

Deon took a deep breath and exhaled. "Yes, sir," Deon replied.

Deon practically ran to the currency exchange to cash the check so he could put that money in his account and wouldn't have all those bounced payments. Deon entered the currency exchange and went directly to the window. He submitted his identification and passed his payroll check through.

The clerk looked over his paycheck and held it up to the light. He looked at Deon suspiciously.

"Why are you cashing this check here?" he asked.

"Why? I always cash checks here or get money orders."

The man gave Deon a sour look. "You work at the hospital?"

"Yes," Deon answered.

"Okay, that's eight hundred dollars. How do you want it?"

"Hundreds, please, if you have it."

The man looked at Deon and started counting the hundreds, minus the eight-dollar check- cashing fee. Deon took the cash and put it in an envelope. He also keeps his check stub, remembering what happened the last time he had cash and it was confiscated.

Deon walked out and walked briskly to the bus stop. He had to go to his branch to make this deposit. Deon waited quietly and cautiously; anyone could rob him, even the police.

When the bus pulled up, Deon boarded the bus and took the fifteen-minute ride to his bank branch. Deon looked at the time: it was 7:55 p.m. Deon exited the back of the bus and ran to the ATM machine. He put all ten hundred-dollar bills into the ATM machine. He then took the receipt: 8:02 p.m.

Deon blew out a sigh of relief. Now maybe he could rest a bit and feel a little bit relieved.

Deon arrived home and tossed his keys on the table. He went to the refrigerator to see what he had for dinner. In the freezer were prepared hamburger patties and frozen meals. Deon grabbed one of the frozen dinners, pulled it from its packet, and made a slit in the cellophane that protected it. He put it in the microwave, setting the timer for five minutes.

Deon turned on the TV. It was CNN or the global news network. Deon tended to his dinner while the program played in the background.

"We are talking about regulating business into the stone ages. Banks pass on the higher cost to the consumer because of these excessive regulations on our financial sectors," said one of the panelists on this discussion.

Other commentators' voices interrupted. "We are talking about guidelines to protect the American consumer from predatory practices."

"What determines what is a predatory practice?" said another commentator. "Being able to do business in the market and getting what the market dictates for what one gets from what service is a free market concept the left just doesn't understand."

Another commentator interjected, "So for a bank to charge whatever interest penalty or fees on consumers is okay provided it is what the market allows or dictates? It's not ethical. To charge a higher interest rate for consumers who have the same credit histories as one who lives downtown and the other in uptown, how is it a fair practice to charge different rates the more advantages to the person living in Upton? That is inherently unfair."

The debate went on, and Deon listened, going back and forth to check on his microwave cuisine. Deon had had enough of the discussion and turned the TV to the basketball game. "Nothing like watching the Whalers and the Birmingham ballers. Deon ate his dinner, then watched the game until the game watched him.

Chapter 12

Deon woke up to the sun shining through the window into his bedroom. The angle of the sun seemed to send all the rays directly into Deon's eyes. He had to get up and see about getting a job. He flipped on his computer and saw an ad for Yummy food delivery. The advertisement stated that he could earn money driving his own car making deliveries for restaurants. "Set your own hours," the ad said. *Perfect idea*, Deon thought.

Deon downloaded the app to his phone and followed the prompt on how to apply to become a Yummy delivery driver. Again, the question came up: "Have you ever been convicted of a felony?" Deon answered no and hoped that his charges would not come up.

Deon completed the application and was instructed to download a picture of his driver's license, registration, and automobile insurance. He took pictures of all three and pressed to send. The app gave him a response: "You will be informed within forty-eight hours if you are approved."

Deon sat down for a moment, thinking about the next thing he should do. *The hope is that the city will release my car, so I can make the money back for my rent.*

Deon called the auto pound. "Hi, my name is Deon White, and my car was impounded two weeks ago. I wanted to know if it has been released?"

"What's the number?" the policeman asked.

"The impound number is 38709332," replied Deon.

"Yeah, the car has been cleared," the police clerk answered.

"How much do I have to bring?" Deon asked.

"Well, that would be the tow charge of a hundred dollars plus thirty-five dollars a day.

That is going to be around seven hundred dollars, he thought. Deon's head hung down in despair for having to pay close to what he'd paid for his car just to get it out of the pound. The evening passed quickly after Deon arrived back at his apartment. Tomorrow, he would find out if he could start as a delivery driver for Yummy delivery.

Deon woke up to a drizzly day. He wished he could just continue to sleep, but that was not an option. He checked his phone to see if he was approved to drive. Just then, an alert rang his phone. It was Yummy delivery. He was approved.

He went into his bank app to see his final balance. He had only eleven hundred dollars in his account. What the hell happened to the other $600?

Deon jumped up and started breathing heavily as he paced the floor while calling his bank.

"Please choose the selection from the menu," said a recorded message. Deon followed the prompt, which kept him jumping from one phone menu to the next. Finally, the automated system asked if he wanted to speak to a representative.

"Yes, please!" Deon screamed at the phone as if the recorded message would hear him.

"One moment please. Your call will be answered in the order it was received."

Deon continued to pace the floor. "What the hell happened to my money?" he snorted.

After a ten-minute wait, an agent answered.

"Hi, my name is Lisa, and who do I have the pleasure of speaking with?"

Tears welled in Deon's eyes. "My name is Deon. Please, can you look at my account?"

"Your last name, please?" she asked.

"White, Deon White," he answered.

"Okay, I have your account in front of me. How can I help you?"

"Ma'am, I had one thousand seven hundred dollars in the bank after an eight hundred dollar deposit and this morning, I show only one thousand one hundred dollars and all these overdraft charges."

"Just one moment," she replied, as he heard her typing into her computer.

"You had nine charges credited to your account when you had a negative balance of ten dollars."

"Wait, ma'am, I realize I had one overdraft yesterday for my utility bill for eighty dollars and my phone bill of seventy dollars. I ran to get my check and cash it, and I deposited that in the bank before the end of the day."

Deon heard her typing on her keyboard.

"Yes, I do see where you did make a deposit. I also see an overdraft for three dollars, five dollars, eleven dollars, another nine dollars, another twelve dollars, and a few others; however, you are still charged the thirty-five-dollar fee for all transactions that overdrew the account."

"Wait!" Deon, yelled, almost began screaming. "I covered all those transactions by a cash deposit, not a check!"

Deon heard a silence on the other end of the phone and again the sound of tapping on keyboard keys.

"I'm sorry, but once those overdrafts hit credit to your account, it is still the thirty-five-dollar charge."

"No," said Deon. "That is not how it works. I am supposed to be able to cover my account before the end of the business day."

"But you made your deposit after 8:00 p.m.," the voice said on the other end of the phone.

Deon sat down because his head was beginning to spin.

"Ma'am, that is over three hundred dollars in overdraft fees when I made an extra effort to cover those transactions. I have been a customer at this bank since I was in high school. I have never had an overdraft my account. Are you telling me that my bank won't back me on this?"

"I'm sorry, sir," she replied.

"I can't believe you won't let your customer cover an overdraft on an account. This is insane."

"Yes, well, they have made some recent changes in the policy. All account holders were notified."

"You all used to didn't do this."

"I know, sir," said the agent. "They removed the regulations, so the bank is within its legal right to charge the overdraft no matter the amount."

"Oh, God," Deon said in exasperation

"You can go to your branch manager to see if they could waive the fees," she replied.

Deon headed to the bus stop. He paced back and forth on the sidewalk. Deon rarely left the house with his hair uncombed, with a wrinkled shirt and wrinkled pants. But today, he did.

Deon arrived at the bank and walked to a desk that stood as an island in the lobby. Deon signed in and sat in the lobby couches that formed a square in front of a large television screen.

Deon waited for what seemed like forever. There was only one teller and a line that was so long it resembled the one at the motor vehicles department. He looked at the offices where customer reps were talking to account holders.

I just wish they would come on, thought Deon.

Eventually, one of the branch managers escorted her client out of the office, and the security police opened the door for the lady and smiled while tipping his hat.

The customer manager picked up the clipboard.

"Mr. White," she called.

Deon got up in a rush and greeted the representative. Deon's demeanor startled her.

"Come on in," she said as Deon walked in and sat down.

Unbeknownst to Deon, she turned to the security officer and gave a concerned stare and nod before coming around to her desk to sitting down.

"Yes, can I help you?"

Deon gave the woman his bankcard and sat back in his seat. He explained the situation to her. She looked in the computer and nodded.

"I understand, Mr. White," she said. "They do sometimes allow deposits to cover transactions until 8:00 p.m., and I see your deposits just went in a few minutes past that."

Deon's eyes went up to the ceiling. "Is there anybody you could talk to override this?"

"Just a minute," she said as she went to her phone. She dialed up a number and waited.

"Yes, hi," she said. "This is Elaine at branch 309. My employee number is 0921. I have an account I need you to look at." She gave the person over the phone all the information, and they proceeded with a discussion. "Okay," she said finally and hung the phone up.

She turned to Deon. "We did see you attempted to cover your charges before 8:00 p.m. However, our system is unable to override that transaction. You would have had to make that deposit before eight."

"So I'm just out almost four hundred dollars in fees alone? This is not fair." Deon's eyes began to water, and his voice began to shake.

The security officer started to make his way to the office as the manager gave him a look.

Deon ran his hand in front of his face. "A neighborhood bank is supposed to help build the community, not penalize its customers so they can't pay their rent," he cried.

"Well, Mr. White, we do have classes that you can take. We offer them once a month to teach you how to balance your accounts."

"I beg your pardon?" Deon said.

The officer stepped into Deon's view. Deon sat back and looked at him.

"Okay, why are you here? I'm discussing a problem I'm having with my account."

The officer stood firmly and put his hands behind his back.

"I'm sorry, Mr. White. We don't have the means to reverse the charges," said the manager.

The officer continued to look at Deon without saying a word. He nodded his head up and down and smiled.

Deon stood up and walked out into the lobby, and the officer followed. Deon proceeded out of the door, feeling like he was in the twilight zone.

"Have a good afternoon, sir," the bank officer said with a laugh in his voice.

Deon stopped and turned, staring directly at the officer. The bank officer grinned as he closed the bank door behind him. Deon felt the hair on the back of his neck stand up. Again his blood began to boil. He was feeling the pressure.

Deon got on the bus and looked at his finances. He could ill afford to lose $400 just like that. Hopefully, Deon could get his car out of the pound and earn money back before the end of the month so he could make that rent payment. He also had to pay back the payday loan store $1,080, including interest. He sat back and shook his head.

Deon got off the bus at the dark underground area where the police pound was located. Deon walked the distance to the trailer where the lot officers were. He stepped in and found someone else sitting at the desk where before it was the lady who laughed at his circumstances.

"Can I help you?" she asked.

Deon pulled out his phone. "I'm here to get my car," he said while giving her his number."

She nodded in agreement. "That will be seven hundred dollars." Deon gave her his debit card. She ran the card and the receipt said approved. She gave the keys to the other lot officer.

"Okay," she said. "Officer Daniels will help you find your car." Deon warily went out the back door of the trailer and into the impound yard. There were hundreds of cars all over the place. Deon walked by the guided numbers until he caught sight of his car. He went over to the driver- side door. The door handle was pulled out but still worked. Deon opened the door from the passenger side to find the radio missing. His glove compartment had been ransacked, and so were the speakers in the trunk. Deon angrily went back to the trailer.

"Excuse me, when was my car brought in, please?" he asked.

She gave him the date and time: 7:40 p.m. the day he was arrested. It seemed the car was pulled maybe five hours after that. *How did they know it was my car? They must have run my license number or something*, he thought.

"My vehicle has been stripped .My radio ,speakers ,glove compartment ,my tire is almost flat Deon complained."

The other policeman walked up. "That is how it was when we got it."

Deon heart thumped. "No. That's impossible."

"Well, look," the officer said. "You can complain to whoever you feel you need to, but that car was pulled in here like that."

Deon could not believe this. He had heard such stories before but brushed them off as just people wanting to complain after doing something they were not supposed to be doing. Now the shoe was on the other foot.

Deon left the trailer and walked back to his car. He put the keys in the ignitions and it begged to start after sitting for more than a month.

Deon tried to start the car again, and his vehicle wailed a little more and then started up. White smoke filled the air. The officer nodded and began his walk back to the trailer.

Deon pulled out of the dirt space, and the car smoked, coughed, and hissed. The right tire was nearly flat. Deon followed the officer to the exit area. The officer scribbled something on a handheld computer, opened the gate, and waved Deon goodbye.

Deon's car rumbled down the road. It sounded like something was wrong underneath, as the front wheel seemed to clunk. Deon had not heard that sound before. He drove up to the avenue following his GPS, trying to find a car shop. Deon made his first stop at what was a reputable mechanic, but after surveying the clinking sound, they told Deon it would cost $400 to fix.

I have to look around, Deon thought as he drove to another location. A fat dark man sitting on some old tires got up and came over to Deon's window. He had a midsized afro and smelled like cigar smoke, and he coughed a lot.

"What can I help you with?" he asked.

"My car is clanking underneath, and I want to get an estimate. Can you fix it and how much?"

"Yeah, I could fix it. No problem with that. I can fix for you, nothing to it. I can fix it for you."

He coughed.

Wow, that was a mouthful, thought Deon. The man talked so fast it was almost like a mumble, but Deon could understand what he said.

"How much?" asked Deon.

"I look and see," the man said.

After examining the car, the mechanic motioned Deon over and said, "All right, let me show you this here." He walked Deon through what was wrong with the ball joints that were causing the noise. "See right here? When they pulled your car, they hooked it up here, and it broke that."

"How much?" asked Deon.

"I do it for two hunned," the mechanic said in that very fast brogue.

Deon laughed to himself. This was obviously a down-home old man. He watched as the man got to work, always smoking those mini cigars all the way down to the very end, then putting it out in his ashtray. Deon didn't want his car smelling like cigars, but at least he was getting it fixed for half of what the big shops were charging.

An hour later, the old man was finishing up.

"All right," he said. "I told you, I got it. If you have any problems with it, bring it back, all right?"

"Thank you," said Deon. "And I didn't even get your name."

"Frank."

That old man was cool, thought Deon.

The evening passed quickly after Deon arrived back at his apartment. Tomorrow he could start as a delivery driver for Yummy delivery.

Deon woke up the next morning to another drizzly day. He went into his new Yummy delivery app and pressed the "get started" prompt. His phone said to wait for an order, so Deon waited. His phone buzzed with the location of the restaurant where he was to pick up. Deon ran to the car as quickly as he could.

Deon followed his GPS navigation to a restaurant called Froggy's. The instructions told Deon to pick up the order inside. The restaurant was lively, with big screen TVs blaring a baseball game. Waitresses dressed in black shorts and green baseball jerseys took orders.

"May I help you?" a voice said as Deon looked up from his phone. She was one pretty girl, with pearly white teeth, a tanned complexion, and brown eyes.

"I'm here to pick up a delivery."

"Oh, okay," she said. "What's the name on the order?"

"Henry," Deon replied, showing her his phone. She looked in the warmer.

"Here it is," the waitress said as she grabbed the yellow bag with what seemed to be dinner for an entire family. She put a large sticker with the frog logo on the front of the plastic bag closing it up.

"There you go," she said with a smile.

"Thank you," Deon replied as he gently took the bag from her hand.

"Bye," she said while waving at Deon.

Wow, she is beautiful, Deon thought as he waved back at her while leaving.

Deon followed the app navigation, which brought him to the address for the delivery. It was a small house in a quiet residential neighborhood. An attractive older woman came to the door with two small children, who came running up to the door too.

"Mrs. Henry?" Deon asked, looking to make sure he had the right person.

"No, Henry is my son," she said. "I'm Mrs. Schultz."

"Oh, okay, yes, ma'am. Well, here is dinner." Deon handed the bag to Mrs. Schultz.

"Thank you very much."

"You're very welcome," Deon responded. He returned to his car and swiped "delivery complete" on his phone. A dollar amount popped up: five dollars. Not too bad. That was five dollars he certainly didn't have before. Another buzz alert vibrated his phone. She left a tip—five dollars again. Not too bad.

Deon drove off slowly and looked at his mounted phone, waiting for another alert for another delivery. The phone buzzed again, and this time it was for Bumpers Bar and Grill. Before the end of the night, Deon had made eighty dollars. *If I could just keep this up, everything might just be okay*, he thought.

The next day, Deon started delivery early. He wanted to take advantage of the breakfast crowd. He started delivering at the Breakfast House, and later at a place called Pounds of Pancakes. Before the morning was over, he had made fifty dollars in deliveries and tips. Later in the afternoon and evening, he had delivered another fifty dollars or so. *Man, if I can keep this up, I will pay everything back sooner than I thought.*

Deon got another delivery from Mickey Dees and went to pick it up. It was a thirty-dollar order for hamburgers meals. *Wow*, Deon thought. *Either this is a party or someone is overindulging.* Deon followed his GPS down winding two lanes roads and twist and turns through neighborhoods. Deon finally arrived at the address, and he went up to the house with this huge bag full of Mickey Dee's burger meals. A young guy answered the door to the sound of music coming from the house.

"Hey, thanks," the guy said as he took the bag from Deon.

"You're welcome," Deon replied. "Have fun."

Deon went back out to the car and checked his phone. He was still waiting on another request. Deon tried to find his way out of the neighborhood and found himself lost through the neighborhood's maze. He also heard that clunking underneath his car again. Deon stopped the car and looked under it to see if anything was obviously broken. Nothing seemed out of the ordinary, he thought as he stood up off the ground.

Suddenly, there were flashing lights riding up to the street.

Deon turned and looked. The lights were coming straight for him. The car stopped, and Deon stood frozen at the driver's side of his cruiser.

"Back away from the vehicle!" the police officer said as he walked toward Deon with his flashlight.

Deon was completely startled.

"Do you not understand what I just told you? Move away from the vehicle!" the voice said strongly."

Deon backed away from his car.

"Is this your car?" another officer asked.

"Yes, it's my car," said Deon.

"Identification, and registration, please."

Deon reached for his wallet.

"Keep your hands where I can see them," the first officer said as they both surrounded him. Deon put his hands up by his shoulders.

"Go ahead and get it," said the other officer.

Deon gave them his driver's license.

The second officer took Deon's ID and went to the squad car. The first officer took his flashlight and started examining the vehicle.

"What are you doing in this neighborhood?" asked the officer.

"I am making deliveries," Deon told him.

"What do you mean making deliveries?"

"I'm delivery for Yummy deliveries," Deon answered.

The second officer closed the squad car door and walked over to Deon.

"Okay, there is no warrant, but you do have recent charges."

Deon remained silent and stood like a stone statue.

"Is that right?" said one of the officers.

"Drug-related," the first officer said while reaching for his handcuffs.

"You know why we are here, don't you? We get calls when you guys get to breaking in cars. Are you connected to anyone else stealing these cars?"

Deon remained silent. A persistent hatred was starting to boil inside him burning the back of his neck.

"You don't have to talk to me, but we get you to talk buddy."

"I'm working. I just dropped off a delivery."

"They will let anybody be a driver, it seems," the officer laughed.

The other officer exited Deon's vehicle. He pulled burned cigar butts out of the ashtray.

"I found these in his ashtray," the cop said.

"Blunts!" the other officer said. "Possession of marijuana!" He laughed.

Deon thought about the mechanic that worked on his car. *He did put out his cigar in my ashtray*, he thought.

"You had no right to search my vehicle," Deon protested.

"What, are you a lawyer now?" said one of the officers.

"All right, you're under arrest," said the other. "Don't resist. Get your damn your hands behind your back."

"What am I being charged with?" Deon asked.

"Possession of marijuana and it's going to be resisting a police officer if you don't shut the hell up." Uncharacteristic of Deon he cursed. What you got a problem replied the officer.

Deon inhaled and gritted his teeth. They pushed Deon down into the police vehicle by his head violently into the backseat. His knees slammed up against the metal partition. Deon was now starting to feel a cold hatred in his heart. The police car drove off as officers tuned in to their car radio:

"The left is in the business of coddling these criminals. We are talking about thugs out in the streets. They are selling drugs, they are in gangs, they walk around with their pants hanging off their butts with no public decency. Yet they are ostracizing our fine police officers who put their lives on the line every day they go out on to these streets. These thugs, they are the epitome of what is wrong in this country. Just recently, an officer was fired for restraining one of these criminals, now you have the NAACP and the racist rainbow coalition putting our officer's life at risk, and this is how the left likes it. These areas are crime-infested and the only cure is to allow our law-enforcement officers to do their job and lock these thugs up. Yes, caller. Thanks for calling WITE."

Deon had no choice but to listen as he headed again to jail.

Deon sat at the desk of the police sergeant.

"Oh, so I see you back again, huh?" the sergeant said.

Deon's face was as hard as a stone. He looked as if he was ready to explode.

"Y'all always come back," the sergeant said in jest. "Possession of marijuana, good! You may be here for a while."

The yellow cell door slammed, and Deon heard the echoed ring in his ear that reverberated down his spine. Deon turned and looked at everybody in the cell. He looked at two guys sitting on a metal seat. They slowly moved aside. Deon sat down. His face and demeanor were hard as stone.

The judge looked at Deon and opened a manila folder on his bench.

"You were just in here," he said in that sharp Southern Confederate general type of voice. "I guess you're pleading not guilty again. Why not just take responsibly for your actions? That's what wrong with you people: no personal responsibility."

Deon remained quiet. Had he had a sword, he would have sliced this judge's head off. Deon had that stare in his face.

"We let you out last time, and this is thanks we get," said the district attorney.

The judge laughed and looked down at the folder. "Marijuana cigarette, cigar, what was it?"

The district attorney spoke up. "Yes it was, sir."

The judge looked at Deon and said, "We're going to find out from the lab what you had, so until then, enjoy your stay. Okay, I set the bond at five thousand dollars."

Deon stared straight ahead. *More pressure*, he thought.

Five days and still in here, Deon thought to himself. He went to his cell, and the door slammed behind him. Five days turned to ten. Then the turnkey came to his cell.

"Get your stuff. You are leaving out."

"Where?" Deon asked.

"Hey, man, either you want out of here or you don't."

Deon retrieved his belongings to find his money again was gone.

Deon stood at the bus stop with three bus tokens given to him upon his release. He boarded the bus and rode the twelve miles it took to make it home. A drunk man was asleep by the window. A nurse was sitting on the aisle. Among the scattered passengers, some were weary and some spry. Deon was depressed.

Deon arrived home and started the trek down the street to his apartment. Deon opened his apartment door and flipped on the light switch. No lights. He threw his keys on the table and felt his way to his room. The lamp from the courtyard was the only light to guide him through the house.

Deon went to his refrigerator. Spoiled food. Freezer completely defrosted. He sat down on his bed. Something else he had to deal with in the morning.

Deon woke from his slumber and looked online on his phone and found he needed to pay $175 from the previous bill, a $20 late fee, and a $50 reconnections charge. *They really know how to stick it to you when you are struggling*, he thought.

Deon checked his bank account; he had to have something left. His statement showed he was overdrawn by $600. The payday loan had hit his account, and now he was going to be way behind on his rent. His car was again impounded.

Deon sat back down on his bed, thinking, *This is as bad as it can get. Should I swallow my pride and call home?* His dad's voice echoed in his brain: *"I didn't raise no fool. You can do this, Son. It comes a time when a man has to stand on his own two feet. Now is that time."*

Deon sat in the office of the property manager. She was on her computer, looking at Deon's payment history.

"You have only been here for four months. I'm sorry, but if you are having problems already, there is not much we can do. I'm afraid I can't waive any of the eviction order. Your eviction date is set for this Thursday. It would be better if you move out before Thursday. That way, it won't be listed as an eviction. Once you have an eviction on your credit, I don't have to tell you how that can hurt you for trying to get another apartment."

"Is there anywhere I could get help?" Deon asked.

"You can try different churches and social service agencies. But they don't help unless you have a job and can produce a pay stub."

"But if I had a job, I wouldn't need help in the first place," Deon quipped.

"Hey, it's not me," said the property manager. "It's the new laws. Work for welfare instead of welfare to work. It's what they're doing. They only pay a percentage based on your check stub. You might want to check on getting unemployment, but that takes a while. The reason why you were terminated will determine if you get unemployment too. They can deny it for illegal activity."

A hot flash went down Deon's chest. He was starting to get short of breath. "Thank you!" he said. "I will try to get everything out so it won't be listed as an eviction.

Deon decided to call Greg up on the campus to get help with moving.

"Sorry, your number cannot be completed at this time," he heard. Deon checked his service: disconnected.

Deon could take no more. He dropped right where he was and cried for a minute. *So this is how it all ends.*

It was now Thursday morning. Deon had used all the money he had stashed away that was not in the bank to pay his phone bill. After all, that was really all he had left.

He called Greg. "Hey Greg, this is Deon. I'm getting evicted give me a call."

Greg called immediately. "Hey, bro, you're getting evicted?

"Yeah, I was wondering if you could help me take a few bags of my stuff and put it in storage at school."

"Where you at? I will be there in a few," Greg answered.

"I'll be at the storage facility. Some things, like my bed, I'm going to have to put in storage. I'll text you the directions.

Deon walked to the storage facility only to find it closed for lunch. He'd sent the directions to Greg as a text message earlier, and speak of the devil, here he was pulling up. "What up, D!" Greg said as Deon came over to the car.

"Would you believe they are closed for lunch? They have a sign in the window saying we will return a one o'clock."

"Well, come on. Let's go back to your place and figure this thing out."

Deon got in the car.

"Why didn't you tell your friends you were about to be evicted"

"It's not like I'm proud of it and want the world to know," said Deon.

"Okay, so we don't mean nothing to you, right?"

"Come on, Greg, you know what I mean," said Deon. "My dad told me I have to stand on my own two feet."

"So, it's all or nothing then, right?" Greg replied in anger.

They pulled up to Deon's courtyard to see people scavenging like vultures over a pile of belongings. Deon got out of the car.

"That's my stuff, all my stuff!" he called out.

Deon's heart sank. People speaking in different languages chattered while picking through his items. Deon was incensed.

"What are you people doing? This is my stuff."

"Then pay your rent," responded one of the residents as he threw back a picture frame he had been hoarding for himself.

Deon's TV had been taken, his coffee table, a small stereo, plants and rubber plants, picture frames—everything he owned had been commandeered and scattered to the wind by his fellow residents.

Deon gathered whatever belongings he could find and files which pertained papers and other miscellaneous items. All his toiletries and towels had been left by the scavengers. Deon grabbed the hefty plastic bags that the eviction crew had thrown his belongings into. All that was left was his mattress and scattered items. He recognized his gray slacks and business shirts scattered about the sidewalk, as he picked them up and put his clothes in the hefty bag.

"Come on, Deon, let's get your stuff and go back to campus," Greg insisted as Deon sat on the sidewalk in a trancelike state. "They took almost all my stuff, my so called neighbors! I never knew people could be so cruel he said dejectedly.

As they rode back to campus, Deon said, "I need to go explain what's going on with my counselor and registrar. I'm not going to be able to finish the semester. I haven't been to class in over a month. Hopefully they will allow me to just get an incomplete until I can get things to straighten out."

"In the meantime, you stay in my room," Greg insisted.

"Okay," said Deon. "I don't want to cause you guys any trouble."

"It's okay just for a night or two," said Greg.

Greg and his roommate accommodated Deon with two thick comforters and laid them down by what was once Deon's desk. The floor was hard, but it did make for an adequate place for Deon to take a rest.

The next morning, Deon sat at Dr. Allen's desk.

"I understand what's been going on," said Dr. Allen. "I mean, you have talked to me about this before. I have no problem giving you an incomplete this semester, but what about next semester?"

"I don't know when I will be returning," responded Deon. "Right now, I have to take it one day at a time."

Deon left the Sportsplex and went back up on the campus, where a protest was starting. Students milled around one of the statues of a Confederate general that stood watching over the history department building. A young activist with a bullhorn was protesting its presence. Deon continued into the university administration building.

Deon sat in the office of Mr. Ross, his counselor. Mr. Ross listened intently to Deon's circumstances.

"Sounds rough what you are going through," said Mr. Ross. "You went out into the world. The devil is everywhere. As parents, we try hard to protect you. Students here at this university are pampered. Most came from suburban middle-class families who have had everything given to them, just wait until many of them have to go out there and live; then they will see too. You have to be very careful. One mistake can set you back ten years, I will grant your hardship request and you will get an incomplete, but you will have to make that up by the end of next semester."

"Thank you, Mr. Ross," said Deon. "I just wish there was some refund I could get. I could sure use it."

Mr. Ross gave Deon his card. "Now might be a good time to call home," he advised.

"Gotta make it on my own two feet," Deon replied.

Deon texted Greg, "Thanks for the invite to camp out with you. I have some business in Upton. Will call you later.

Deon caught the bus back to the wards. He couldn't feel right about being homeless on the campus, sleeping from room to room, but maybe that would be better than walking the street with nowhere to go.

Deon walked down the boulevard toward the hospital. He stopped at a bus station and fell asleep in a chair with his head against the window. A security guard woke him up and told him he had to leave. Deon continued to walk through the night.

The morning sun rose as Deon peered out into the unforgiving world. Deon walked to the area social services agency.

"Excuse me," he said, "who do I see about getting some help?"

The social intake person guided Deon to the line. "Over there," she said, pointing to the end of a line. Another long wait.

Eventually, he sat down at the desk of a social worker.

"Okay, sir. I'm Mr. Alfred. And you are?"

"Deon White, sir."

"Okay," said Mr. Alfred. "What brings you here this afternoon?"

Deon went through the story of where his journey had taken him thus far.

"So, I see you are in a great deal of trouble," said Mr. Alfred.

"Yes," Deon replied

"Unfortunately, we don't have anything to help you. When you are even charged with a crime, it disqualifies you for almost everything. Do you know if it is on your background check?"

"Yes, it is," Deon answered.

"We can put your name on the list for the shelter. You have to sign up early, because beds or cots fill up quickly. As far as the employment, you are going to have to find a job somewhere, somehow. Don't you have any friends that can help?"

"No," replied Deon. "I have to handle this on my own."

"Indeed. I am very sorry. I can give you a room voucher for one night at the YMCA. You can get a shower and so forth. They will provide you with a room for one night only."

Deon thanked him for the voucher and asked for directions.

"Oh, the Y is right down the street," said Mr. Alfred.

Deon walked to the YMCA and went to the front desk. "I have this one-night voucher," he said as he presented it to the desk clerk.

"Okay, did you bring anything?"

"No, nothing."

"Okay," said the clerk. "Well, here, let me give you a key."

Deon took the key and went to a room that had just a bed and shower. Deon looked at the made-up bed. He pulled back the covers, and it wasn't too bad. Deon checked the bathroom and found bottles of soap.

He quickly took off all his clothes and went into the shower with every piece and bottle of soap he could find. He rubbed the soap over his body and all over his clothes. Then he wrung the clothes out and saw the dark, murky, dirty sweat coming off his clothes. *They must have smelled bad as well*, he thought. He had been wearing the same clothes for two days.

After he wrung out his clothes, he hung them over the rails in the bathroom, hoping that in the morning they would be somewhat dry and not nearly as offensive. He went and sat on the bed, lay down, and went to sleep.

There was a way out of this predicament, possibly by calling home, but Deon remembered the echo of his dad telling him, "You got to stand up on your own two feet, Son." And so it was that Deon wandered for days, aimlessly going back and forth, trying to pick up a few dollars by running errands for vendors and sleeping on the floor of the city shelter whenever he could get in. How would have anyone have believed that he was now homeless?

Deon woke up on the cold floor of the shelter. The place smelled bad. People you would see on the streets and would call bums were now sleeping right next to him. Mentally ill, most of them. Deon started to think about his own sanity. *Is this where I am supposed to be?*

Deon stood up and made his way to the bathroom. He looked in the first stall and found a homeless person sleeping in there. Deon went to the second stall. Fortunately, he could use this one. Deon tried to wash his hands after he finished. The trickle of water was enough to make them wet, but he was happy to notice a hand sanitizer dispenser on the wall. *Thank goodness*, Deon said to himself.

Deon walked over to the security and social workers. "Will y'all be servicing anything today?" he asked.

"They supposed to pass out bags this morning in about a half hour," a worker responded.

Deon was hungry, but he knew what breakfast was going to be like here: warm milk or six- ounce juice, a Pop-Tart, and a boiled egg. Beggars can't expect smorgasbords.

Deon noticed a van pulling up to the facility. The security guard made his way to the back- door entrance. An older lady in her sixties came in with another worker.

"Hi, I'm Sister Joseph Mary," the social worker said.

"How are you, Sister Joseph Mary? I'm Deon."

"Do you need any help?" he asked.

"Well, I do have lots of boxes in the van that needs to be brought in," she said.

"Yes, ma'am, right away," Deon answered. He walked with the social worker and security guard to the van. It was the breakfasts in little brown lunch bags, containing precisely what Deon had envisioned. Deon helped unload the van as Sister Joseph Mary looked on. She stopped Deon as he walked past her with a box in his hand.

"I don't think I've seen you down here before," she said to Deon as she helped him with the door.

"I know, I just arrived."

"Come here," she said

"Yes, Sister," Deon replied.

"Do you know where the community center is? Here is the address." She handed Deon a card. "I would like to talk to you further."

"Thank you, Sister, I appreciate it." After breakfast was completed, Deon searched for the directions to the center and found it was not far from the hospital. There was a sandwich shop, a train station, a small church, a Laundromat, and then the community center. Deon went in to find the same guy he saw with Sister Joseph Mary.

"Hey, how you doing?" Deon said.

"Hey. I remember you from the shelter this morning."

"Yes, do you work for the Sister?" Deon asked.

"Yeah, part-time," he responded.

"Is Sister Joseph Mary here?"

"Yeah she's here, hold on," the guy said. He got up, walked to another office, and knocked on the door slightly.

"Sister," he called. She was apparently on her way out at the same time because they met at the door. "This gentleman is here."

"Oh yes," Sister Joseph Mary said. "Give us a moment, Jesus."

Turning to Deon, she said, "I asked you to come by, and we were to discuss your circumstances."

"Yes, Sister, it has been a terrible journey."

Deon explained his circumstances for what he knew was the umpteenth time. She listened carefully and nodded in agreement or compassion.

"Well look, what we can do now is pray. Pray that Jesus will protect you and comfort you through your trials," she said. "Give me your hands."

Deon put his hands in her hands as they both closed their eyes.

"Our Father who art in heaven …" They both recited the Lord's prayer.

When they had finished, Sister Joseph Mary said, "You seem like such a very nice young man, and I appreciate you eagerly trying to help me today. When do you go to court?"

"October 18th" Deon replied.

"Okay. I'm going to run your background, and I will see about getting you to help out here. It is a voluntary job, if that's okay. I can get you a very modest room. But that is after the background check, and I am sure you understand."

"Yes, Sister Joseph Mary, thank you so much. Can I come back tomorrow? Will that be okay?"

"Come by about 10:00 a.m. I should have things ready for you then."

Deon stood there with tears in his eyes. "Thank you so much," he cried.

"You're welcome," she said.

Deon left the community center and wondered what he was going to do with the remainder of his evening. There was nowhere to go. He didn't have but three dollars in his pocket. He was hungry, but he'd learned to live with that. He decided to take the three dollars he had and catch the bus to the campus.

Deon arrived at the dorms and went to Greg's room.

"Hey Deon, what's going on!" called Mike down the hallway.

"Hey Mike, where's Greg?"

"He's around here somewhere," said Mike. "How's that thing working out for you?"

"It's getting better. Got some things lined up," Deon told him.

"You look tired, bro."

"Yeah, kind of," Deon replied.

"You still need a place to stay, dude?"

"Just for the night," Deon responded.

Michael led Deon to a janitor's closet in the hallway.

"They won't catch you here," he said. "I'm the only one who's got the key. This cool for the night?"

"Yeah, it will do."

Mike and Deon walked out of the storage closet, went to Mike's room, and grabbed some old blankets and a small blow-up mattress.

"Man, this will work," Deon said as they secretly went back to the janitor's closet. Deon put the inflatable on the floor.

After everything was inflated and situated, Mike stood up and looked at Deon. "How is that case coming?" he asked.

"I will find out on my next court date."

"You get an attorney yet?" asked Mike.

"Man, I can't afford an attorney," Deon told him.

"Have you tried legal aid?"

"Yeah. They don't take criminal cases," Deon replied.

"Well, you good here. Just don't snore too loud. You might get caught."

"Thanks, bro," Deon said.

Mike put up a fist. Deon bumped it.

"Later."

The next morning, Deon and Greg met in Greg's room.

"So, you have no attorney?" Greg asked as he slammed down some books on his desk.

"No, not yet."

"When is your court date?"

"On the eighteenth," Deon replied.

"You have got to find a lawyer man. My uncle has a law firm. I should call them. I will let you know."

Deon shook his head in appreciation. "Got to go, man," Deon said. "I got to see a man about a horse."

Greg looked at Deon. "Be careful, man."

Deon took the bus to the community center. Sister Joseph Mary was busy as usual, trying to arrange food donations in the back of the center.

"Hi, Sister Joseph Mary," Deon said as he walked into the room.

"Why, hello, Deon. How are you? Oh, let me show you to the place I have for you."

Deon and the sister walked down a long dark hallway behind the community center walls. It looked like a maintenance hallway for the community center and other connecting establishments on the street. The smell of old paint hung in the air. They came to a door halfway down the hallway and went in.

It was a small room with a twin bed in the corner, a place for a hotplate, and a small sink, with a green carpet on top of a concrete floor. A small TV sat on a milk crate, much like the one he had before being evicted. Just two electrical outlets. It was perfect.

"You will need to get yourself one of those little refrigerators," she said. "I might be able to find you one. Now remember: I can only let you stay here provided you are helping out."

"Thank you so much, Sister Joseph Mary," said Deon.

"This is your key to the door off the alley, so be careful."

They both went back up to the center.

"I need you to fill these bags," she said. "If you could help me fill these with this list of items?"

Deon looked at the items on the list. Each was in a large pile in the middle of the room on a table. Deon put one piece of each into individual brown bags, filling them and putting them away.

Jesus walked in. "Hey, you want to help me deliver these to the seniors?" he asked.

"Yeah, sure," Deon replied.

Deon and Jesus filled the community van with the bags Deon filled.

"Sister Joseph Mary, Deon and I are going to go deliver these," Jesus called out.

"Yes, go ahead," she responded.

Deon and Jesus rode in the van to several places where seniors were living alone in subsidized housing, dropping off bags and talking to senior residents.

"Hey, thanks for letting me ride with you," said Deon.

"Ah, no problem. I know it can get tough just packing bags. The one thing for sure with Sister Joseph Mary is that you will *work* for her. Don't act like you don't feel like doing something, because after that, she won't help you at all."

"Yes, I can tell she is a tough lady. I take no one's kindness for weakness," Deon replied.

When they arrived back at the community center, Deon noticed a new desk that he had not seen before.

"I need to talk to you two in my office, please," she said to both of them.

I wonder what it could be? Deon said to Jesus.

"Don't worry. I don't think you are getting fired," Jesus said with a laugh.

"Okay," said Sister Joseph Mary. "We are going to have a massive influx of people coming in this Wednesday, and I'm going to need you guys to help intake all these people. We have forms they are to fill out, and then we interview them with the social workers to see what assistance we can provide for them. So be ready tomorrow. Also, we are having a Wednesday-night Mass. I'm inviting you both to come."

"Thank you!" they both said.

"Here, I have two free coupons for the hamburger place across the street, if you guys want them."

"Thank you, Sister," Deon said as he took the coupons.

"Well, see you bright and early tomorrow."

Just as Sister Joseph Mary said, by eight o'clock in the morning, everyone was at the center. A long line of women and children were standing outside on a misty day. Social workers helped applicants complete forms.

"Deon?" called Sister Joseph Mary. "Could you assist in getting these applicants to fill out the forms? Here, you use this desk, please."

Deon went and sat down at the new desk. One applicant after another needed help in filling out the application. Some of the mothers spoke no English. There were girls with their children holding on to their shirttails with runny noses. Deon noticed Erica, the girl he remembered from the hospital. Deon swallowed a massive lump in his throat.

Erica? Deon said to himself. He took the next applicant but kept his eye on Erica. As soon as he got the opportunity, he went over to her.

"Erica?"

She turned and looked at him with her pretty brown eyes and honey brown skin. Her son, Eric, stood looking up at Deon, and holding his mom's hand.

"Oh, hi," she said as she grabbed hold of her son's arm to make him sit down.

"Can we talk for a second?" he asked.

"Sure," she replied.

Deon led Erica to a table in a break room.

"How did you end up here?" he asked.

"I got no place to stay," she said. "My mom is on drugs, and I don't know where my dad is. Nobody could take me and my son in. I was staying with my aunt, and her boyfriend started making advances toward me. When I wouldn't give in, he told me I had to pay him to stay there. It was at the Dell apartments, and there was like eight people in a two-bedroom house doing drugs and up all hours of the night. I couldn't even take my son to school because of what was going on, with tricks and everything else. I just got a part-time job, but I still have to get out of there."

"You want to get something to eat?" Deon asked.

Erica looked at Deon. "You don't have the money to be spending on me," she replied

"No, it's okay. I can afford a hamburger or something."

Deon went to Sister Joseph Mary. "Sister, I need a few minutes. Is it okay?" "Yes, how long?" she inquired.

"I could be back in a half hour."

"Go ahead. I know you haven't had lunch," she said.

Deon, Erica, and Eric walked down the sidewalk to the Burger Hut and ordered the special meal of two large burgers and fries with the coupon Sister Joseph Mary had given Deon the day before.

"I thought you were working at the hospital?" she said.

"I was. Some things happened. I'm not working there anymore."

"What happened?" she asked.

"I got caught up in a sweep at the basketball court and charged with drug conspiracy."

"Oh, man," she said. "So, what are you doing now?"

"Right now, I'm just working at the community center voluntarily. I'll try looking for other jobs."

"Are you going to be all right?" she asked.

"Yeah. Sister Joseph Mary gave me a place to stay until I can get through this thing."

"What about school?" she asked.

"That is on the back burner for now," Deon answered.

"How's your hamburger?"

"Tastes like a regular old hamburger to me," she said. "The fries ain't too bad."

"Actually, I was asking Eric here." Deon laughed.

"He's okay. He loves french fries," she said.

"Yeah, I like mayonnaise on my fries," said Deon.

"Gross," she said

"No, it's delicious. Just mayonnaise, salt, and pepper."

"Oh my. Please don't eat that in front of me." Erica laughed.

Deon thought she was so pretty, but she looked like she had been through a few things. She couldn't have been much taller than five feet. To Deon, she seemed like a little baby doll.

"Where are you going to go to tonight?" he asked.

"I'm going back to my friend's house. I have to find something soon before the state takes my son and puts him in foster care."

Deon's heart sank as he heard her talk about what she would have to go through. She was a nice young lady. They started to walk back to the community center.

"All I ever wanted was a small country house with a porch swing, in the country, and away from everybody, just me and my baby. It is my dream," she said.

Deon returned to work and found everyone in a conference with Sister Joseph Mary.

"Okay, here's what is going on," she started. "We have four three-flats where we provide apartments for single mothers and their kids. When the office closes at five, I want all of us to walk over there, and I am going to give you guys a tour of our residences."

Five o'clock came around, and Deon met with Jesus in front of the community center.

"Have you been to these buildings?" Deon asked.

"No, not all of them," Jesus replied.

"Okay, gentlemen," Sister Joseph Mary said as she came out of the door. "Let's go."

They stopped by the first brownstone. It had three floors, and it had nine apartments in the building. It was a nice-looking building made of brown brick. Apartments all came with a lovely bay window. The inside had a brown carpet on the floors, and the walls were painted light green. They proceeded to the second floor and knocked on the door of the building manager. A heavy- set man wearing Duluth jeans and sporting a bald head opened the door. He looked to be in his forties.

"How you are doing, Sister Mary?" he said to her, leaving out the *Joseph*.

"I'm great, Mr. Lester," she responded. "We have some new tenants we are interviewing for the most recently vacated apartments."

"Yes, ma'am, Sister Mary."

"I would like you to meet Deon and Jesus. They will be bringing you supplies, just like the last guys did."

They continued to look over the building. One mother had her door open. Her eyes seemed welled up with tears. *I wonder why she seems so upset*, Deon thought.

"Hi Sister Joseph Mary," the mother said, bowing her head when speaking. Deon could not tell whether she dropped her head because she was being polite or for lack of confidence. But something was troubling her, and it seemed the feeling was exacerbated when Mr. Lester walked past. *Something was up with that*, Deon thought.

"We have three more buildings to see before five o'clock, so we better skedaddle," the sister said.

Deon, Jesus, and Sister Joseph Mary went to the next brownstone. Indeed, it was identical to the previous one. This building was under the same manager, Mr. Lester. Although he didn't live in the building, he was still responsible for building maintenance.

"How many buildings is Mr. Lester responsible for?" Deon asked.

"These two," replied the sister. "We will make a trip to the other properties tomorrow, but primarily, these are the ones we use the most."

They walked back to the community center and went to her office.

"Okay, tomorrow, we must screen applicants for apartments. One thing they are strict on is males living in the brownstones. If they have men staying over, we assume the men are living there, and that is against the regulations."

"So, the father is not allowed to stay with them? Isn't that like creating separation of families?" asked Deon.

"I know what you are implying," responded Sister Joseph Mary, "and I tend to agree. However, the state feels that if the man is in the home, he should be working, and if he is, then there is no need for assistance."

Jesus looked at Deon.

"I guess that makes sense," Deon said.

"So, we will see you guys tomorrow," said the sister.

Deon arrived at his desk the next morning to see Jesus looking disturbed.

"What's going on?" he asked.

"Oh, nothing. Just family matters."

"Is everything going to be okay?" Deon asked.

"I don't know. Depends on the wind," he answered.

The community center doors opened, and Deon saw Erica walk in.

"Erica, hey, how are you?" he asked.

"I'm okay," she said.

"Do you need anything?" he asked.

"You got some of those school supplies left over? I need some for my son," she replied.

"Yeah, I have a book bag and supplies for him. Hold on."

Deon went to the supply closet and got a book bag with a picture of pro basketball players on it. Here you go, Deon notice the gold cross and chain around her neck. What church do you go to? I was raised catholic.

"I went to Mass once in my life," she said. "It's kind of spooky to me. I wish I could go to my church."

"What's the name of your church?" Deon asked.

"Fall River Apostolic Church," she said.

"That's nice," Deon answered. "Never been to an apostolic church before. One day maybe we can go?"

"Are you asking me out on a date" she asked.

"I don't know. How does one have a church date?" Deon answered.

"Nothing wrong with going to church," she said. "How about this Sunday?"

"That would be great," he told her.

"Okay, I can meet you at the visitor's tables. Church starts at ten."

"All right, well, I know you have to get that book bag over to your son's school, so I will see you at church on Sunday."

"That would be fine," she said as she continued to walk up the street. "Bye."

When Sunday came, Deon dressed in his gray and white shirt he salvaged from his eviction. He took the bus to the address of the church and got off right in front of it. He took the bus to the address of the church and got off right in front of it. It was a large church. It would seem to be impossible to find Erica in this place; then he saw her holding her son Eric's hand by the visitor's table, just as she said she would be.

"Hey, so glad you are here," Deon said

"I told you I would be here," she said, smiling. "You ready?"

They went into the church, found three seats together, and sat down. The choir marched single- file into the church, wearing long blue and purple robes, singing as they walked. They took their place in the choir seats behind the ministers and deacons of the church, who sat in big chairs on the altar like they were kings.

A soloist walked forward from the choir and stood at the microphone, and he began singing:

Never would have made it

Never could have made it without You.

I would have lost it all,

But now I see how you were there for me,

And I can say,

Never would have made it,

Never could have made it,

Without You.

I would have lost it all.

But now I see

How You were there for me,

And I can say,

I'm stronger, I'm wiser,

I'm better, much better.

When I look back

Over it all, you brought me through.

I can see that you were the One

I held on to.

And I never would have made it,

Oh, I never could have made it,

Never could have made it without You.

Oh, I, good God, Almighty …

"This is my favorite song," Erica whispered. She became emotional. Deon had heard the song before and thought it was beautiful and moving. The choir was magical. It had over one hundred members, and their gospel singing reverberated throughout the church.

Some parishioners sang, and some became overly emotional. They fell upon the floor and started chanting and slurring their words, which was considered speaking in tongues. Women cried and waved their handkerchiefs in the air. Some fell out and had to be helped by nurses.

The sermon by the Reverend Jordan was riveting. He preached on keeping the faith even when there seemed to be no way out or when things seemed impossible, and how the faith of a mustard seed had the power to move mountains.

Erica sat next to Deon and barely said a word. She remained focused on the service. It seemed that she was very comfortable and assured with Deon sitting there, like they were a couple.

After the service, Deon and Erica stood outside the church and watched other parishioners drive off in their cars.

"I really enjoyed the service, Erica. Thank you for inviting me."

"You're welcome," she said. "Hopefully we will again. I have to meet my ride. I will see you later."

Monday morning, Deon waited for the community center doors to open at nine. He remembered what Sister Joseph Mary said about having to interview applicants for housing assistance. The line outside was getting longer and longer as women with their children held by the hand waited outside the community centers doors. The doors opened as Sister Joseph Mary unlocked them.

"I want you to show some of these mothers the apartments," she told Deon, "but only the ones who have their vouchers. Others will have to wait until approval; just take their information. In addition, we are trying to get people registered to vote, which is going to be difficult because most of these applicants are transients. Also, we are going to need help on Election Day for state and local elections at Mother of God."

"Is that the only place? Seems like last time we had four locations," asked Jesus.

"Well, not anymore. They passed a referendum to cancel early voting and closed three of the four polling places in Upton. There is only one now. You can expect some very long lines if people come out at all, and this is a state election," Sister Joseph Mary answered.

Deon nodded in agreement.

Families poured into the center, took their numbers, and took a seat. They knew the procedure all too well. The talk radio program Deon had listened to before reverberated in his memory.

"These people who are on welfare, the welfare that you and I have been paying. It is free for them to continue to have babies, and their kids are growing up and failing every year. They are passing these kids with social promotion, now they are out here crying discrimination, and when you, a hard-working American who supports family values, plays by the rules, and who tries and is qualified to get the job, they do. It's called affirmative action, and I'm telling you, folks, it's the deep state of social welfare that these people thrive on. The very existence of the welfare system is created for the survival of the liberals and people from the left who encourage this and encourage more women to have more babies, so they can get more money. They are getting supplemental housing, nutritional assistance, free medical services. They are getting their nails done and hair weaves with welfare money that you are paying for. You, the hard-working Americans who work hard, are subsidizing these people and all their entitlement programs. Where does that leave us? America was once great. Will we ever be great again? Or are we going to be a Third World socialist country?"

Deon sat at his desk and screened applicants for affordable housing vouchers. "Number twenty-one," Deon called from his desk.

"Hi," the woman said as she sat down. Her daughter was toddling along with her, and another child pulled at her shirt. "Sit down!" she instructed them, pointing. Her nails were beautifully done. She handed Deon her blue-green voucher and the letter that was attached to it.

"What's the name?" he asked.

"Margarita Lopez," she said in a heavy Spanish accent.

"Do you need someone who speaks Spanish?"

"I understand," she replied.

"I see you have your voucher."

"Yes," she replied.

"Where do you work?"

"At G Mart, just part-time."

"Okay," Deon replied. "I am going to have you talk to my coworker Jesus. It would help. Is that okay?"

"Si," she answered as Deon noted that on her paperwork.

Just then Jesus walked up.

"Hey, Jesus, could you help her?" asked Deon. "She has her voucher, and I processed her paperwork already, but make sure she understands, right?"

"Sure, I got it," Jesus replied. "You want to come with me?" he said to her in Spanish.

Deon went back and sat at his desk to take the next housing applicant. So many single mothers, so many kids. It wasn't long before the hour passed.

Deon and Sister Joseph Mary gathered the voucher holders together to view the apartments that were to become available. They walked together with kids in tow to the brownstones, and Deon assisted as they all entered the front of the building. Sister Joseph Mary gave them the tour, explaining the rules and regulations of the building.

Deon noticed Mr. Lester peering from a darkened enclave that surrounded the hallway entrance to his office. His eyes peered out like a wolf peers at its prey at all the women passing down the main second-floor hallway. A smirk covered his face.

His eyes fell upon Margarita. Deon caught his glare at her, and he could see Margarita noticing but trying to ignore it. The tour of the building continued, and eventually they met back out in front of the building. Sister Joseph Mary gave them the times they could arrange to move into their new apartments.

Later that afternoon, Sister Joseph Mary met with all those who were authorized to move into the building. The women were asking questions.

"Will there be someone to walk the kids to school start at eight thirty? I got to be to work before eight," one resident asked.

"We do have before-school programs where the kids can be dropped off here at eight o'clock. That is the earliest that we have," Sister Joseph Mary answered.

"See," the lady interrupted. "It's damn near impossible to work and get your kids to school. They won't adjust my schedule to take them."

Sister Joseph Mary looked at her and smiled. "I'm sure we can find a parent who has kids who are walking to school or will come here before school. You will have to look around and find a way, and Jesus will help with a prayer to get through these issues."

Deon listened intently. *I wonder if I could open this up a little early for the kids*, Deon thought.

After the meeting, Deon went up to Sister Joseph Mary.

"Sister, can I talk to you for a minute?"

"Yes," she said as she assisted the ladies who were piling out with their kids.

"I don't mind opening at seven for these mothers to drop off their kids before work," said Deon.

"I understand your concern," replied the sister. "But there might be liability issues. Since we are a community center operated and funded by the state, I cannot allow the building to open before 8:00 a.m."

"Wow," Deon said, shaking his head. "It makes it so difficult to do the simplest things."

"Yes, that is right," she said. "Tomorrow we will assist in helping the mothers move in. We will be supplying them with the food boxes we put together earlier to start. I told them their move-in time is eight to eleven, okay?"

"Yes. Thank you, Sister."

Jesus walked up to Deon. "Hey, you know that lady you transferred to me?"

"Yes. Margarita, right?"

"Yeah, well, she is working but doesn't have no papers though. You know they are coming down hard on the undocumented immigrants."

"How did she get a voucher if she is undocumented?" Deon asked.

"They base it on if they have a job or not."

"How is she able to get a job being undocumented?"

"It's a huge need, especially below the minimum wage"

"Seems like she would have some family to live with."

"Don't stereotype," Jesus replied. "Not all immigrants live twenty to a house as you might think."

"Or from what I have been told," Deon quipped.

When the day was finally over, Deon locked the back entrance to the center. Sister Joseph Mary stood at the front door, ready to lock up.

"We will see you bright and early tomorrow morning, okay, Deon?"

"Yes, Sister. I will be here."

It was seven-thirty in the morning. Deon was waiting outside the building for the new residents to move in. One mother noticed Deon from the day before.

"Hey," she said to Deon while holding on to her son. "I got to get to work. If I am late, I will be fired. It is so much pressure I am put under. I must get my son to school, but he can't be on the campus until eight. Could you please watch him, then drop him at the school across the street for me?"

"Yes, ma'am. I can do that for you."

"Thank God. I really appreciate it."

Another mother asked, "I'm sorry, but can you do the same for me? I can get daycare for him and drop him off at school next week. That's going to cost me one hundred dollars extra a week."

"Girl don't you know it," said the first woman.

"No problem, ma'am," said Deon. "I will take the kids to the park until school starts. Can't do it every day though."

"We know, honey. Just one step at a time, but bless you, hon."

Deon walked with both boys to the park and let them play on the swings until the students were permitted on the school grounds. There was an old white-haired man sitting on a bench that sat on a concrete platform about two hundred feet away. There was an older kid playing with his galactic laser.

"Mr. Deon, can I get on the slide?" one of the kids asked.

"Yes, go ahead," Deon told him as he sat on a wooden seesaw. Deon watched the boy on the concrete platform continue to pretend to shoot aliens with his galactic alien laser.

Suddenly, speeding up the grass in the park came a police vehicle. It screeched to a halt directly in front of the kid with the laser gun,

"Drop it! Hands up!" an officer screamed.

The kid was startled and frightened. He didn't know what was happening. Then came the sound of two gunshots, and the little boy lay there in a pool of his own blood. A young girl screamed as she ran over to the concrete platform.

"My brother!" she screamed. "Oh my god, Mama!"

"Get away from him!" yelled the police. "Get your hands up!"

"No!" she cried. "My brother! Mama!" she screamed.

The police officer pointed his gun at her. "Get back, I said. Get back and get down on the ground!"

"No! You shot my brother!" she cried.

Another police car arrived. The officer got out and pulled his weapon.

The girl continued to cry, "Omar wake up! Please don't be dead! Please, Omar!"

The police officer went to the girl, but she fought back. The officer slammed her to the ground, bursting her lip against the concrete. The officer put handcuffs on her and proceeded to handcuff the shot boy as well.

Deon and the boys looked on in horror as Deon tried to shield them from seeing what was going on.

"You people need to move on," said an officer. "This is a crime scene."

An ambulance showed up and put the handcuffed boy on a stretcher.

"Are you with them?" a voice called out. It was another police officer.

"No," said Deon. "I am here watching these two boys until it's time to go to school."

"Are you their legal guardian?" the officer asked.

"No, I am not. I do this for their moms who need to go to work."

"Were you aware that this kid had a gun?" the officer asked.

"I didn't see no gun. I saw a toy," he replied.

"Are you being a wise ass?" asked the officer.

"No. I'm answering your question," Deon said while looking at the officer without dropping his eyes.

The officer walked away, saying, "Okay this is a crime scene, and you need to clear the area."

Deon called the kids and walked toward the school. The school was opening, and Deon went to the receptionist. "I was dropping these two boys off for school," he said, "and they witnessed something that they might need to see a councilor about."

"What happened?" she asked.

"A kid just got shot in the park by police," Deon told her.

"Oh my God. At the other end of the park?" she asked.

"Yes, ma'am."

"Thanks for letting us know," said the receptionist.

"Yes, ma'am"

Deon's heart was hardening. He went to work and sat at his desk, not saying a word to anybody about what had happened. There was talk all around the community center about it.

After work, Deon went to his room. His TV played while he ate a sandwich he had just made. The cable news stations were full of opinions.

"This kid was probably out there selling drugs as they always do. Police officers put themselves in harm's way every day in these neighborhoods. This is just another ploy by the left, refusing to take responsibilities for their own actions."

"Breaking news! A video has been released of the incident, and I want to warn you this is graphic. It clearly shows the boy playing with what looks like a gun from here, and then in the next few seconds you see the police car pull up, the door opens, and the officer, you can see him there firing two shots into this kid as he stood there. Also, the boy's sister runs over, disobeys the officer's order, and is arrested. The officers had received a call about someone with a firearm. "This is obviously a cold-blooded murder," one of the news panelists said as they watched the video.

"My question to you is, why he was playing with a gun?" asked another.

"It's a toy gun. You are supposed to play with a toy gun," said another panelist.

"Where are the parents? Why is he in the park playing with a gun instead of being in school?" another panelist asked.

"Middle school doesn't start until eight thirty in the morning," replied another panelist.

"He should not have been outside playing with a gun," said another.

"Again, you keep saying he had a gun. It was a Star Wars light laser. It seems only inner-city kids get killed in a park by police for playing with a toy laser."

"Now there they go using the race card," yelled another panelist.

"I never mentioned anything concerning race," the panelist said.

"Yes, but we know what you are trying to say. Race has nothing to do with this incident. Had the boy followed the police orders to drop it, he would be alive today."

"You expect an eleven-year-old kid who is doing nothing wrong to be able to follow a loud command in less than three seconds?"

"The officer only had three seconds as well," yelled another on the show.

"I'm sick of everyone ganging up on police" said another.

Deon shook his head. The response from the panelists did not shock him anymore. Deon's heart was hardening.

The next morning, Deon went to the brownstones to assist the mothers who were moving in. He saw Mr. Lester enter the building from the side entrance, almost in a clandestine manner.

I wonder what is up with that dude? Deon thought as he waited in the morning sun, which was getting hotter by the minute. He looked down at his watch. It was eight thirty. Deon noticed a young woman with her two kids getting out of an old used blue Skylark. She had two large Hefty bags full of belongings. It was Margarita.

"Good morning," Deon said as he assisted with both her big heavy bags.

"Thank you," she said in her heavy accent as she tried to gather her kids together. "Come on," she said.

They walked through the main entrance and proceeded down the hallway. Deon noticed a young woman walking toward them. It was the same young woman Deon had seen the day before looking upset. She looked upset now as well, except more so this time. Her eyes welled up with what seemed like tears, and they were puffy.

Deon walked past the darkened hallway of Mr. Lester. Out the corner of his eye, he noticed the office door slowly close. Deon turned and looked at the young woman scampering down the hall. He started putting these incidences together and decided something was going on.

They walked to Margarita's new apartment. She tried the key, and the door opened. Deon walked in. No one had painted, it seemed. The carpet on the floor looked new; it hadn't been worn that much. For the most part, the small one-bedroom apartment was excellent.

So, there are already two beds here, Deon thought to himself.

"I must get a bed for myself," Margarita said in broken English as she looked around the apartment.

"I will see if I can find another bed for you," Deon told her.

"Thank you," Margarita said, smiling.

"I am to bring back some supplies for you later. I'm on my way back to the center now. I should be back later this afternoon," Deon said to her.

"Okay," she said, smiling, while her kids played with the Hefty bags on the green-carpeted floor. "Thank you again."

Deon returned to the center and went to his desk. He began looking around for a request form that had to be submitted to Sister Joseph Mary. Deon looked up as a young woman sat at his desk.

"I need your help," she said softly.

Deon looked up from his desk. It was the same girl he had noticed in the apartments, the girl who always seemed bothered and upset. This time she was shaking a little.

"Are you okay?" he asked.

She paused. Deon stared at her with deep concern in his face.

"Can you get me out that building?" she asked.

Deon looked at her. "What's going on? First, your name is?"

"Vanessa," she replied. "I need another building. I mean, I know beggars can't be choosy, but please," she insisted.

Deon eyes dropped in thought. He knew it had something to do with that building manager.

"I don't want to say nothing, because I don't want to lose my apartment," she added.

"Why do you think you might lose your apartment?" he asked.

She looked at Deon. "Can you just help me please? Whatever you can do."

"Let's take a quick walk," Deon suggested. He grabbed a box with food and supplies that he had to drop off. They walked together up the street toward the apartment building.

"Listen—I notice that something is going on, right?" he asked. "Just straight up tell me what's happening."

"Let's just say he can have you put out and ain't nothing the center can do about it, and he makes sure he let all these girls know that." She stopped and looked at Deon. "That's all I'm going to say, because I have done been out there with nowhere to go and with my kids, and I can't go through that no more. I mean, I got a little job, and I'm building up."

"I can tell the sister, and she can make something happen," Deon suggested.

"No, please don't," Vanessa said. "It could backfire. I have seen it happen. She can't do anything anyways. He don't work for her. Mr. Lester oversees who gets section seven housing. He's employed by the state, and he manages who lives in the building or not, and they know what he is doing, and they are laughing about it. They call it perks. I ain't for giving nothing up, especially to nobody like him, but he be pressuring all these girls."

Deon looked at the building as they walked toward it.

"Just see if you can find me another building," she said, "and please let me know, 'cause I'm scared for my kids. I got eleven- and twelve-year-old daughters."

Deon nodded in agreement. "I will look today and let you know."

"Thank you!?" she said as she turned and gave Deon a serious but appreciative look. She walked the other direction as Deon entered the front door of the building.

Deon went up to the first floor to Margarita's room. He knocked on the door, and it was already ajar. Deon put his shoulder into the door while holding on to the box full of essentials. He heard some mumbling in the room. Mr. Lester had Margarita pinned against her living room wall. His bulking body was shadowed and covering her completely. He turned around startled and, grinning at Deon, walked out of the apartment. Margarita's face looked hurt and troubled.

"Sister Joseph Mary wanted me to bring you this box, and I have another for you. I will be bringing that back in a few minutes. Everything okay?"

Margarita looked at Mr. Lester, who had made his way out of the front door and stood in the hallway. He had his clipboard with him to give the appearance he was there for business. Deon saw all through that.

"Is everything all right?" he asked again.

She looked at Deon. "It's okay," she replied. "Thank you for the box."

"I have another box I will bring later," Deon said as he continued to look at her, knowing what was going on.

"Thank you," she said, looking very upset and shaky.

Deon left the building, not knowing what to do. If he went to the sister and she made an issue of it, he would have no proof. The women were not going to call the police for fear they would lose their apartments. The building manager was in with the owners. What could he do? Just wait and see what happened.

Later that night, there was a knock on Margarita's door. Her kids were sleeping in the front room. She opened the door, and there was Mr. Lester.

She stepped back from the door. He investigated the front room and saw her kids asleep. He looked at her. She looked away, and he nudged her toward the bedroom. The door closed behind them. Expletives were uttered, Spanish words pleaded in the darkened room. Commands and demands. Muffled sounds. Whimpering and crying, then silence. An hour later, Mr. Lester left the apartment, all smiles.

The next day, Deon and Jesus sat in Sister Joseph Mary's office as she walked in and sat at her desk.

"Today I have been informed that deportation officers will be coming to the center and reviewing the records of all our cases. It's frightening what is happening. Needless to say, there are probably going to be some issues with tenants as far as their paperwork."

Deon looked at Jesus. "What do we do?"

"Comply with everything," said the sister. "It's out of our hands."

Deon and Jesus left the office and strolled to their desk.

"I'm scared," Jesus said.

"Why, what's up?"

"I got family members here and all over, you know what I mean."

"Yeah," Deon replied. "Is all your stuff straight?"

"Oh yeah," he said. "I was born here".

Just then, deportation officers dressed in black entered the community center. They marched to Sister Joseph Mary's office.

Deon and Jesus looked at each other. "Here we go," they both said at the same time.

Ten minutes later, the officers came out of the office with Sister Joseph Mary trailing them.

"We need to go over to the brownstones," she said.

They all walked down to the brownstones. There was an enforcement van parked out in front of the complex. Officers were walking in and out of the building. Deon noticed Margarita crying as she tried to hug her crying children with her hands handcuffed behind her back.

"Margarita!" Deon called out as he and Jesus walked up.

"They take me," she cried as her children were led away by another officer. Jesus spoke to her in Spanish. The officers proceeded to put Margarita in the van and shut the van door. Deon stood speechless with Jesus.

"What did she say?" he asked.

"She said they were taking her kids; that is all she kept saying. The kids go one place, and they are taking her somewhere else."

Damn, Deon said as he looked at the metal enforcement van. His heart became ever harder.

Deon sat in his room watching cable news. A debate was on about undocumented workers.

"These people come into the United States illegally, crossing the border unchecked. There are thousands of these people, and they are not the best of the population. They come here and start gangs, and they are burglarizing and selling drugs, they are murderers and prostitutes, and they are bringing this to our country and cities, and the liberals house them, and give them sanctuary, and with our tax money support these lawbreakers and menace to society," one panelist stated.

"I disagree," another panelist interjected. "These are hard-working individuals just looking for a better life in this country, as it says on the Statue of Liberty."

"That is for those who enter this country legally," another commentator said. "These people are leeches, and they get free education and free healthcare and housing assistance. What about Americans first? What about those hard-working Americans who play by the rules? Where is their amnesty?"

"The initiative now is to build a wall," the host of the program stated. "What do you think about this?"

"Yes, I am in favor of a wall being built on our border. We must keep these people out of our country because we are being infested by these people."

Another panelist spoke up. "So, you have women and children who are sacrificing everything to get here for a better life for their families and are frightened every day of being rounded up and deported. Crimes are committed against immigrants; they are afraid to call the police or call for help for fear of being arrested and deported and their families separated."

"As they should," interjected another panelist. "If you are here illegally, you should have no rights afforded to you by the constitution," he said. "How easy was it to forget Heather Woods, who was killed by one of these illegal aliens?"

Deon continued to listen as he fixed himself a ham sandwich and popped open a soda before taking off his clothes and calling it a night.

Chapter 13

Dion was told by Sister Joseph Mary to take some necessities to some of the residents in the residential brownstone. Walking up the sidewalk, Deon noticed a man working at the side door of the building. He had dreadlocks down his back, brown khakis, boots, and a gold, black, and green shirt.

"What's up, sir," Deon said to him as he walked past.

"Hey, mi bredda, how everyting wid yuh?" the man said in a thick Jamaican accent that was so strong Deon could barely understand what he said.

"Yes, sir. Just got to drop these off to this lady here,"

"Yea, mon," the man replied.

"Yes, sir," Deon said as he walked up the stairs. He looked down the hall at Mr. Lester's office. It didn't appear anyone was there, but who knows what could be going on behind his door.

Deon proceeded to the apartment of the old lady and knocked on the door.

"Yes?" she answered.

"Hi, ma'am, it's Deon from the community center."

An old woman came to the door. She needed a walker to get around the room. She was heavyset, and she wore a black wig on her head. A ceiling fan blew a stale smell of mold and mothballs around the house.

"Hi, dear," she said. "You can bring them in right here. I sure thank you, young man." She blew out of her mouth and wiped the sweat from her head underneath the wig on top of it. "I just need to sit down for a minute." She seemed exhausted.

"Do you need help?" Deon asked.

"No, I'm doing okay, baby. I'm fine. Whew! It is hot in here," she said wiping her forehead with the back of her hand again.

Deon looked around. "No air conditioner?" he asked.

"Yes but it don't work so good. My grandchildren be here and they be hot, I loves my grandbabies she said."

"I will let them know at the center," he said.

"Okay, dear," she responded and smiled.

Deon walked down the hallway and peered toward Mr. Lester's door as he walked out of the building.

He saw the Rasta man again. "Hey, brethren yuh sey yuh wuk up at di community center?"

"Yes. I'm Deon."

"Me Preacher," the man said.

Deon gave him a handshake. "You work here?"

"Yea, mi contract wid di city fi handy man wuk fi all di buildings," the Rasta man answered. "Yuh doing community service?"

"Yes, sir, I'm trying to get things straight before going to court."

"So weh yuh live?"

"Right now, Sister Joseph Mary gave me a small utility room to stay until I get on my feet."

"So yuh need a job now?" the Rasta man said abruptly. "Mi give yu mi numba, gimme a call lata irate?"

"All right, Preacher. Thank you."

Deon walked back to the community center. There was another woman with her two kids waiting to get an apartment. The children stood obediently beside her. Deon sat at his desk and took her information.

"The first availability is next week," he said. "Come back on Tuesday and see what we have," Deon told her while handing her an appointment card.

"Thank you," she replied graciously.

Deon escorted her and her kids to the door. As Deon started away from the glass door, he noticed a young lady and her son walking into Mr. Lester's building. Deon stopped and looked closely. It appeared to be Erica. *Oh my God, I hope that isn't her*, he thought. But yes, it was.

Deon's heart raced and his eyes got big as he started to hyperventilate. Deon ran up to the apartment building, stepped in, and heard the voice of a social worker showing her the apartment. Dion looked down the hall and saw a smile on the face of the apartment manager, Mr. Lester.

Deon's jaws tightened and his fists clenched. He knew what Mr. Lester was thinking, and Deon knows damn well he was not going to let anything happen to Erica.

Deon waited outside of the brownstone, staying out of sight, until Erica came out.

"Erica, I need to talk to you," Deon said, startling Erica. She turned to Deon as she came through the door.

"What are you doing here?" she asked.

"Erica, I don't want you to move into the building!" he said.

She looked at Dion. "What are you talking about?"

"Look," said Deon, "the resident manager here, he's raping the girls in this building."

Erica looked bewildered yet stern. "Well, I don't have much of a choice," she said. "It's either here or stay in a shelter." She saw the look of concern on Deon's face

"He's going to come by your room at eleven o'clock at night. He's going to corner you."

"Okay, so I won't open the door," she replied. "Ain't nobody gonna rape me. I can't give up this apartment. I won't have nowhere else to go, and even this apartment is on a month-by-month basis."

"What if I get you an apartment?" Deon asked.

"How are you going to get me an apartment, and you don't have a place for yourself?"

Deon said to himself, *I have no job, and I barely have no place to stay, but I got to do something to get her out of that building.* To her, he said, "If I get you in another building for six months, would you do that?"

"I don't need to take anything from you," she said. "I make it on my own."

Deon stopped for a second and looked at Erica.

She added, "Everybody has a reason for what they do, Deon. So what's yours?"

"It's no secret that I want nothing awful to happen to you," he said, "and I am looking for nothing in return."

Erica knew Deon liked her, but for what other reason would he want to help her?

Right about that time, Deon and Erica stopped and noticed the dark shadow of a person looking at them from inside the building. He knew who it was. He looked back at Erica.

"I'm going to get you out of here," he said.

Deon sat in his room, thinking about how he was going to get Erica out of that building. He thought about talking to Preacher, remembering their earlier conversation. Deon thought about all the marijuana smokers at Mid Union. It is a huge risk he thought, but Deon knew he might be able to get away with selling marijuana on campus since most students seemed to received privilege from police that he would never get in Upton. Deon counted his money and found he had about sixty dollars. That was a long way from having the money to help Erica.

He went over to Preacher's house. The Rasta man came to the door. "Wah gwaan mi brethren? Cum ina."

Dion walked in and saw Preacher's wife preparing dinner as she stood at the stove, putting ingredients in a potboiler. "Nice. What is that?" Deon asked.

"Pressure cooker," replied Preacher. "It soften the meat up."

"Looks and smells so good," said Deon.

"Yea, mon," Preacher said.

"I need to talk to you about something," Deon said.

"Okay," Preacher responded.

The Rasta man and Deon went to the next room which was decorated with Jamaican statues and pictures of Bob Marley on the walls.

"I have a situation where someone needs my help. I have a friend of mine, and she has a five- year-old, and right now she doesn't have no place to live. They're going to give her this apartment with the city in a building where she would have to fight for herself, you know what I mean?"

"Yuh ah talking abou dat bloodclot dat works dere?" Preacher asked.

"Yes," Deon replied, after making sure he understood what Preacher asked. "I don't want her in that building. That building manager is a rapist. I was hoping from our conversation that you had a job or something for me. I need to make some money so I can get her out of there."

"Yuh hab nuh place fi yuhself, buh yuh waan tuh help har?" "I know," Deon replied with tears in his eyes.

"I have some friends on campus that I can sell to. I only have 60 dollars and if you could trust me to turn over a few bags, I know I can make some money, can you help me Preacher"?

"No worries." Preacher reached under the end table, which held a bong-styled lamp. "Dis four hundred dollars bagged up. Yuh git half. Bi mindful ah wah yuh duh. Guh eena peace, bredda."

Deon called Greg.

"Hey, Deon, what's up?"

"Hey, man, can you come down and pick me up and take me to campus?" Deon asked.

"Yeah, sure, Deon. When?" Greg asked.

"Whenever you get the chance."

"I can come now," Greg replied, trying to figure out what might be wrong.

"Okay. I appreciate it, Greg."

Greg picked up Deon at the center. Deon had packed his weed bags in his scrotum.

"Hey, man, what's been going on?" Greg asked.

"Are those fools up on the yard?" asked Deon.

"Yeah."

"Look, I got a few bags of bud I need to get rid of. You know what I mean."

"Thanks for letting me know," Greg quipped.

I can't believe I have now stooped to being a drug dealer, Deon said disappointedly, but I really need the money". "It's only bud Greg said, I don't think that classifies you as a drug dealer". "I think the police would disagree" Deon added. "Well one thing is for sure, you will sell out quickly on the campus and with much less chance of being caught, gotta be careful though", Greg assured.

They arrived back to campus to see students gathering at the school canteen.

"What's going on?" Deon asked as Greg walked up beside him.

"Everybody is watching the pro football league draft. Isaiah Islam is supposed to be drafted first-round," Greg said.

The television blared, "The Southerners draft Isaiah Islam in the fourth pick of the round one of the pro league draft." There was Isaiah on TV with his suit on. His family cheered and his mother had tears in her eyes as Isaiah made his way to the podium to accept his new professional kersey and number.

"I am truly grateful," he said as he spoke to the crowd. "All the hard work and dedication has paid off, and I am going to give my best to this organization."

Isaiah shook hands with the coach as he was given the number thirty-three jersey. Everyone in the canteen cheered as he put on the team hat.

"Thank you," said Isaiah, "and I want to give a shout out to all those at Mid Union University who helped to make this moment possible." Everyone cheered and clapped.

"Wow," Deon said, "that is a guaranteed five million signing bonus. He is now a millionaire."

Greg and Deon arrived back at the dorm room.

"I see my old bed looks the same," said Deon. "What happened to the hard chairs?"

"Those are long gone," Greg laughed.

"Look, man, I have to finish these bags."

"How many you got?" Greg asked.

"Twenty twenties," Dion replied.

Greg called Michael and Andrew. They came by with their friends and bought all Deon had.

"You guys are lifesavers," Deon said to them.

Deon went back to see Preacher.

"Mi si yuh sell out," Preacher said.

Deon breathed a sigh of relief.

"Got a long way to go," said Deon. "I need another four hundred. I can get it sold right away."

Preacher handed Deon a package. "Dis mek eight hundred. Si mi wen yuh a finished."

Deon blew another sigh of relief.

"Thank you, Preacher."

"No problem, Bredren." There was a whistling sound on the stove. "Cow foot in the pressure cooker," Preacher said.

"Cow foot? Really?"

"Yea, mon. Like life, whole heap guh inna. An di pressure breaks ih dung. But tings can cum out gud."

Deon thought about that pressure cooker. His feelings for Erica, losing his job, the news, and what was happening on campus—a pressure cooker seemed to be the right metaphor.

Deon arrived back at his room and hid his bags in a sock. *As long as no one is coming here for weed, I should be okay*, he thought. *Sister Joseph Mary should not even think this is going on here. Let's just hope this works out.*

Deon sat at his desk the next day, looking at the clock, waiting for lunch. He'd had no money for breakfast but had a coupon left for the Burger Hut.

"You want to go to the Burger Hut with me?" Deon asked Jesus.

"No, I'm good. I have a sandwich from home," Jesus replied. The clock showed one o'clock as Deon made his way to lunch.

He noticed a crowd gathering at the Burger Hut. Police cars flew around the corner with lights and sirens blaring. Deon walked up closer and saw a big man arguing with the police.

"Man, why can't y'all just leave me alone? I ain't bothering nobody."

"Sir, you are being arrested for selling items out here in front of this establishment," said an officer.

"But I always set up my table out here. Been doing it for years"

"Well, we're telling you can't," said another officer. The owner of the burger hut, Mr. Singh came to the door.

"Mr. Singh, did you call them? You could have told me. I would have moved," the big man said.

"No, I didn't call," Mr. Singh responded.

"We don't have time to discuss the matter, sir," said the officer.

"Look, I will just move then," the big man said.

"I'm sorry," the officer said. "It's too late for that."

"Aw, come on, man. Damn. I can move. Why it got to be all this?"

Other officers moved closer in. The big man stood back and put his hands up a bit higher than his shoulders.

"Hey, man, I ain't did nothing. Don't be puttin' your hands on me."

The officers grabbed at the big man. One officer grabbed him around the neck. The big man staggered while as many as six officers grabbed him at once.

"You choking me! You choking me!" he could barely yell. He fell to the ground. "Let me go, you choking me!" His voice grew weaker until no sound came from him at all. A crowd gathered and started to intervene. "Hey man y'all ain't got to do all that, he saying y'all choking him!" people in the crowd yelled. Two officers walked towards the gathering crowd. "You people need to leave the area!" he said loudly while grabbing his Taser." "We aint got to go nowhere, we got the right to be here!" yelled people in the crowd.

The officers held him there until there was no more movement from the big man. They handcuffed him while he was on his stomach. Blood ran from his lips and nose. Other police cars arrived and ordered everyone to clear the area.

Deon turned and saw Isaiah Islam. "Hey, Isaiah, what you doing down here?"

"This is where I'm from, the hood," Isaiah said. "I live right up the street in that bungalow." He pointed to a small one-story modest flat.

He just signed a multi-million-dollar contract. I know he will be moving his family out of here, Deon thought to himself.

"Did you see what happened?" asked Deon.

"Yeah I saw it, crying shame," said Isaiah. "Happens all the time down here."

"Damn. I hope Big Mike is okay."

"Yeah, me too," Isaiah said. "He been out here with his table since I was in middle school."

"I imagine you will be moving with your family up out of here soon," Deon said.

"I ain't no millionaire yet," said Isaiah. "Too many of us leave and don't reach back. Plus, my grandma loves that old bungalow. We probably won't be going anywhere."

"Good to see you here, Isaiah. I got to get back to the community center," said Deon.

"Assalamu alaikum," Isaiah said as he turned to walk away.

"Wa-Alaikum-Salaam," Deon replied. He headed back to the community center.

After work, Deon went back to his room and chilled out for the evening. The ten o'clock news came on the television.

"Today in Upton, an assailant whose street alias was Big Mike was killed by police after being apprehended and arrested for selling stolen goods in front of this restaurant on 77th Street. Officers put duty in front of danger in subduing the suspect, according to arrest reports. There is a video of the altercation between police and the assailant people knew as Big Mike. As you can see, he had a card table with CDs and movies on them, and he was told he was being arrested. You can see him arguing with police before he was taken down by officers. Michelle Wesley reports ..."

The reporter began, "This is Mr. Singh who owns The Burger Hut carry-out. Mr. Singh, can you tell us what happened?"

Mr. Singh said, "Big Mike sells his movies and costume jewelry and perfume oils out here. We never had any problem with it; we never called the police. The police never told him to leave. They told him right away he was under arrest. They argued, and now he dead. It's a shame."

The news immediately cut to another scene and another person interviewed.

"This guy they call Big Mike is always here selling illegal movies and merchandise. The police expected him to move along. When confronted, however, this man resisted, and this is the outcome. Thank God none of the police were injured."

Then another panel discussion:

"Again, these people have no respect for the rule of law," one panelist said.

"This man is dead now for selling CDs and perfume in front of this establishment."

"Which is illegal," interrupted another panelist.

"First, there is no evidence his items were stolen, but even if so, it is a misdemeanor infraction. Should he have to die because of that?"

"This assailant died for fighting the police," another panelist said.

"We are watching the same video; he did not fight with police."

"He resisted arrest by not complying with the police. What is so hard about following police demands?"

"Standing for your rights is not noncompliance and should not mean a death sentence."

"The video showed Mike was a big man of over three hundred pounds. What do you want the police to do?"

How about using some de-escalation instead of killing someone?" another panelist asked. "You can clearly hear him saying 'You're choking me' as many as ten times."

"If you follow police demands and be respectful, things like this don't happen. It's pretty simple really."

Deon sat there shocked.

Deon awoke the next morning and was glad it was the weekend. Deon gathered his product and tucked it safely away in his pants, then he called Greg.

Greg answered. "What's up, Deon? You got some customers waiting for you."

"I'm coming that way in about an hour," said Deon. "I can meet you at your room."

"Call me when you get here—no text, call," Greg insisted.

"Will do," Deon replied.

He turned on the TV. It was the public education channel, and an old rerun of *Mr. Roger's Neighborhood* was coming on with its jingle, "It's a beautiful day in the neighborhood, a beautiful day for a neighbor, would you be mine, could you be mine?"

Deon turned the channel.

Deon arrived back on campus and noticed a massive gathering of people protesting at the Confederate statue. He called Greg to say that he had arrived, and they met on the main campus grounds.

"What is going on?" Deon asked Greg as they walked toward the gathering protest.

There were armed police officers, and there was a group of skinheads with military-style weapons wearing combat boots and army camouflage. Some of them had on army helmets. They all chanted, "You can't erase history. Blood and earth! Hail to the Confederate general and the Confederates who died for our rights and your rights." Confederate flags flew on makeshift poles stabbed into the ground. The crowd got larger, the chants grew louder, and the applause was constant.

Deon and Greg walked around the outside of the mob. Many protestors spat on the ground as Deon walked by and began hollering racial epithets.

On the other side were other protesters trying to shout down the Confederates with chants of "No Nazis!"

The local radio stations and TV stations were there. Deon walked toward the student union, remembering that he wasn't up there clean. He had a few bags of flowers on him, so Deon stepped back so that he wouldn't get caught up in an arrest in the protest.

"Let's get the hell out of here, Greg said as he pulled on Deon's arm.

I'm right with you," Deon agreed as they walked away.

They arrived back at the room. "Hey, man," said Greg. "I am sorry about all this going and this campus protest."

"You don't need to apologize for the actions of others."

"Yeah, I know, Deon, but it's really embarrassing," said Greg.

For me too," Deon added.

Deon and Greg pulled their chairs together.

"Is the door locked?" Deon asked.

"Hold on," Greg said as he went to the door to make sure.

"Okay, I have all of these. Twenty-five dollars each," Deon said.

"Those look like good buds. I also want to talk to you about your case. Let me get Andrew over here." Greg called Andrew, who came right over.

"Hey, Deon," he said as he entered the room. "What did you get?"

Deon showed Andrew his wares. Andrew smelled the bud though the bag.

"Man, that is strong. How much for these?"

"Twenty-five dollars," replied Deon.

Andrew went into his pocket and pulled out a bankroll. "Give me ten," he said as he put down $300.

Greg went into his wallet. "Here, give me two. Tell Mike to come by," Greg said as he took his two.

When Mike arrived, he said, "Hey, Deon, what's up? I see you got that sticky icky." He laughed. "How many you got left?"

"Just two more."

"Here," Mike said, handing Deon fifty dollars.

"Damn, sold out in thirty minutes," Deon said.

"You should have brought more, man," Greg said. "What is going on with your case?"

"Nothing yet," Deon answered.

"I talked to my uncle about your situation. He has a law firm. He told me he would look at your case, but he would have to have the retainer fee of at least two thousand."

Deon shook his head. "I can't come up with two thousand dollars, man."

"Let's take a ride over to his office and talk to him," Greg suggested.

"Maybe you can work something out.

"Is he open on Saturday?" Deon asked.

"Yes they keep hours on Saturday" Greg answered.

Greg and Deon stepped back onto the yard as the protesting of the Confederate statue continued. A student in camouflage spoke over a loudspeaker: "We don't have slavery now. That is something that happened two hundred years ago, get over it!" Defending our American heritage is not racist! It is they who always bring up race. It is they who still use the race card. It is they who are the racists! They want to silence you for standing proud of who you are. We will not be silenced!"

Deon and Greg made it to the parking lot, got in Greg's car, and took the ride over to Greg's uncle's law firm—again, a tall shining skyscraper. Deon and Greg rode the elevator to the third floor.

Boyd, Schmidt, and Anderson Law Partners was the sign that hung on the wall. "Can I help you?" said the receptionist.

Greg spoke up. "I'm here to see my uncle, Scott Boyd. I'm Greg."

She got on the phone and chatted with the person on the other end. She hung up the phone and said, "He will see you guys now."

Deon and Greg followed her to his office and found him sitting at his desk.

"So, you must be Deon," said Scott as he shook Deon's hand. "Greg kind of told me what has happened. It's a situation where it is complicated to defend, because it is the defendant's word against the police. We would have to establish that you were not involved. The best way to do that is to demonstrate that you are a law-abiding citizen. Are you working right now?"

"No. I was fired a month ago."

"That is what happens. It's a trap that is set up. Certain politicians want to show they are tough on criminals and so forth. I'm sure Greg told you I will need the retainer before I can even begin. I would like to help you otherwise, but I would at least require that to have any wiggle room at all."

"I will try to come up with it," Deon promised.

"When is your next court date?" Scott asked.

"Next week," Deon responded.

"You will need a continuance," Scott said. "They may not give it to you depending on who is representing you at that time."

"It's a court-appointed attorney," Deon replied.

"Yeah, they want a shut case. I can give you my card and number and see what you can come up with before your court date."

"Thanks," Deon said as he stood up.

Scott stood up to shake Deon's hand. "Tell you what. Give me the case number, and I will take a look, okay?"

"Thank you, Mr. Boyd. I greatly appreciate it."

Greg and Deon got back in the car. "You need a ride back into town?" Greg asked.

"That would be cool," Deon replied.

"Well," Greg said as he drove, "maybe you can make that retainer with the trees you are selling. I can come down and pick you up."

"No," Deon said. "I don't want to put you in jeopardy. I got a few stops to make. And I can be back tonight."

Deon stopped at the Rasta man's house. Deon put the money down for what he previously sold.

"Mon, weh yuh guh sell suh fass like dis bredren."

"Me have friends, Preacher," Deon replied, trying to speak in the patois accent.

Preacher laughed. "Yuh gud mon." He gave Deon many more bags.

Deon counted the bags and took a deep breath.

"Yuh mek wi both rich," he laughed.

"Thanks, Preacher."

"No problem mon."

"No wait till drum beat before you grine you axe." "What do you mean?" Deon Asked.

Be prepared for all eventualities. Preacher answered.

Deon arrived on campus to see the campus police riding around. *Must be police day*, Deon said to himself. Deon called Greg, who was in the dorm.

When he finally arrived at the room, Greg said, "Hey, come on in. Everything cool?"

"Yeah," Deon replied.

Greg turned on the TV. A news program was on with a breaking news alert.

"A protest has started at the capital in Allendale where defenders of the Confederate flag were protesting the effort to have Confederate statues to the Civil War removed. A group calling themselves the Sons of Dixie protested with sidearms and assault rifles. Most were singing the song 'Dixie.' In opposition was a group calling themselves the EAF, which is an acronym for Eliminating All Fascism, which over here as you can see are the ones wearing all black shirts and hats. A lot of vitriolic exchanges are going on here. There have been some battles between the two groups."

"Man, this stuff is spreading," Greg said.

Deon looked on and breathed a sigh of dismay. "I just want to get rid of these bags and get back to Upton."

Greg and Deon watched TV and waited for Andrew and Mike. There was the knock on the door.

"Hey, it's Drew," said a voice from the other side of the door. Deon let him in.

"Where's Mike?" Deon asked.

"I think he's gone, man. I don't know where he went," Andrew answered. "What did you get?"

"Same thing as yesterday," Deon replied.

"Cool. That bud you had yesterday was the truth, man. Twenty-five?"

"Yeah," replied Deon.

Andrew went into his pocket. "I got a hundred."

Deon went to what was once his desk and pulled out four bags that he had already taken from his pants.

"Cool, man. Thanks. How long are you going to be up here?" asked Andrew.

"Until I'm sold out," Deon told him.

Greg's cell phone buzzed.

"It's my friend Brianna, she wants 6 bags, she's coming over," Greg said. And so it went for the next hour, and Deon was sold out.

"I'm done," Deon said to Greg.

"Good," Greg responded with a sigh of relief. "I don't want to get caught any more than you do. You need a ride back to the hood?"

"Yeah, that would be good, since I'm not carrying anything but money. But from experience, that can be a bad thing too. Hopefully, I will have that retainer by Monday," Deon said.

"My uncle is cool," Greg answered. "I'm sure he's going to step in for you. We are a close family."

They arrived at the community center. "Hey, be careful, bro," Greg said as Deon got out the car.

"Hey, man, I got to make it while I can. Be safe on the drive back, dude," Deon replied.

Deon went to his room and turned on the TV before grabbing a cup of ramen noodles he put in the microwave. He flipped the channel until he found a news program talking about the flag controversy.

"I tell you, Bill, this organization out there called EAF needs to be classified as a terrorist hate group. They are using terrorist tactics of destruction and are no different than ISIS or any other terrorist group," said one of the panelists.

Another commentator spoke up. "I agree, Bill, many these people have no idea what they are supposedly protesting. They dress in all black and use vandalism and destruction of property."

"Just a minute," said another commentator. "They were protesting the statue of a Confederate soldier."

"Again, you people on the left are tolerant when a group like this breaks the law but had there been a group that vandalized a statue of Martin Luther King, then that would not be tolerated. The left is full of hypocrisy."

"Surely you are not making a comparison between a Confederate and Dr. Martin Luther King!" another voice echoed out.

"What I am saying is that people have the right to a Confederate historical monument the same as there is a right for there to be a statue of Martin Luther King. Typical liberal hypocrisy along with the usual media bias."

Oh, boy, Deon said to himself as he ate his roman noodles and watched the program. *What is going on in this world?*

It was a quiet morning, as nothing particular was occurring—not just yet anyway. Deon turned and looked down toward the apartment buildings. He noticed a woman and a young child on the front doorstep of one of the buildings. It was Erica.

Deon walked down to meet her. "Erica!" he said as he walked up. He was speechless. He didn't know what to say.

"Deon, I don't have much choice," she said. "It's either here or stay in a shelter. We have been through this. I know you are concerned. I will be all right."

"I'm going to get you out of here," Deon replied.

Deon went to his room and looked up apartments for rent. He knew of a nice area some distance away. He knew where she worked; maybe he should find a place out in that direction, he thought.

Deon mapped out an area and went on a walk. He saw the bus that could get him to that neighborhood. The bus arrived, and the ride seemed to be five miles or so away. The area was two- and three-story brownstones that lined both sides of the street. At the end of the block, there was an apartment building that held about thirty units.

Deon went inside the rental office.

"Hi, can I help you?" the lady behind the desk asked.

"Yes, ma'am. My name is Deon, and I really need to talk to you about an apartment."

"Okay," she responded. "You can fill out an application."

"Okay, thank you," Deon replied. He took the application and filled it out with his information.

The lady looked over the form. "For employment, you put self-employed," she said, questioning.

"Yes," Deon replied. "Let me explain, please."

Deon sat down and began, "I currently work at the Upton community center, and I have a friend who is the mother of a five-year-old boy. She presently is assigned a subsidized apartment; however, the manager in charge of section seven rent subsidies puts her at risk."

"What do you mean?" the lady asked, looking suspicious.

"I mean, no one has come forward yet, but there are vulnerable tenants there, and the manager who is in charge of the units takes advantage if you understand what I mean."

"Has no one reported this?" the lady asked.

"They are all afraid of losing their apartments and being put back on the streets," Deon answered.

"I see," the lady said. "Does she have a job?"

"Just part-time," Deon answered. "Do you have a month-to-month lease?"

"No, only six months and yearly," she replied.

"Is there any kind of way if I pay six months in advance that she could get an apartment here?" Deon asked.

"That might be possible, if she can bring some check stubs, because these units are not subsidized. They recently took that away," she responded. "I would need those check stubs."

"Okay, I will tell her," Deon replied. "Can I look at one of the apartments?"

"Sure, we actually have a furnished apartment available," she said as she stood up and grabbed a key. They walked out of the office and down a brightly lit hallway to an apartment on the second floor toward the side of the building. She opened the door. It was a one-bedroom furnished apartment, which was small but nice.

It is quaint and comfortable, Deon thought. It had a balcony on the side, hardwood floors, and a small tiled kitchen.

"How much per month is this?" asked Deon.

"This is for six hundred," the lady replied.

Deon thought about the $3,600 he would have to come up with. Could he be a fool? He needed money for his own case, and he was out here trying to save some girl who probably didn't want to be saved.

Deon arrived back at his room and thought about Erica. Did he want to help her only for selfish reasons? Then he thought about Mr. Lester cornering her and putting his hands all over her. Deon put the money away and went out front to the street. Down underneath the train overpass were about four guys and woman on their knees with their hands behind their heads. Police cars and a police van arrived. They were handcuffed and led into the police van.

"Hey, don't I know you?" a voice over Deon's shoulder said.

Deon turned around. "No, I don't think so."

"Remember down at the court that day?"

"Oh yeah," Deon said. "Were you there?"

"Yeah, we all went in the wagon."

"So, what's been up, dude?" Deon said while acknowledging he remembered.

"Plenty much," the guy said as they shook hands in the organization's handshake. "So, they got you going to court on what date?"

"This coming Thursday," Deon replied.

"Mine is Wednesday. I'm Raymond."

"Deon," Deon replied.

"I going to go on ahead and take the case," Raymond said. "I can't fight them. It's my word against them."

"That a felony though," Deon said.

"Along with the rest of them," Raymond replied.

"That's how they do it," Deon said. "Throw everyone up against the wall, then charge everybody. Leave it to you to prove yourself innocent."

"You work down here or something?" Raymond asked.

"At the community center for right now," Deon answered. "Be careful, my brother. I got to roll."

"Later, D," Raymond replied.

As Deon walked away, a police car pulled around the corner, stopping by Raymond.

"Hey, Raymond, how about a talk, bro," one of the policemen said.

"About what? I didn't do nothing."

"Nobody said you did. Get in," the officer ordered.

Raymond, looking like he had no choice, got in the back seat. The police car pulled away.

"Tell us what you know about the G-thang involvement in the Forty-Ninth Street shooting," one of the officers ordered.

"Hey, man, I don't know what you are talking about," Raymond answered.

"Oh, you don't. You know your G-dog Meechie? He says you know all about it, you guys taking that twenty thousand in that drug money hold up. The Mad Cobras not too happy about that," the officer said as they continued to drive.

"Where y'all taking me?"

"Somewhere you are familiar with," the officer replied with a sinister smile.

The police took Raymond on a twenty-minute ride, pressuring him to give up information.

"How about we let you out here?" one of the officers asked.

Raymond looked around. It was Mad Cobra territory.

"Man what y'all trying to do? You going to let me off here?"

"You can't tell us what we need to know, this is where you get out at."

"Man, I'm not getting out this car," Raymond responded.

"Oh yes, you are, right here," the officer ordered as he got out the front seat and opened the back door of the detective car.

Raymond looked terrified. "How y'all going to do this to me?"

"Like this: get the hell out. Enjoy you walk back to Upton," the officer responded.

Raymond exited the police vehicle and cautiously looked around as the police left him standing on the street. Raymond walked briskly, trying to hid his face. Cobra members pointed and watched him as he tried to be inconspicuous. Moments later, Raymond was accosted between two brownstones. "What's up, G-thang?" he heard a voice say as a shot rang out. All things suddenly turned black. He felt his presence spiraling toward a light, then a cold sensation all over his body and oblivion.

❧

The next day, Deon called Greg.

"Hey, man, I was wondering if you could do me a favor. Can you come down here? I really need to talk to you in person."

"Yeah man," Greg replied. "What's going on?"

"Nothing. I will tell you when you get here. Meet me at the community center."

Deon waited until he saw Greg's white Cougar pull around the corner. Deon jumped in.

"What's up, man?" Greg asked. "You in trouble or something?"

"No, but I do need your help," Deon replied. "Look, I have a friend who lives in that building. She just moved in. The building manager oversees government assistance, and he is a rapist. I want her out of there."

"Come on, man," said Greg. "How do you know he's a rapist?"

"I work in the community center and talk to the residents. Let's just say a lot of these women are in compromising situations, and let's just say he takes advantage."

"Oh, okay, but what's that got to do with you?" Greg asked.

"Like I say, I have this friend who just moved in, I looked to find somewhere else for her."

"You want me to help her move?" asked Greg.

"No, I can handle that if it comes to it. I just want to show her something I found." Deon told Greg to drive down to the brownstone. Deon got out and went to the front door, pushed the combination, and went into the building. He walked down the hallway to her door to find Mr. Lester talking to her through the partially open door. Deon stood back and looked at the back of the man's head like he could cave his skull in.

"Excuse me," Deon spoke up.

"Yeah, what's up?" Mr. Lester said.

"I need to see Ms. Williams," Deon replied.

"Well, I'm talking to her right now," snapped Mr. Lester.

"Well, this is from Sister Joseph Mary," Deon said while looking at Mr. Lester and staring him down.

Erica spoke up as she fully opened the door. "I do need to talk to Sister Joseph Mary. Is she there now?"

"Yes," said Deon.

"Okay, let me get my son," Erica said quickly.

Deon turned toward Mr. Lester. "All right?" he said while staring in the man's eyes. Mr. Lester was infuriated. "So, what are you trying to do?" he forcefully said to Deon. "Nothing," Deon responded as he turned toward the hallway to wait for Erica. She closed her door with Eric holding her hand.

"Okay, well, we will talk about any problems with the apartment later," Mr. Lester said and stormed off.

Erica did not respond. She walked holding the hand of her son toward Deon as they walked together to the end of the hallway. Deon opened the door for Erica and Eric. Greg looked on as they approached the car.

Deon opened the back door of the car, and Erica and Eric got in. Deon also sat in the back.

"What, am I the chauffer now?" asked Greg, laughing.

"Excuse me, but where are we going?" Erica asked.

"I'm sorry, Erica, this is Greg, who was my roommate at Mid Union," Deon said.

"Hi, Greg," she said as he turned to shake her hand.

"I'm sorry, Erica, but I need to show you something," said Deon.

Erica remained silent as Greg pulled off.

"Okay, what's the address?" Greg said to Deon.

Deon pulled up his phone. "Here we go," he said as he gave his phone to Gregg.

"You didn't answer me before, Deon," Erica insisted. "Where are we going?"

"I just want to show you something," said Deon.

They arrived at the apartment building. She looked up and around, and Eric did too with his big eyes, wondering what was going on.

"Come on," Deon said as everyone got out of the car.

"Beautiful block," Greg said as he looked around.

They walked into the building and found the building manager.

"Hi, Deon," she said exuberantly.

"Hi! How are you?" Deon said. "I wanted to introduce you to Erica, my friend, and this is

Greg, my ex-roommate at Mid Union."

"Yes," she said. "How are you both?"

"I'm good," replied Erica. "What is this all about, Deon?"

They walked down the hallway to the door of the apartment.

"Here's the key. You guys look around, and I will be in the office," the rental agent said.

"Thank you so much," Deon replied.

The three of them stood in the living room area, looking at each other.

"Deon, look, I appreciate you trying to help me, it is really sweet, but I ain't working full time, and I can't pay no full rent, so …"

"It's okay," said Deon. "I'm going to give them six months in advance."

"What?" Erica responded in surprise. "You ain't even got nowhere to stay yourself, unless you feel like you would be living here too."

"No, I would not be," Deon replied.

"Then why you are doing this for me? There is always a catch."

"Erica, I do like you very much, but to be blessed, things must be done the right way and for the right reasons. No pressure."

She looked at Deon with a glimmer of softness in her eyes, but skepticism as well. "Damn, they don't make them like you no more, Deon," she said.

"All right, so move here, please. You are closer to work, and the school is right down the street. I'm going to pay the rent up for six months, so it would be the same as it would have been in the last building. All they need is your check stubs. After six months, I will help again with the rent or whatever, but I just want you here and not there."

Deon looked at Erica with pleading in his eyes.

"Ok, I'll do it," said Erica, sighing with exasperation.

"Great!" Deon replied.

Greg came out of the adjourning room. "Hey, man, this is nice," he said.

"Yeah, she says it will do," Deon answered.

"Okay, let's do it!" said Erica.

All of them walked to the manager's office.

"I have three thousand six hundred dollars cash, or I can get a money order," Deon said.

"We will need a money order," the building manager said, "and please don't forget those check stubs."

They all piled into the car and headed to the Super Mart. Eric was playing and pointing and naming everything he saw.

"Smart guy," Greg said as Deon smiled.

Greg pulled into the Super Mart, and Deon went to purchase the money order while everyone else shopped around.

Man, I hate standing in line, but hey, patience is a virtue, he said to himself. Finally, Deon was at the counter purchasing the money orders. The clerk printed them and gave them to Deon, and Deon put them in his wallet.

Deon ventured into the store to find Greg and Erica, but he couldn't find them anywhere.

"Hey," said a small voice.

Deon turned around as Erica walked up.

"Hey, I had to get a few things, wipes and stuff," she said.

Greg drove them back to the previous apartment in Mr. Lester's building.

"You get your most important stuff, and I will help you with the rest later," said Deon.

"Okay," she said. "Everything really still in bags."

Deon and Erica went to her apartment and started putting things back into the Hefty bags that she had.

"I hope we can get the hell out of here before that damn manager gets here. He gives me the creeps," she said.

Deon looked at her. "Yeah, let's get the hell out of here. Did we get everything? Essentials?"

"This is everything," she said. "Come on."

Deon grabbed all the bags from her.

"No, I got it," she said.

"No, Erica, just gets Eric." He looked over his shoulder toward Mr. Lester's door. *I hope he does see me*, thought Deon.

They all made it down the steps and loaded everything into the back of the car. They drove to the other apartment, and Greg and Deon helped her with those three large bags with everything she owned. They went to the building manager's office.

"Come on in," she said.

"I have the money orders here for you," Deon said with a smile.

Greg and Erica looked on.

"The check stubs?" she inquired.

"They are online. All I have to do is print them," Erica said.

"Okay, well, we can do that for you here," she said as she led Erica to one of the office computers. Erica pulled up the information and printed her pay stubs for the past month.

"Here are your keys," the manager said, smiling as she gave them to Erica.

"Thank you so much again," Deon said to her.

"Oh, no problem. We are good until February of next year."

Deon and Erica stood in the living area, facing one another again.

"Okay," Deon said. "This is it. I'm going back over to the campus with Greg to try to put some things together."

"You be careful," Erica said in a caring way.

"You got something to eat and everything?" Dean asked.

"I'm fine, Dean. It's all good. Thank you."

"Call or text me if you need anything," Dean said to her as he looked deep in her eyes.

"Bye," said a little voice.

"See you later, little man."

Chapter 14

Greg and Deon drove back to the community center.

"So, let me get this straight," said Greg. "You took the money you were going to pay for a retainer and gave it to Erica for an apartment?"

"I didn't want to see her get hurt," Deon said. "I really like her, Greg."

"Man, you really have screwed up," said Greg. "My uncle was ready to work with you."

"I got a few days, Greg. Hopefully, I can make a couple of scores."

"Yeah, well, let's hope so," Greg answered.

Greg dropped off Deon at the community center. There was a small group of men standing by the Burger Hut. They walked up to Deon. "Yo, what's up, G," they said as they gave the organization's handshake to Deon.

"One of our brothers was executed yesterday," one of the men said.

Deon did not respond. "Five O dropped him off in another territory last night, so we got to fix that, know what I'm saying?"

Deon thought about his conversation with Raymond the night before. Deon wondered if it was

Raymond they were talking about. "Let us know if you hear anything," the man said.

Deon nodded in agreement as he continued on his way to his room. *This is how these shootings get started. Another brother killed, another gang incident*, he thought. Deon had something else on his mind: *Got to go talk to the Rasta man.*

Deon sat in the Rasta man's meditation room. Preacher was sitting in a lotus position. His locks were swerving from side to side while his closed eyes faced up at the ceiling. The sound of reggae played in the background.

"Gud ting yuh did bredren," he said to Deon.

"What thing?

"Yuh hab ah gracious heart," he said as he tossed two buds on the floor like dice toward Deon. "Did yuh fine har ah place tuh liv?"

"How did you know, Preacher?" Deon asked.

"Sum tings mi kno. Yuh blessings will cum," Preacher said.

Deon nodded slowly, accepting the fact that Preacher seemed to be clairvoyant.

"Preacher, I need another re-up. I need two thousand," he said.

The Rasta man sat back in his lotus position.

"Nuh problem," he said.

The Rasta man went to a book on the shelf, pulled out three bundles, and gave them to Deon.

Deon took the product and placed it in his pants. "Thanks. Hopefully, I will see you tomorrow."

"Yea, mon," said Preacher.

His wife came to the room. "Yuh hungry?" she asked. "Wi ave fish tea eff yuh lakka. Mi hab ah cup yuh can tek."

"Thank you," Deon said as she poured him a helping in a Styrofoam cup. Deon took a sip of the fish tea and had to ask to sit down for a moment. "Damn, this is so good!"

Preacher and his wife laughed.

"Bi safe out deh, keep ah chrang meditation tuh mount zion, I Selassie I," the Rasta man said as he put his index fingers and thumbs together, making a diamond shape in front of his heart.

"Yes, Preacher, me will."

Deon left Preacher and started his careful walk back to his room. He stashed some product and extra cash and then locked up and made his way to the bus stop, where he stood waiting for nearly twenty minutes. The bus finally came. After another long ride, Deon arrived at the campus.

Andrew saw Deon and called out, "Deon. Hey, man, where you been?"

"Just trying to make it. You need anything?" Deon asked.

"Yeah, sure, man. I can get on the horn and let people know you are here. In the meantime, you can give me two." Andrew went into his room and invited Deon in. Deon gave him two bags. Andrew chatted on the phone and then came back over to Deon.

"I got a few dudes coming over. They say they want four bags."

Greg finally called back. "Where you at?"

"At Andrew's" Deon replied.

"Be down in a minute."

"Who was that, Greg?" asked Andrew.

There was a tap on the door. It was Greg. "What's up, man!"

"Hey Deon," said Greg, "you make some of that money back?"

"I'm getting there," Deon said.

"I talked to my uncle about what happened," Greg told him.

"What? Why did you do that?" asked Deon.

"Hey, man, he understood. He thought you did an honorable thing."

"He thinks I'm a damn fool," said Deon.

"Yeah, he believes that too." Greg laughed.

Everyone was starting to gather in front of the TV to watch the start of the pro football season. The announcers from the game were broadcasting.

"Good evening, ladies and gentlemen, welcome to Pro Football Tonight for the matchup between the Southerners and the West Coast Raiders, and Ed, I know this is going to be a great matchup today, especially for the first-round pick at running back for the Southerners, Isaiah Islam. One of the best running backs to come out of college this year, and this will be his pro football debut, and what can we expect, Dan?"

"I hope he shows out," Andrew said.

There was a tap on the door, and two guys walked in as Andrew stood up.

"What up, bro?" he said.

"I'm Brent. You got four?"

"Yeah, right here," Deon said as he pulled four bags.

"That last you had blew our heads off," Brent said.

"This is good too," Deon replied.

Another tap on the door. More customers. Again, Deon sold out quickly.

"Isaiah Islam gets the ball at the thirty-yard line, makes a fake up the middle for nine yards, and that's another first down," said the announcer on the TV.

"Damn, he's killing it!" Greg yelled out.

"He is really a good guy too," said another person in the room.

Everyone passed vapes, beer, and chips as the game went on. Isaiah had a fantastic game, receiving the game ball for the winning touchdown.

"Deon, are you going to stay the night?" asked Greg.

"No, I need to get on back home. I have to work tomorrow at the community center."

"Hold on, let me get my keys," said Greg as he reached for his jacket.

Greg drove Deon home. "All right, man, I will see you hopefully tomorrow," Greg said as he pulled off.

Deon sat in his room and looked at the television, wondering if he would be able to make the rest of the money tomorrow. A text came over the phone. "Hi, thank you for your help, it is sweet of you. Be careful out there," it read.

Deon jumped out of bed. It was Erica—the first time she had ever texted him. Deon responded, "You're welcome."

Tuesday had come, and Deon still did not have the $3,600 he needed to secure the attorney. He could only hope that the public defender had done his due diligence.

Deon stood up in court. His public defender stood next to him. The arresting officer was standing next to the state's attorney.

"Judge Herman Nimitz presiding," the court deputy said.

"Are we ready to proceed?" the judge asked while looking over some files on his desk.

"Yes, Your Honor," the prosecution said. "We have the statements from the arresting officer, Richard Charlotte. This defendant has been sighted numerous times at and around this location participating in illegal activity. He was arrested and charged for the drug conspiracy and gang activity."

The judge looked over to Deon's court-appointed attorney.

"Mr. Kilpatrick?"

"Yes, Your Honor. My client has stated he is not guilty and that he was not carrying any drugs at the time of the arrest".

"Is that it?" asked the judge.

"Yes, Your Honor. I have explained to the defendant his options in his defense."

"Your Honor!" called a voice from the back of the courtroom.

Deon turned around and saw Greg's uncle.

"I am an attorney for the defendant," he said, walking up to the bench.

"State your name, counselor."

"Scott Boyd your honor, defense attorney for Boyd, Woods, and Anderson law offices. Mr. White conferred with me over the weekend, Your Honor, and I have decided to take his case— with Mr. White's permission, of course."

"Your Honor, is this necessary?" the state's attorney complained.

"The defendant has the right to provide his own council if he feels that he is not being adequately represented," Mr. Boyd interjected.

Judge Nimitz looked dismayed. "Mr. White," he asked, "what is your official request to the court regarding your council?"

"I would like Mr. Boyd to represent me, Your Honor," Deon said.

"I certainly hope this isn't a waste of the court's time. We will have a continuance one month from today. That should be adequate time," the judge said, peering over his bifocal glasses. "Okay, court is adjourned."

"Thank you," Deon said to Mr. Boyd. "Why did you try to help me?"

"I don't know," he answered. "Call it temporary insanity. I heard what happened. You got a big heart or you are a big fool—either way, I got your case. Let's get out of here so we can talk."

Deon and Mr. Boyd found a café in the building and stopped for a cup of coffee.

"Look, try to come up with that retainer," said Mr. Boyd.

"I have five hundred now," Deon told him.

"Okay, I'll take that." Then he added, "Tell me something. How are you coming up with this money?"

"I have friends that give me odd jobs. I'm not paying rent while I am at the community center."

He looked at Deon like *you got to be kidding me*. "I just wanted to see how well you can lie,"

he said. "I know Greg, and I know you. Be careful."

Deon nodded and smiled. "Yes, sir."

"I just want to let you know what the penalty is for this, depending on the amount of drugs found on that court, which would determine your minimum: it could be five years or even ten. This cop, Officer Charlotte. I understand his shift is 3:00 to 11:00 p.m. So, were you out in the neighborhood at night?"

"I was working at Masonic—hospital security," Deon replied.

"Why did you lose your job?" asked Mr. Boyd.

"I got locked up," Deon replied.

Mr. Boyd shook his head. "What time was your shift?"

"Three to eleven-thirty," Deon told him.

"And that was between February and the end of June. You weren't there very long—all this happened in June?"

"Yes, sir."

"Is there anybody up there who can verify for you?"

"Yes, Captain Suh and Officer Kevin Daniels, Mike Evans, all of them."

"Was there a sign-in sheet?"

"No. We sign-in on the computer, electronically."

"Okay. Come up with that retainer, please."

"Yes, sir," Deon replied as Greg, and Mr. Boyd stood up to leave.

"Go home get some rest, then get me my money," said Mr. Boyd, "and I will see you when you have it."

"Thanks, Mr. Boyd."

It was Friday afternoon as Deon walked into the shiny building on his way to Mr. Boyd's office. It had been a challenging two days, but Deon had been able to accumulate a thousand dollars more toward his retainer. The lady at the receptionist desk called Deon, and he went to Mr. Boyd's office.

"Hello, Deon."

"Hi, Mr. Boyd. I have the money for you here."

"Okay, thank you, sir," he said as he counted the money and then handed it to the receptionist.

"I will have the other five hundred in a few days," said Deon.

"No problem. I see you are trying to hustle up the money. I will start preliminary proceedings."

"Thank you, Mr. Boyd."

"Don't thank me until you get the remainder of that retainer, and we win this case," Mr. Boyd said with a smile.

"Yes, sir. I will be working on it. Thank you," he said.

Greg gave Deon a ride back to Upton, stopping up the block from the community center.

"Man, I got this funny feeling," said Greg.

"Like what?" Deon asked

"I don't know, man; I think you should come home with us where you will be okay."

Deon got out of the car. "I know you understand this," Deon replied.

"Yes, but damn, man," Greg said in response, "be careful."

Deon went to his room and turned on the television.

"This is breaking ten o'clock news! In the shooting case of Darren Davis, the police involved were cleared of any wrongdoing this afternoon by the police commissioner. Darren Davis was the young man who was shot when charging police after not responding to the repeated request of the officer. There is currently community outrage that is brewing because of the incident."

Deon continued to listen as residents of the community expressed their fear and anguish at the shooting of Darren Davis. His family was all over the television demanding answers. People were being interviewed in the street—loud, angry voices. "They shot him for nothing!" screamed one woman. "The police out here killing us and ain't nobody doing nothing," she said. "Our lives matter!"

Deon lay on his bed, tired. Time to call it a night.

Deon arrived back at the campus the next morning to find everyone heading to the canteen.

Deon called Greg. "Hey, man, where are you?"

"I'm right over here, dude," Deon heard Greg's voice say.

"Where is everybody going?" he asked.

"To the canteen to watch the game," Greg said. "Isaiah is playing."

"Oh, that's right. It's a Saturday game today," said Deon. He added, "I want to sell a couple of these bags."

"I'm right ahead of you," Greg said. "Come on, let's go to my room, if you don't mind watching some of the game on my regular TV."

Deon and Greg went to the dorm room and set up for people coming by. Greg turned the game on as Andrew came by the dorm room.

"Hey, dudes, what's up?" he said as he walked into the room.

"What's up," Deon said as they bumped fists.

"I got about one hundred dollars here," said Andrew.

"Cool. Here's four," Deon said as he handed Andrew the bud.

Soon others came by the room, and in no time, Deon again sold out.

The television played as everyone gathered around it. It was the beginning of the game, and the announcers introduced the national anthem. The camera spanned the Southerners players. The camera focused on one player who remained seated during the anthem while all other players stood with their hands over their hearts.

"Why is he sitting?" the announcer asked.

The camera continued to zoom in on an angry young face: the face of Isaiah Islam. Another player joined Isaiah and held his hand while taking a knee. Another player stood beside Isaiah and held his other hand.

The game started. The Southerners had the football. The TV camera panned over to Islam, who was having a discussion with the head coach on the sideline.

"I wonder what this discussion is about," the broadcast announcer asked.

"I don't know, Tom," said the other announcer. "Perhaps it's about the anthem."

Isiah put on his helmet and ran into the game. He then began to mount up the most running yards any rookie halfback had ever gained. Scoring three touchdowns and thrown a touchdown pass, he gained two hundred yards on just eleven carries, as everyone stood in awe of his performance. The Southerners won the game 31 to 17 to the complete applause of the crowd.

The postgame show had Isaiah interviewed from the locker room as he sat with his head bowed.

"Fantastic game today, Isaiah," said, one reporter. "Could you please tell us why you chose not to stand during the national anthem?

"Our team had a breakthrough game, and you are asking me about the anthem?" Isaiah answered.

"We would like to know if you were saving your legs for the game or ...?"

"No, I was not saving my legs. I find it difficult to continue to stand and not protest the brutality and deprivation that permeates our communities across this country."

"So let me understand this correctly," said the announcer. "You are protesting before the game?"

"That is right. I reserve the right to do so. Someone needs to take a stand against injustices in our community and unprosecuted deaths of unarmed brothers who have been profiled and killed by law enforcement all over the country."

"So, you are protesting at the beginning of an important football game. Don't you feel that your focus should have been on the game?"

"My focus was on the game, as you saw."

"Don't you think protesting during the national anthem is unpatriotic?"

"No, I do not," Isaiah responded.

Deon and the entire room were silent. No one could believe this was happening. Reggie, who had walked in earlier, sat shaking his head.

"I wonder, does he know the repercussions of what he is doing?" Reggie asked rhetorically.

"I applaud him for this shit," Andrew said. "I did see the video where that kid got shot. He was not a threat to anyone."

Everyone stopped and looked at Andrew.

"Are you okay over there?" a girl asked. She could not believe she'd heard Andrew say that.

"Andrew, I can't believe I'm agreeing with you," said Reggie, "but it's going to be a hurricane of a blowback."

Sounds of milling about started outside. Voices growing louder and more audible.

"Can you believe that fucking nigger?" one voice yelled out.

Another voiced yelled out, "Send his ass back to Africa for disrespecting our flag!"

"Oh hell, it's started already," said Greg as everyone slowly walked out of the dorm room and out to the main campus. A crowd was brewing.

"I can't believe he would disrespect the United States of America and all that it stands for. Isaiah Islam hates America. He hates the greatness this country stands for!" sounded someone on a loudspeaker.

Camouflaged groups invaded the campus yard, spitting in the direction of Deon and anyone like him. The campus fraternity that had been making the offensive chant the previous semester was there as well, all congregating under the statue of the Confederate general.

The crowd grew louder and more hostile. The minority conservative group that Deon remembered from his sociology class walked cautiously around the others who were protesting, obviously concerned that maybe they should not be there.

One voice hollered out at the minority conservatives, "These are your people!"

The protesters screamed at them.

One of the minority conservatives spoke up. "We disagree with the actions of Isaiah Islam. We feel it reprehensible to disrespect our flag, no matter the reason," he yelled.

"Then you need to tell the rest of your people!" yelled voices in the crowd while others applauded.

"I'm thinking it's time to take you back to Upton," Greg said with a look in fear in his eyes.

A voice behind Deon and Greg spoke, startling both of them. A camouflage conservative spoke with menacing blue eyes.

"You are the leftist types who enable these people," he said, peering at Greg. Deon, normally reserved could not quell his boiling temperature. After everything he had been through, he was going to be damned to let this jackass talk to him any kind of way.

"Hey, man, ain't nobody said nothing to you." Deon spoke up.

"Yeah, well, I'm just telling you, why you don't go back to your ghetto, because you are only here because of some affirmative action, you fucking racist."

Deon started for the throat of the guy, but Greg held Deon back.

"No, let him fucking go," the guy said as other camouflage conservatives came up smiling with so many familiar smirks on their faces.

"No, let's go, Deon. Let's just get the hell out of here."

"You better fuckin' leave!" the voices said as Deon and Greg walked away.

"I got to get you home," Greg said. "This isn't about free speech at all right now."

Deon and Greg walked further away from the expanding crowd and toward the dorm parking lots.

"You know what, man, I think I will take the bus."

"No," said Greg. "I'm taking you."

"Right now, for your own safety, you should just go to your room and chill out," said Deon. "Being with me might put a red dot on your head from some of these people. Just let me get the bus back to Upton. I need some time to think myself."

"Okay," Greg said with the brotherly concern on his face. "Be careful, dude."

On the ride back to Upton, Deon sat in the back of the bus listening to AM talk radio on his phone.

"Isaiah Islam is the enemy of America. He sits and disrespects our proud tradition, our sacred tradition, a show of respect to those who fought and died in this country, so this thug can have the right to spit in the face of every hard-working God-fearing American. And to think this professional football league would tolerate this disrespect. And what are they supposedly protesting? Police brutality. The same police who are sworn to defend the law and put themselves in harm's way every day not know whether they will be coming home or not. You hear about this guy who was resisting arrest and died because he was fat and unhealthy more than anything else. What about the one police officer who recently was killed? You don't hear about that, do you? We are at a place in this country where we have given allegiance to the so- called football player and teams and not the sacredness of or flag."

He switched to the phones. "Go ahead, caller, you are on line number 2."

"Yeah, Ed, this is Scott from North Town, I am so sick and tired of hearing these people rallying against police officers and our flag. This guy is a millionaire. What could he know about any of this?"

"You are right, Scott. These guys are millionaires. They are not pimps on the street, although they probably could be."

"Well, Ed, I'm tired of all the complaining by these people. If you wouldn't resist and followed the police demands, you have nothing to worry about."

"You're right, caller. I agree with one hundred percent. Thank you for your call, Scott. Let's go to Kevin. Hello, Kevin, you are on AM 90."

"Thanks for taking my call. I am calling for a boycott of pro football if this unpatriotic ass continues to play. If you want to protest some bull crap, do that on your own time. I am watching the game to be entertained not to hear a bunch a crap about how these people are being mistreated and profiled. Well, if thirteen percent of the population would stop committing ninety percent of the crime, then you wouldn't have to worry about being questioned by police. I'm telling you, Ed, it's a bunch of crap."

"Couldn't agree with you more, James. It is truly a disgrace. These people are complaining about being profiled by police. Then stop committing all the crime then and stop acting like an uncivilized thug. They complain about stop and frisk; well, if you don't have anything to hide, you don't have any worries."

"I agree with you, Mike. You are a great American. Thank you for your call."

Deon exited the bus and looked up the street. Small crowds were gathering as the evening started to settle in. Deon had to stop by the Rasta man's house to drop off his money. The avenue looked busy, as people were walking all over the neighborhood. There was an uneasy tension in the air; pressure was building.

Deon walked over to Preacher's house and knocked on the door. The smell of good cooking was coming out of the house again.

"Come in, mon," the Rasta man said to Deon as he opened the door. Deon looked in the kitchen.

"Pressure cooker," Deon said as he smiled at Preacher and gave him the money.

"Yes, me cooked dis time." The pressure cooker started to whistle.

"Jamaican oxtail stew again?" asked Deon.

"No. Cow foot," the Rasta man answered.

Deon stared at the pressure cooker while the Rasta man looked at Deon.

"Yes, the pressure build up, brethren."

"Will it blow, Preacher?" asked Deon.

"If it don't release no steam, den yes. Come by tomorrow to re-up. Be careful out dere, brethren. Pot 'bout to blow."

Deon stepped outside and noticed more commotion going on down the street. He passed a lady walking up the neighborhood.

"The police got off for killing Big Mike. It just came on the TV," she said

"What?" Deon said. "That's impossible! He screamed repeatedly, 'You're choking me!'" "Hey, them cops just got off!" she answered angrily.

Deon walked faster up the neighborhood to the main boulevard. He walked down to the end of the street where everyone was congregating. Deon's anger and resentment turned to bitterness, as he was unable to restrain himself from is normally subdued demeanor. He stood up on a porch step.

"Yo, everybody, listen up! This has been going on in our neighborhood for too long. This has to stop! We need to come together and stop this."

A crowd started to gather.

"We know Big Mike did not deserve to die at the hands of the police like this!"

The crowd chanted back, "Yeah, that's right!"

People began shouting expletives, and others started milling around in the street. Suddenly, the police came around the corner. An officer stepped out of the vehicle with his club in his hand and a loudspeaker.

"This is an unlawful assembly! Unless you're prepared to go to jail, leave this location immediately!" he demanded.

More police cars arrived, and people started screaming.

"To hell with the police! To hell with the cops!" they screamed.

Police cars showed up, and they all started out of their vehicles with the clubs in their hands. Some had their hands on their guns. The crowd was agitated but began to back off.

Deon continued speaking to the crowd.

"We've had more than four incidents. First Malik Edwards, shot and killed after putting his hands up ! Then Omar Little shot and killed in the school park for playing with a toy laser! We know, Big Mike! He sold CDs up at the Burger Hut and in front of the thrift store. The police killed him. Then we had Raymond Evans, who was set up by the police. He was shot and killed. The police are not even charged; they won't have to even go to court to be judged by their peers."

Deon continued. "The police department continues to protect these cops. Some of these are racist cops. They don t come here to protect you and me. They come here to make war on all of us under the premise that this is a high crime area. They come in here and set us up. One person has drugs, so they charge everyone in that house, on that street, or in the park or the car. They leave it to you to prove your innocence. They know you can't afford good representation and then you cop to a charge to stay out of jail so that you won't lose your children or lose your job. However, if you cop to that felony, you won't get no job anyway. In the meantime, they are throwing you out of your car. Talking to you like an animal. Laughing in your face!

"They are picking up brothers and dropping them off in hostile neighborhoods for them to get killed. Then comes the cycle of retaliation, causing some to shoot up our communities. They are setting up drug houses to set up so-called dealers but contributing to folks getting shot, for gangs retaliating against each other, against your brothers and sisters, and we counter, and the cycle goes on.

"Bad choices, yes, but what can we do? Black lives don't matter. Our children don't matter; they are poisoning our kids. They are laughing in our face, and they are laughing right now. We need to take our community back. They got us scared to catch a bus, to walk in our neighborhood."

The crowd erupted in cheering voices and chants of "Black lives matter."

Deon continued. "We matter to nobody else. Yes, our community has problems, but this is one problem we cannot let continue. How can the community expect to become law-abiding when we have lawlessness by the people who are hired to protect us?"

The crowd grew bigger. It seemed thousands of people gathered in the streets. They began to march, with many of them hollering, "To hell with the police!" Some went into the store and took posters without buying them and started marking on them with black markers, making signs protesting police brutality. Thousands of people from the neighborhood continued to flood into the street, from adults to kids.

The police returned this time with wagons. Residents shouted insults at the police as the police presence continued to increase—most with riot gear of shields and batons, tear cannons, and stun guns. People start to march. News trucks drove in—channel 5, then channel 7. News reporters began to fill the streets.

Police on loudspeakers ordered the protestors to disburse. Down the street was a loud explosion. A car had been set on fire. The mews cameras moved to capture the incident. There was the sound of a window shattering, hollering, yelling, chaos.

Deon amazingly heard his cell phone ring. Deon stepped off the porch and found a secluded space between buildings.

"Deon, is everything all right?" It was Erica.

"Hold on," Deon yelled back at the phone. He tried to run to a quiet place. He found the wall in a doorway.

"Deon, this is Erica. What the hell is going on down there?"

"It's going crazy, Erica! Are you and Eric all right?" Deon screamed into his phone.

"We're okay! Why don't you come over?"

"Thank you, Erica. I will try to make my way there to make sure you and Eric are safe."

"Be careful, Deon. Call me when you are on your way."

Deon went back out to the streets, where people were screaming, "Black lives matter!" Deon started to notice people from everywhere on the globe pulling up, many with signs that they had made to protest police brutality. More and more arrived from different college campuses. Tear- gas canisters fired off into the crowd. People were running and choking, screaming in loud angry voices. A student yelled in Spanish in his bullhorn, balled fist raised in the air.

The protest began to grow violent as the police in riot gear fanned out into the streets. Residents were screaming, "Hands up, don't shoot!" Tear gas started to fly through the air, and children began coughing and covering their eyes as people started running.

Deon smelled the tear gas and started to run away, rubbing his eyes and coughing. He noticed the Sun department store down the street. Residents had crashed the windows of the store, and people were grabbing whatever they could.

Deon stepped in the store. "Hey, man, come on. Let's not take stuff. That is exactly what they want to say about us—that we are about rioting and looting. This all they want to see so they can serve this as the example!"

"This ain't your place," yelled one of them. "They are making their money off you too. We are taking this, unless you think you about to stop something, which you ain't. What, you the police or something? Are you one of them?"

Deon just looked on with dismay and shook his head no. Residents went after the big-screen TVs. They smashed windows and continued to take everything in sight.

The crowd was growing even more massive, screaming and hollering profanity. Police in helmets lined up shoulder-to-shoulder and started to march forward like soldiers. Deon moved farther away from the store, turning to look and see police apprehend the looters.

Deon's phone rang again.

"Deon, this is your mother. What is going on there?"

"A lot of protests going on, Ma."

"Are you out in the streets with these people? You get out of there right now!"

"Ma, I'm okay. Don't worry!" Deon screamed in his phone.

"You listen to me, damn it! You get out of those streets before you get killed!"

"Ma, I'm okay. Don't worry about me. I will be okay!"

Deon noticed one officer he thought he recognized. He stopped and stepped a little closer, squinting to be sure of what he was seeing. He recognized the police officer. It was the same guy in the auditorium with the camouflage hat and the ultra-conservative opinions. Deon also remembered him from the statue removal of General Lee protest. *Is he a police officer?* Deon thought. *Oh my God, he is!*

The police proceeded to throw people against the wall and pepper-spray them as they screamed from burning eyes.

Deon jogged down the street, trying to make his way toward the brownstones. Residents clogged the arteries of every road leading there. Deon looked up the street and saw many cars of men wearing red, white, and blue hats. Some walked with torches. There were a few hundred of them, and as they walked, more joined in. Some had automatic weapons across their shoulders.

"Bold Power" they yelled

Scores of others joined as they walked the quarter mile toward the thick of the protest. Their voices began to carry over the screaming voices of the others. Community residents and college students turned to watch as they walked forward.

The crowd of protestors was taken aback. "The Bold Alliance is the fucking Klan!" one blond protester yelled to the group of college students he was with.

"Hey, fuck you," a guy with an EAF shirt on said as they walked straight toward the oncoming Bold group.

News cameras followed the events. The Bold Alliance stepped out front with their semiautomatic weapons across their chest. Insults and epithets were hurled. American flags were flying as they held them up with chants of Bold power.

Demonstrators chanted the names of Malik and Big Mike and "black lives matter" as they sat on the sidewalks, refusing to move. Others joined hands with them and took a knee.

A group of young people with black ski masks on their faces came out swinging fists at the armed group of Bold nationalists. The chants of "Bold power!" continued to rise in the air. The police riot team stepped in and formed a line in front of the Bold Alliance. They stood there with their riot shields like an offensive line in front of a backfield.

"I can't believe the police are protecting them," yelled the protesters." "This is why we can't trust police" Deon yelled. "Yeah why don't you shut the fuck up" a Bold Alliance member said while walking up to Deon's face. Deon's mind went singular, the thought of Malcolm X oration referring to those who turn the other cheek, and others to "preserve your life, it's the best thing you got, and if you got to give it up, let it be even-steven," repeated in his mind. Standing up to this vile, foaming at the mouth racist in front of him, Deon's blood boiled from all he had been through, the laughter and sarcasms of the police, the loss of his job, car, apartment, homelessness. The bigotry of talk radio and hatred politics he watched on television news stations begin to release itself in a rage like the whistling hiss of a pressure cooker. The subdued and normally passive Deon fled, what remained was nothing too nice. No more turning the other cheek and nonviolence bullshit he said to himself. Deon threw a body shot and an uppercut to the chin of the Bold member knocking him spread out in the street. "You fucking Nigger yelled another Bold member." Deon felt the punches of fist wailing on him as Deon turned and swung back, connecting with the chins of numerous Bold boys before other protestors intervened. Deon ducked low to get away from the fray while holding his injured jaw from the punches of the Bold Alliance.

The police sprayed tear gas into the protesting crowd as the Bold Alliance stood behind them. "You will not replace us!" they chanted. "You will not replace us! Go back to Africa!" they yelled. "Build the wall!" they began to shout.

Shots started to ring out, and people scrambled in every direction. The police line started to move forward, taking small steps. The protesting crowd started to move backward. The Bold Alliance crowd moved slowly behind the police line. "Black lives matter!" was chanted louder and louder from all different groups of protestors. In response, the Bold Alliance group help up watermelons.

Suddenly, a group of young activists flanked the police line. They charged into the Bold Alliance. Fists started flying. There were sounds of fighting and mayhem.

Armed Bold Boys cocked their weapons. The police intervened and grabbed the protestors, throwing them to the ground and zip-tying their hands behind their backs as the Bold Alliance stormed in and started kicking the protestors in the head. They cheered as police apprehended a dozen black men and grabbed them by the back of their heads, pulled them to the sidewalk, and knelt on their backs. Blood poured from the nose and forehead of one protestor as she sat subdued on the street with her arms bound behind her back.

"Bring a wagon!" yelled one police officer.

"There is none available, but we have two mounted horses," cried out another cop.

"What is the procedure?" asked another cop.

"Zip-tie them all together and lead them by horse," said another.

As many as ten men and women with their hands zip-tied behind their backs were zip-tied together and marched through the street like cattle, much to the delight of the Bold Alliance.

Deon heard the sound of car tires screeching up the road, followed by screams from the crowd. He ran toward the commotion. A car had plowed into a group of demonstrators; people were lying all over the street. A young woman had been mowed down. Blood ran from her head and mouth as she lay motionless on the ground. A camouflage-dressed driver jumped out of the car, throwing up his middle finger as his Bold brothers came to rescue him.

"Oh my God!" a woman's voice called out as Deon saw her grab the young lady under her arm, holding her bloody head.

"You sons of bitches!" a man cried out as the crowd slowly started walking toward the Bold Alliance line. The police arrived at the scene and again shielded the Bold Alliance from the crowd. Paramedics soon arrived to help the people who were hit in the street. Deon happened to look toward the brownstones and saw that one of the buildings was in flames.

Deon ran to the brownstone. Smoke filled the fourth floor of the building and billowed from the windows. Deon continued to look up to see if there was anyone in those windows. He heard the voice of a woman yelling, "Help!"

Flames filled the front staircase. A woman ran down the stairs through the fire coughing and covering herself up. "There is a lady upstairs!" she cried. "I know her she had two grandkids. Deon remembered the woman he had dropped off supplies to a month before and remembered her stating her love for her grandkids."

The building became engulfed in flames. *Maybe I can get up from the back stairwell*, Deon thought. He ran around the side of the building to the fire escape. The ladder that was supposed to be let down to the ground was not there.

Deon continued around the back, and suddenly there was a police officer coming around the building.

"Hey, hold it there!" said the officer.

Deon turned, saw the police officer had his hand on his gun, and stopped in his tracks. Deon looked at the officer with disdain, after everything he had been through with police, there was a rancor in his heart. "There is a lady and her two kids on the fourth floor," he told the officer. "There may be a way up there around the back. We got to get them out of there!"

The officer replied, "Let the fire department and first responders handle this." He started squawking into his radio.

Deon looked up to see if he could hear the woman screaming for help again. Then there was an explosion. Deon hit the ground. He turned and saw the officer hit the ground too.

"We can't wait got to get them out of there," Deon insisted.

"No, wait here," the officer demanded.

Deon started running into the back door. The police officer chased after him.

"Help!" cried the voice of the woman inside. The back stairwell was engulfed in flames.

"I'm going up there. Arrest me now if you got to," Deon said to the police officer.

"You are not authorized to make a rescue like this," said the officer.

There was another smaller explosion, and the fire went out for a moment. The flames on the stairs died out from the short blast and seemed to give Deon a path forward. A song reverberated in his memory, the one the choir sang when he went to church. The lyrics and the music to the tune played loudly in his mind: "Never could have made it, without you …"

Deon made his way halfway up the back stairs. The officer remained at the back door, demanding that Deon not to go further. "Hey, I told you, this is a fire department matter!" The officer ran up to the bottom of the stairs. Smoke began to billow down the stairs.

"Hold on," the officer said as he carefully made his way up the stairs. He passed Deon on the stairs and said, "Okay, I'm going first."

"Stay down," Deon said.

The officer looked at Deon and shook his head in agreement. He continued to stay low and proceed up the stairs. Deon followed behind him.

"Hold on," Deon said to the officer.

The officer stopped. They both moved carefully to the third flood. Deon went ahead of the officer, as he saw a break in the smoke and flames.

Suddenly, there was a loud crack. The stairwell gave way. Flames, embers, and sparks flew up. Deon dove low and held himself by rail that remained.

"Hey!" called the officer.

Deon was able to focus and see the officer hanging by where the rail broke off. He was dangling three stories up. The fire was all beneath. Jagged wood and window glass littered the ground thirty feet below.

Deon braced himself with the dangling wooden rail. He extended his hand to the officer. The gospel song "Never Would Have Made It" played loudly in his mind again.

The officer grabbed Deon's arm and pulled himself up using his other hand on the broken guardrail. They both stood up and looked at what had just happened. The sound of screaming came from one of the apartments above.

"We got to get them out of there. I should go forward," the officer said as they continued.

"No, I got it. I know the hallways," said Deon.

Deon walked up the burning stairs to the fourth floor. He put his hand on the door. "The door is hot," Deon said to the officer. "If I open it, we going to get a backdraft."

"Okay, I'm going to open this door, and you hit the floor," the officer said to Deon.

"Okay, go ahead," Deon told him.

The officer opened the door. At first, nothing happened. Then suddenly, an explosion of burning wood shot through the door. Both the officer and Deon hit the floor and covered up. The fire cleared, but the hallway was full of smoke.

The officer began to cough. He took a handkerchief out of his pocket and covered his mouth. Deon ran to the apartment and knocked open the door. He looked in the front room where there had been screaming from the window. However, there was no one there. The entire apartment was full of smoke.

Deon heard the crying of a baby in the background and found the child in a room, crying. He grabbed the boy in his arms and took him to the hallway, where the officer waited.

"Is he okay? I can't find the others," the officer said while covering his mouth from the smoke. "They may have left him behind," the officer said.

"I'm going back and checking," Deon yelled.

"No!" The officer yelled at Deon. "It's too dangerous! I'm coming with you."

There was a louder explosion.

Deon turned back to the apartment.

"Damn!" yelled the officer. "Look, I'm taking him downstairs. Hurry up and get the hell out of this building!"

An eruption of flames blew out a window at the other end of the hallway. The little boy screamed. He began coughing hard. The police officer covered his mouth with the handkerchief and tried to head down the smoky, fiery, dark stairwell. He made it outside and ran to a safe open area on the grass. Other gathered around.

"Is he okay?" the residents asked in exasperation and fear.

"Everybody back away so he can get some air," ordered the officer.

"Put something under his head," an older woman suggested. She found some clothing, rolled it up like a pillow, and put it under the baby's head.

"What about the others?" another resident of the building asked.

The officer looked up at the Brownstone. The fire had started to engulf the roof. He looked around: no sign of a fire crew.

"Here, please watch him. Make sure he is okay," the officer said as he made his way back into the burning building.

Deon kneeled low while coughing into his hand. His eyes burned as he tried to cover his face with the shirt that he had taken off.

"Help me please, Jesus," came a whispered cry that Deon barely heard. How could he hear a whisper coming from the apartment when he was still outside in the hallway?

"Is there anyone there?" Deon yelled down the hall

"I'm in the bathroom," a voice whispered, like the sound of someone choking.

Staying low to the ground, Deon followed the voice. The gospel song "Never Would Have Made It" continued to play in his head. The lyrics "I'm stronger, I'm wiser" echoed in his brain. Through the sound of fire and the darkness of the smoke, the charred feeling in his chest and the sweat pouring off his body, the song continued even louder in his head as he moved forward.

The apartment filled with smoke. Deon could not see an inch in front of his face. Nevertheless, he heard a voice, and he knew he had to follow that.

A light underneath a door seemed to be shining through the smoke. Deon went to the door and opened it. He could see now just barely as he squinted and tried to focus his eyes.

There she was, unconscious with her grand daughter in her arms scrunched inside the bathtub. Deon shook her. No response. He shook the little girl. No response.

Deon heard the songs in his head, as though the one-hundred-person choir was right in front of him.

Just as he remembered, it was the heavyset woman with the wig on her head that he brought supplies to the month before. She looked to weight about two hundred fifty pounds, but Deon knew he had to get her and her grand baby out of the building. He reached down and grabbed her, lifting her upon his shoulder.

The verse from the song "I'm Stronger, I'm Wiser" rang in his head as he lifted both of them. Using his legs in a squat position and unable to see, Deon was guided by something that led him to the front door of the apartment. The hallway was black but for the bright flames that pierced the darkness. Deon took measured quick steps, holding on to both of them tightly.

The stairwell had flames shooting up both sides of the wooden steps. Deon took a deep breath. Again, the song "Never Would Have Made It Without You" sang in his mind. With every step he took, he felt stronger.

Deon continued down the steps, unable to see them as he stepped. Then he felt the touch of a hand on his elbow, the pulling of his arm, and the voice of the officer yelling, "I got her!"

Deon felt arms trying to comfort him and lead him away to the grass. The little girl was still in his grasp. Deon fell to the ground at the orders of the people trying to assist him.

"Stay down!" they said.

Deon coughed.

"Get him some water somebody!"

"I got a bottle," a man's voice said.

Deon took a sip of the water and, automatically, his throat cleared. Deon rose to his knees.

The grandmother caught her breath and started coughing as residents went to assist her. The officer went over to the little girl, "She's not breathing, move back everybody please!

"I got you," a woman said. "I'm a nurse."

"Thank God," the police officer said as he tried to give chest compressions. The woman took the officer's handkerchief, put it over the little girl's mouth, and gave her a quick blow. The little girl began to cough.

"Oh, thank God" the officer said. "Give her some water or something!" he yelled.

"It's okay. She is going to be all right," the woman who gave her the breaths said. She reached down and felt the girl's pulse.

Other officers and EMTs arrived at the scene.

"What happened?" asked one of the other officers and a news reporter who happened to be there.

"The building was on fire, and these people were caught on the fourth floor of the building. I was able to pull the little boy out, but this other guy who went in the building with me stayed behind to try to find his grandmother and sister. He just brought them down over here."

"They all look like they are going to make it," the nurse said to the officers and reporter.

"Where is this guy?"

The officer stood up. "He was just here. Where did he go?"

Deon lay exhausted on his single sized bed looking up at the ceiling in his make shift room from a janitors closet. The sweat and the smell of smoke diffuses though his pores. The horrors of the night rattle in his brain as the sound of firetrucks, police cars and ambulances, breaking glass, explosions, car alarms, gunfire, looting, screaming voices of protesters, the profane sounds of anguish and pain and death, echo through the night. How did this all come to be? How it is that people who would otherwise hug and high five one another after a home run, a jump-shot, or a touchdown could be at each other's throats? How could it be that this demonstrable hate for one another always persisted but hid itself, cloaked in a façade of superficial equality and civility as people appear to go along happily in their great American lives? Could this division be stoked by those who have invested interest, like so many media host and politicians and could it be that this divisiveness lay dormant in the soul of society like a bear in hibernation, but now is awaken and hungry ,ready to devour whatever is edible to feed its bigotry and hate. Is it just one incident or a culmination or accumulation and scaffolding of injustices that brings forth such hate and derision? How did we get here thought Deon as he lay in retrospect while continuing to stare at the ceiling. Has it always been this way…? Deon's phone rang.

"Hey, Son, is everything all right?"

"Yeah, Dad, I'm okay."

"All right, Son," his dad said. "I trust you will make good decisions."

"Yes, Dad."

"Okay, bye," his dad said and hung up.

Dad was always to the point, straight no chaser. Deon fell off to sleep.

His clock radio awoke Deon the next morning with the talk radio program it was tuned to.

"The riots that occurred yesterday and last night have a ring of anarchy from the left. Therefore, they burned cars in the street, attacked police, and broke store windows. Peaceful protestors on the other side. The video played the scene at a department store being looted and people carrying out TVs. This is the left in this country. They hate and refuse to follow the law, and they are looting and burning down neighborhoods and attacking those people who uphold and cherish the second amendment arriving to show their support for what America stands for only to be assaulted by bottles and objects thrown at them."

Deon turned off his radio and turned on the TV.

"Breaking news report: The President is making his remarks. Ladies and gentlemen, the President of the United States."

"Good morning. I would just like to address the protesting going on right now in places that have seemed to spread. These are nothing more than troublemakers. It started in one place, and now it is spreading. I want to let the police departments know we will do everything we can to assist you at this time. I have seen the feeds coming out of the cities, and I am seeing these people burning cars and looting stores. These people are animals, I am telling you. But we are going to get to the bottom of what is going on there."

"Mr. President?" a reporter called from the room. "What about the Proud Power group that was there?"

"Look, there were good and bad people out there. Good and bad people."

"Mr. President, are you saying there are good Bold Alliance members?"

"I'm saying there are good and bad people. In addition, I believe they have a permit and the others did not. Therefore, everyone has a right to free speech."

Deon looked on in disbelief.

"Mr. President, after last night, and after we have discovered that the Proud Alliance group was responsible for several deaths, could that be grounds for labeling this group a terrorist organization?"

"Well if you're going to talk about terrorist organizations, you would have to include this

Black Lives Matter movement. I think it is a bad thing. So, we are going to look and see what happened exactly. We will know more in three to seven days."

"Mr. President, another reporter asked? What about Isaiah Islam's refusal to put his hand over his heart during the national anthem at the game yesterday?"

"I think it is a disgrace. He disrespects our flag, our country. He should be snatched off the field and suspended or kicked out altogether. As I have said before, these Muslims are a threat to this country. They are terrorists, and so are Black Lives Matter, and that group EAF should be investigated."

The TV switched to a political talk show. Deon noticed Sheriff Black among the guests. He wore a cowboy hat and a thick goatee and mustache that looked glued onto his pecan brown skin. The news feed showing community people ransacking a store ran repeatedly while he spoke.

"I tell you, I don't know who is running the plantation down there. You have apparent criminals here stealing and looting. All of them should be found and charged with felony theft and burglary; there is no excuse for it. These people are against the police. These people make false police complaints. These are the people who feel they are entitled because they get taxpayer-funded assistance and don't have to work." "I agree with everything you are saying, Sheriff," the reporter said. "Every one of these protesters should be arrested and charged to the fullest extent of the law the Sheriff urged.

Another guest on the show, Eric Elis, said, "You know these people are always referring back to slavery and lynchings that occurred. Just as many others were lynched or killed by angry agitators as slaves were. It is just the same today, as more people are killed by their own people. Then they want to blame the police who come to work every day and put their lives at risk to do their jobs. There is something definitely wrong in this country when a community of thugs and criminals vilifies the police. What should happen is that all the protestors out there should be held for their personal responsibility. If you are a part of this mayhem and riots in the street, you are complicit in the death of the young student and the fires and everything else you are responsible for last night."

Deon looked at the TV program shaking his head. *Man, you can always find an Uncle Tom-ass nigga.* Deon sat up and silenced the TV as he lay back.

The morning sunshine gleamed off Deon's eyes as he looked out over the decimated neighborhood. He heard a buzz from his phone. It was a text from Erica.

"Are you okay?" the text asked.

"Yes," replied Deon. "Are you and Eric okay?"

"Yes," she replied. "We haven't left the apartment."

"I will be over later," Deon replied.

"Okay," she responded.

Crowds were still in the streets. Police cars screamed down the road past the community center and stopping in front of one of the rent buildings. Deon walked in that direction as many police vehicles pulled up to the building. *I wonder what happened.* Deon thought while making his way there.

He noticed a coroner's ambulance stopping next to the building. The officers appeared to be going to the second floor.

A middle-aged woman with her son came up to Deon.

"What happened?" he asked.

"It looks like the bastard who ran the building," she quipped.

"What about him?" Deon asked.

"If something happened to him, he had it coming. He has been raping his tenants for years," she said as she strolled away while watching what was going on.

Soon, a gurney entered and later exited the building. A sheet was over the victim's head. Deon looked across the street and noticed the woman named Vanessa who had complained to Deon earlier about Mr. Lester, sitting on a bus bench coolly smoking a cigarette with an accomplished look on her face.

The afternoon passed. Toward evening, a bullhorn blared in the streets as the sound of protesting continued.

Deon went back to his room and showered. *I need to check on Erica*, he thought. He dressed and started the long walk to her apartment. It took a long while without any bus service, but finally, he arrived at her building and knocked on her door. He noticed someone peeping thought the door peephole.

The door opened slowly. She stood in gray and white shorts; her room was dim. Deon walked in and glanced around. She stopped and sat on her living room chair. Deon looked at her, and she looked straight at the TV set.

Deon sat down on the sofa and stayed silent, waiting for her to speak. She didn't talk, so finally, Deon broke the ice.

"What going on?" he asked.

She gave Deon an angry but soft look. He stood up and walked toward where she was scrunched in her chair. He looked in her eyes.

She stared back at Deon and said, "All the time the protest was going on, I heard nothing from you."

"I'm sorry," Deon said to her. "Is Eric okay?"

"He's in his room asleep."

"Come here," Deon said, holding his hand out for her to take it. She stood up, and Deon took her hand. He walked her over to the bed and lay down with her, holding her in his arms. She cuddled close and tight as Deon wrapped his arms around her. She felt security and safeness. They both dozed off to sleep.

The light coming through the window awakened Deon. He had held her in his arms the entire night. He turned and looked at her soft, pretty face, her sweet little hands, and her beautiful smooth brown legs and little feet, and his heart melted at that moment.

Deon opened the door to Eric's room. The boy was still asleep in his bed with his posters of football and baseball players fastened to the wall. Deon closed the door.

He went to the kitchen and opened the refrigerator to find four eggs and a few sausage links. He looked in the cabinet and found some Quaker grits.

Deon quietly cooked the sausage in a frying pan while adding a little water. He scrambled the four eggs together with a few sprinkles of cheese he found in the refrigerator door while watching the grits he was making in the microwave. Finding butter in the refrigerator, he mixed it into the grits while stirring, making the grits a light yellow.

Walking back to the front room, he found Erica still sleeping. He went back to the kitchen and fixed her a plate, then grabbed a glass and poured in some orange juice from the carton that sat on the top shelf of the refrigerator. Deon found a platter to put everything in. He carried it to the living room and lay the plate on the end table.

"Erica," Deon called to her in a whisper.

She turned and looked. "Hey," she said. "Good morning." She rubbed her nose while cuddled in the spooning position in which she had slept in Deon's arms in all night.

"What's this?" she asked.

"Breakfast, from the food you had in the kitchen," Deon replied.

"For you?" she said sarcastically.

"No, sweetie," Deon responded. "It's for you and Eric when he wakes up."

She sat up in the bed. There was no headboard, so she sat with her back against the wall.

Deon put the platter on her lap. She looked at Deon as if she wanted to cry.

"Thank you," she said with a sniff of her nose.

Deon watched as her beautiful soft hand grabbed her fork and mixed some of the eggs into her grits. Deon picked up the remote control and turned on the TV. He remembered her mentioning that she liked to watch *Good Morning America*. Deon turned the station and put the remote on the bed next to her. She touched Deon on the shoulder in appreciation.

"Should I check on Eric?" he asked.

"No, let him sleep," she responded. "We can warm it up for him in the microwave when he gets up."

Deon sat down on the bed next to her. He touched her leg closest to him. He softly scooped up her pretty foot and massaged it softly.

"Ooh," she said as her head went back against the wall. Her eyes closed, and her fork fell to the plate clinking. "Deon, what are you trying to do to me?"

"Nothing. Just relax," Deon said.

"Are you trying to make up for not calling me? If so, then it's working." She smiled.

"No, I'm just glad you are here, and safe," Deon answered while taking her other foot in his hand.

"Thank you for staying the night," she said.

Deon looked at her and smiled. "Nothing happened last night," Deon said with a slight laugh.

"Oh yes it did," she answered, smiling.

The door opened to Eric's bedroom. He came staggering out.

"Hi," he said to Deon as he walked over to the bed to sit next to his mother. Deon looked at the both of them sitting next to each other. *Beautiful*, he said to himself.

Deon got up, went to the kitchen, and began to warm up breakfast for Eric. They both sat there and ate together.

"I need to get over to the community center," said Deon. "Thanks for the best night of my life."

Deon made his way to the door. Erica put her tray on the end table and followed Deon.

"Why do you have to live there?" she asked. "You can stay here."

"I don't think that is the right example for Eric right now," Deon said.

She exhaled disappointedly. "It's dangerous out there. I feel so much better when you are here."

"I do too," Deon told her while looking into her eyes.

"I understand," she said. "Call me, text me, something, okay?"

"I will," Deon assured her.

He reached for her and hugged her. Her head fit perfectly on his chest and under his chin. He kissed the top of her head. She looked up at Deon. Deon bent down slightly, and very slowly they both came together with a soft kiss. They looked into each other's eyes.

"Okay, I'll see you," Deon said as he let go of her hand and slowly walked away.

"Bye," she said as she put her hand on her heart. She watched him walk down the hallway. Eric came to the door and stood beside his mom as Deon walked down the stairs. She stepped back and closed the door quietly.

That Monday morning, Deon sat in the waiting room of his attorney's office. Greg was there too, pacing the floor.

"What's up, dude?" Deon asked. "You are more worried than I am. Dang."

"It's a lot going on, man," Greg told him. "You haven't been to the campus. It is ugly up there. A lot of students are going home; they don't feel safe."

"Come on in, Deon," the receptionist said.

Deon and Greg went into Greg's uncle's office and sat down, exhausted.

Mr. Boyd walked in. "I have some interesting news," he said. "We have found a large number of officers participating in what I would describe as ultra-right-wing media sites. The officer that arrested you has made some rather bothersome statements on that site, along with pictures of him and other officers in front of Confederate flags and others holding nooses."

He continued, "We found these just recently, and we are looking into public records of police complaints. "That officer has over one hundred complaints the past three years." We have submitted this to the police department, but no response as of yet. If we do not hear anything by tomorrow, then we are going to the media. We know they are going to call it fake news and the dishonest media. Hey, let them go ahead, but they are going to have to deal with this legally."

He added, "I have also made some discovery. You were working the second and third shifts at the hospital, and I was able to get the time sheets to prove it. If the officer says he has seen you during the times you were working, this whole thing will be tossed out. We have a conservative judge, and I am sure he has an opinion on the most recent occurrences. In the meantime, I need you to check your balance before we go to trial." He looked at Deon.

Deon went into his pockets and pulled out the wad of money. "A thousand," Deon said as he put it on Mr. Boyd's desk.

"We will see you in two weeks," said Mr. Boyd. "Try not to worry, Deon. It's going to work out."

Greg gave Deon a ride back to Upton.

"I got to meet with the sister," Deon said as they sat in the car in front of the community center.

"I will be glad when all this is over, and you are back on campus," said Greg.

Deon got out of the car. "I appreciate it," he said.

The community center line led out of the building and around the corner. Deon went into the center to find Jesus, Sister Joseph Mary, and an office worker Deon had never met trying to help everyone in line.

"Thank goodness you are here," said Sister Joseph Mary. "We really need your help."

"Okay," Deon said as he started to make his way to his desk.

"Let me talk to you in my office really quickly first," the sister said to Deon.

Deon followed Sister Joseph Mary into her office. She turned to Deon and said, "We have no way to help these people. We have had four of our buildings vandalized and two burned. Our shelters are at capacity. I really do not know what to do. All we can do is give out these food boxes for now and referrals to other social agencies throughout the city."

"What about the people who have no place to go?" Deon asked.

"I don't know," she responded. "I have inquired about opening Immaculate Conception just so people can have somewhere to go."

"What did they say?" asked Deon.

"Father said he would have to get back to us on that," the sister replied.

"What? Why?" Deon was shocked.

Sister Joseph Mary sighed. "They are afraid the property would be destroyed to let everyone in."

Deon looked at her stone-faced.

"Unlike Pharaoh, do not harden your heart," Sister Joseph Mary responded.

Deon spoke to the women and children in his line one at a time. All had horrific stories to tell. They were the ones burned out, with no place to live.

"Until we hear something else from the city to address the problem," Deon told them, "all we have currently is boxes of food and referrals to other agencies in the city."

Most said thank you. Some got angry.

Deon looked down to see how many more box vouchers he had left. When he looked up, a middle-aged man with a pale complexion and bald head sat before him, looking at him with piercing blue eyes.

"Yes, sir?" Deon said as he sat back.

The man looked at Deon and shook his head. "So, this is where you work?" he asked.

"I beg your pardon?" said Deon.

"I beg yours," the man responded. "It seems you do better running into burning buildings."

Deon sat stone-faced again. "Oh. Okay," Deon responded.

"Hey, what kind of detective would I be if I didn't find you?" the man asked. "Why did you leave?"

"I don't know," Deon answered. "I guess I went to try to assist someone else."

The man nodded. "I understand you used to work security at the hospital."

"Yes," Deon replied.

"You know, I have to accept a service award which really should belong to you," he said.

Deon looked at him. "I don't deserve anything. I'm sure others would have done the same."

"Then why didn't they?" he answered curtly.

Deon remained silent.

The officer passed Deon a card with his name on it. *Officer Brown.* "Get in touch with me if you need anything."

"Thank you, Officer," said Deon. "I appreciate it."

The officer tapped the table three or four times with his finger. "All right, have a good afternoon," he said as he rose up from his seat.

Deon nodded again in a show of gratitude and then moved on to the next person in line.

The clock showed four o'clock, and the line was slightly shorter. Sister Joseph Mary called Deon into her office.

"I just got approval from Father Ryan to open the doors to people who have no place to stay," she told him. "Also, there is a Mr. S. L. Wright who needs assistance. He lives in the countryside about thirty minutes from here. We are trying to get him into a senior living community. In the meantime, he needs food and diapers. I was wondering if you could drive out there to see him."

"No problem at all," Deon replied. After all, it was a chance to get out of Upton, just for a while.

✦

Deon loaded up the van with boxes of food, soap, and essentials. He pulled off listening to AM talk radio.

"What in the hell are they so angry about? They get rent-free houses, free food, free education, and emergency care services. Where is the injustice? The injustice is me having to pay my taxes to these people who live off my dime. I am sick and tired of it. In addition, all I hear is black lives matter. Well, my life matters too."

Deon continued to listen as he rode south of Upton, viewing the nice countryside that Deon hadn't seen since taking his trip home last Christmas. Finally, he arrived at the old man's house.

"Hey, young man."

"Mr. Wright, how are you doing?" Deon asked as he brought boxes of food into the first room, which smelled like mothballs. "Have you been okay?"

"I'm okay," the old man said. "Could use some help around here."

"Like, what do you need?" asked Deon.

"Well, my plumbing is stopped up. It gets cold in here," said Mr. Wright. "I been in this house for over forty years. I ain't been able to keep it up. Wish I could rent this old place to someone who want to take care of it."

Deon looked around. It wasn't a bad house—a small three-bedroom ranch with a fireplace in the living room, a front porch, and a swing. It sat back off the cul-de-sac with a nice front, side, and back yard. Deon looked outside quickly at the porch, which looked like it might need to be replaced and certainly needed paint.

"I like your house, Mr. Wright," Deon said.

"Would you be interested?" the old man asked.

"Maybe. I will let you know," Deon replied.

Okay, well, don't take too long. I'm eighty-seven years old."

Deon got back into the van and looked at the old house. It had some definite possibilities. *It would take ten thousand dollars just to whip it up in some shape*, Deon thought. *Anyway, I will keep all that in mind.*

Deon arrived back at the community center. Sister Joseph Mary was arranging supplies to assist those people affected by the protest.

"Oh, Deon, thank the Lord," she said when she saw him. "We have cots we are putting out here, and we have blankets."

He asked, "Is the city helping with the relocations?"

Sister Joseph Mary shook her head. "You have to understand, the state and city are run by people who don't take kindly to people down here in Upton. They wonder why they should use tax money to help people who vandalize their own communities. They look at it as the people in the community's fault. So far, no assistance from the state or city."

Deon had heard as much on the talk radio. He looked at his cell phone, noticing numerous messages from Erica.

"I need to go just for a while," he said. "I can come back."

The sister looked at him kindly and said, "It's already nearly seven o'clock. Just call it for this evening. And I will see you in the morning."

"Thank you, Sister," said Deon.

As Deon headed out, Jesus said, "Hey, where are you going?"

"I got to go over Erica's," Deon explained.

"Oh yeah, that's essential," said Jesus. "Family first."

Deon stopped for a moment. *Family? No*, he said to himself.

"Hey," Jesus called out, "you need a ride? It isn't too safe walking the streets. It will take me ten minutes to drop you off up there. Just wait a minute."

Jesus dropped off Deon at Erica's apartment. He knocked, and the door opened slowly. Deon walked in. Eric was playing with his toys, and Erica was looking at Deon solemnly. She jumped onto Deon's arms and kissed him passionately.

"You are not leaving tonight," she said sternly.

"I missed you," she added as she continued to kiss Deon. Then she went off to get Eric ready for bed.

"You need help?" Deon asked.

"Aww, you so sweet. No, I got it."

Deon could hear the water run in the bathroom as she gave Eric a quick shower before putting him into his bedclothes. Deon went into the kitchen and started washing the dishes that rested in the sink, putting up dishes that sat in the drain.

Erica came back into the kitchen while Deon was putting away dishes. She hugged him from behind.

"Thank you," Deon said as he turned and hugged her. She wrapped her arms around him, and he took her to the bed in the living room. He held on to her as if nothing could separate them. His hands touched her trembling body, and he hugged her tightly. Her head fell back in her pillow as she brought Deon on top of her by the back of his neck. They lay together trembling in a passionate inseparable embrace. He held her in his arms all night long.

The morning sun shined through the window, and Erica's beautiful brown skin sparkled as she opened her eyes and looked at Deon.

"I got to go," he said.

"I know."

"I don't want to leave," he added.

"Then don't," she replied. "Why do you need to get away from me?"

"I don't want to get away from you," Deon replied. "I just want things to be right."

She looked up at the ceiling.

Deon took her hand. "Trust me on this. Everything we do seems right. I just need to straighten out some things first."

"Please, Deon," she said. "Don't say anything more. Just make sure you are okay. And let me know. Please."

"I will," Deon replied.

Chapter 15

The week had passed, and now came the day of truth. Deon put on his white button-up shirt and tie while looking in the mirror. This is the day I am going to be a convicted felon and go to jail for drug conspiracy, or I will walk out the courtroom vindicated, Deon thought.

His cell phone rang.

"Hey, you okay?" Greg asked when Deon answered.

"Hey, Greg," said Deon.

"We are waiting for you out front," Greg told him.

"Thanks. I will be out there in a minute."

Deon hung up the phone and looked in the mirror. Then his cell phone dinged. Deon looked; it was the Rasta man. "Peace bi yuh journey bredren, chant ah psalm pan yuh way."

Deon went out of the building where Greg waited in the car by the curb.

Deon got in the front seat. "I feel like I'm going to an execution."

"Think positive," Greg responded. "From what I understand, it's all going to be okay."

They arrived at the courthouse building. Deon and Greg walked through the metal detectors. Courtroom E 3, Deon said to himself as they walked into the courtroom. The room was filled with defendants on the left side and prosecutions witnesses on the right. The court deputy instructed everyone where to sit. The cases went through the docket. Most findings were guilty, as most accepted plea deals.

"Hey, Deon let me talk to you a second," said Mr. Boyd. "Look, I want you to relax and just tell your story to the judge, okay?"

Then came the call: "Case number 100651983, defendant Deon White."

Deon stood up with his attorney. The judge looked disdainfully at Deon.

"Council," he called.

Deon's attorney and the state's attorney gathered at the bench. Deon wondered what was going on. Deon's attorney returned to the table.

"The judge is upset at the fact there was no plea deal," Mr. Boyd said. "He admonished me for letting this come to trial. I told him you were not guilty and want no record and to clear your name."

"Will the jury for this case be called in, please?" the sheriff's deputy instructed.

The jury came in and took their seats; there was just one person who Deon could consider his peer.

The prosecution made its opening statement.

"Ladies and gentlemen of the jury, the state's attorney will prove the defendant was actively involved in the crime he has been charged with. I know many of you have seen the lawlessness that has recently occurred in Upton, a direct result of the criminals in the streets who have taken over neighborhoods making our schools unsafe with gang activities and drugs. The defendant has been charged with conspiracy and gang affiliation to distribute and sell drugs. He has had and additional arrest since being charged. The defense is going to try to paint this defendant as an upstanding citizen attending college, member of the church, and etcetera. We will discover that he is just another one of these people who need to be held responsible for the crime in these neighborhoods—crimes that the police department officers put their lives on the line daily to protect and serve those law-abiding citizens in that community, and possibly your community as well. Thank you."

Deon's attorney stood up.

"Ladies and gentlemen of the jury. Mr. White is indeed an upstanding individual in the community. He has demonstrated over the past fourteen years an impeccable reputation in school and college with his teachers, professors, and people who know him in the neighborhood. What has happened, and what we will prove, is Mr. White, on a sunny Friday afternoon, put his clothes in the Laundromat and then went outside while his clothes were washing, and while watching a basketball game on the city park courts, was apprehended and arrested for no other reason than profiling. He was not at all involved with any gangs nor the selling of drugs. He could have taken time served and a felony conviction or accepted some plea deal, which a lot of others have done because they could not afford counsel or just to not go to jail. Some anticipate the option of having their charges expunged later, but Mr. White, because he knows he is right and understanding the gravity of the situation, has chosen to fight these charges. I am here to prove his innocence—that the practice of sweeping and charging numerous individuals who happen to be in the area is what Mr. White has encountered. We will show that Mr. White is entirely innocent of the charges against him. Thank you." Deon's attorney sat back down next to Deon.

Okay, here we go, Deon thought

"The state calls Officer Charlotte to the stand." The officer looked at Deon with that familiar smirk that Deon detested. He put his hand on the Bible and swore the oath.

Suddenly, there was a commotion at the courtroom entrance. Deon turned and looked and saw Sister Joseph Mary, Officer Brown in full uniform, Jesus, Mr. Thetu, Captain Suh, Reggie, Andrew, and Erica walk into the courtroom and sit on the defendant's side. The judge watched them come in and sit down. He called Mr. Boyd and the prosecutor to the bench.

"Who are these people?" he asked pointedly.

"These are character witnesses for the defendant, Your Honor."

The judge shrugged. "Fine. As you wish," he said disdainfully.

The state's attorney started his questioning. "Officer, state your name and rank with the police department."

"My name is Officer Edward Charlotte. I have been on the force for fifteen years. I am a sergeant."

"I would like to thank you for your service," the state's attorney added. "How long have you been on the beat in Upton?"

"Over five years."

"On the day in question, please tell the court what happened."

"I received a call of gang and drug activity at the south playground," the officer said. "Knowing that this is a high crime area, I called for four cars. When we arrived, we found these gang members in the park in open air selling narcotics. We stopped and took control of the area, arresting all involved."

"Was the defendant among those arrested?"

"Yes," the officer responded.

"Did you find any narcotics or other illegal substance on the defendant?"

"No, not on his person, but I have seen him involved with these groups in the past."

"How does the gang operate in the park?"

"Everyone is given a role," Officer Charlotte explained. "Some are lookouts, others hold the product, others distribute."

"And you have seen the defendant not only this day but other days involved in this activity?"

"Yes," the officer answered.

"No further questions," said the state's attorney.

Deon's attorney stood up.

"Officer Charlotte, when you arrived at the park, what was going on?"

"As I mentioned before, gang members in open air selling."

"Is it not true that there was a basketball game going on?" asked Mr. Boyd.

"Yeah, that's what they always do, play basketball."

"*They*? Could you clarify who are the *they* you are referring too?

"Objection!" called out the prosecutor.

The judge looked at Deon's attorney. "Sustained," he said. "At the time you arrived at the park, where was Mr. White?" "He was along with all the rest of them," the officer answered. "So you are not sure?" Deon's attorney asked.

"He was there with the rest of the gangbangers."

"You say you have seen the defendant out there all the time."

"Yes, I have," Officer Charlotte answered.

"Well, Officer, how can you be sure if you have seen him out there before if you cannot identify him from the day of his arrest?"

"Objection!" "Sustained."

"Officer Charlotte, isn't it possible that a person could just be watching a pickup basketball game and not be involved in any activity even though he or she would be scooped up along with everyone else?"

Officer Charlotte laughed. "Yeah, they always say they are not doing nothing …"

"Officer Charlotte, how many were arrested on that sweep?"

"I believe we took twelve of them off the street, including the defendant."

"How many had drugs or illegal narcotics on their person?"

"There were two, I believe."

"And how much illegal narcotics was found?

"I'm not sure. Around ten grams?"

"Ten grams? That's all?"

"They were bagged and ready to be delivered, and the defendant was complicit with those individuals. I have been on the force enough to know who the players are."

"What kind of drugs were discovered on the day of the arrest?"

"I believe it was heroine."

"In your professional opinion, would that warrant the charges of conspiracy to distribute with ten others who were on that court?"

"Yes, it would," Officer Charlotte said. "It is time we stop coddling these criminals."

"Could it be, Officer, that my client had nothing to do with gangs or drugs, that he is an innocent bystander caught up in this sweep?"

The officer laughed. "Yeah, sure, they are all innocent. I'm sure you will paint him as a pillar of society."

"Officer," asked Mr. Boyd, "what time is your regular working shift?"

"My shift is 2:00 p.m. to 11:00 p.m. Most of the time I work till twelve."

"And this is the time you observed Mr. White previously conspiring with gang members?"

"Yes, that is right."

"Have you ever seen him selling drugs between these times?"

"That is correct."

Attorney Boyd pulled Deon's timesheets from work and submitted them to the judge and Officer Charlotte.

"This is Mr. White's electronic timesheet from where he was working security at Masonic Hospital."

Officer Charlotte shrugged. "Okay."

"Can you please read the timesheet for the months of March, April, and May, the month before Mr. White's arrest?"

"It says he punched in at two thirty and got off at eleven."

"Yes, but look at his actual hours," said Mr. Boyd. "He worked overtime nearly three days a week until twelve or even one o'clock. Could you explain to the court how you witnessed Mr. White conspiring or otherwise with drug dealers and gang members as you say he did when he was actually at work?"

"I don't care what this sheet says. What I am telling you is I have witnessed him on many occasions collaborating with these gang members. My job is to get these gangbanging thugs off the street."

"Thugs, sir?"

"I'm not here to be politically correct," Officer Charlotte said.

"I understand, sir."

"It's funny how you people always try to use the race card," said the officer.

"No one mentioned race here, Officer Charlotte."

"We arrest because of gang activity." Officer Charlotte looked at the judge, looked at Deon's attorney, and started laughing. "It's funny how you guys try to twist things around with fake stories. The fact is that eighty percent of your crime is coming from thirteen percent of the population in this country. Those are facts."

"And we see how they arrive at those statistics when innocent people are charged and convicted," said Mr. Boyd.

"Objection!" yelled the prosecutor.

"Sustained!" said the judge

"One moment, Your Honor." Mr. Boyd's legal assistant, who whispered something in his ear, gave Deon's attorney a legal brief.

"Your Honor, may I approach the bench?" asked Mr. Boyd.

"For what purpose?" the judge asked.

"I have new information pertinent to this case."

"Let's proceed, counselor," the judge said, shaking his head in refusal.

Deon's attorney continued. "Officer Charlotte, are you aware you have just been accused by the Department of Justice for racist activity and for planting evidence?"

"Objection!" called out the state's attorney.

"Sustained!" roared the judge. "Counselors, I will see you at the bench, please."

The prosecutor and Deon's attorney met at the bench.

"What in the hell are you trying to pull?" said the judge to Mr. Boyd. "I will have your ass debarred."

"This is from the Justice Department, Your Honor," Mr. Boyd said calmly. "Officer Charlotte, along with four other officers, were charged yesterday with racist activity and civil rights violations for planting drug evidence on defendants, and they must have evidence to support the charges."

The state's attorney said, "This is obviously an attempt to slander our leading witness. It's unconscionable."

"Did you have anything to do with this, counsel?" the judge asked Mr. Boyd angrily.

"I beg your pardon, Your Honor?"

The judge was beside himself. His eyes began to water, and his skin was turning red with anger. "I swear, if I find out you had anything to do with these ridiculous accusations against police officers in this city, there will be repercussions—like recommending disbarring you. You understand?"

"As you wish, Your Honor," Mr. Boyd answered.

The judge looked up at the courtroom. "I'm going to call a continuance until tomorrow at 9:00 a.m. on the docket," said the judge. "Court dismissed. I want to see all of you in my chambers."

Deon's attorney grabbed his briefcase and walked into the chambers with the other attorneys. There was a discussion behind those doors, and Deon wished he knew what was going on. Sister Joseph Mary and all of his character witnesses came over to Deon.

"Don't you worry about a thing," said Officer Brown. "We all have your back."

"Thank you so much," Deon replied, nearly crying at the support he was receiving.

About a half hour later, Deon's attorney walked out with the other attorneys. Deon and his attorney met in an empty meeting room.

"What happened?" asked Deon.

"The arresting officer's being investigated for hate speech on supremacist websites. They have copies of his video and posts," said Mr. Boyd.

Deon remembered he had been told that they'd found this when they last met.

Mr. Boyd opened up his Chromebook and went to a livestream. It was a news report. A picture of Officer Charlotte showing him putting his hand over his heart in front of a Confederate flag, holding a machine gun with the words

Koon Killer on the stock, and posters and stickers with statements of Nigger Beware and Jews Will Not Get in Our Way. Other pictures showed him and other officers mimicking a hanging, with a photo of one officer with black shoe polish on his face. The livestream reported:

"Officer Charlotte of Upton has been investigated for racist posts and with planting evidence, as recorded by an undisclosed home security camera that clearly shows Officer Charlotte placing a bag with a white substance under a sofa to later be collected by another officer. The residents were charged with drug possession and conspiracy to distribute."

Deon looked up at his attorney. "Wow," he said.

"I don't see how they can proceed in light of these accusations of the arresting officer."

Erica, Michael, Andrew, and Reggie met Deon outside the courtroom. "Hey, man, are you going to ride back to campus with us?"

"He's coming home with me tonight, guys," said Erica, quite comically.

"Ooooh, okay!" they all replied in unison.

"Okay," Deon replied with a slight smile on his face.

Deon and Erica arrived at her apartment. Deon turned on the TV to the news channel.

"That's enough of the news, don't you think? Besides, I have to pick up Eric from school," she said.

They both went to pick up Eric from school and walked back to her apartment.

They all sat together and watched *The Avengers* with Eric. Soon they were all snuggled together and sleeping in the front room as the TV played through the evening.

The next day, Deon stood in court next to Mr. Boyd for the start of his continuance. The court deputy summoned the court. "All rise. Judge Nimitz is presiding."

"Be seated," the judge said. He looked tired and worn out, like he hadn't gotten any sleep in a while. His hair or toupee seemed uncombed and stood up on his head.

"I would like to see both attorneys in chambers," he said.

Attorney Boyd looked at Deon. "Okay, here it is," he said as he stood and grabbed his briefcase. Both attorneys went into the judge's chambers. Deon sat at the defendant's table, trying to remain calm.

After a few minutes, the attorneys exited the chambers, and Mr. Boyd came and sat down next to Deon, whispering in his ear, "The judge is considering his options due to the recent news about the arresting officer."

"What did he say?" whispered Deon.

"We will know something in just a minute," replied Mr. Boyd.

Judge Nimitz returned to the bench. "Circumstances that have recently been established to have occurred involving the arresting officer, Ed Charlotte, require me to make a decision about this case. Will the defendant stand, please?"

Deon stood.

"I had every intention, if you were found guilty, of giving the maximum punishment allowed by law," the judge told him. "Since the arresting officer's credibility is in question, however, I can only say case dismissed."

"Yeah!" Deon's friends clapped and yelled from the back of the courtroom. Deon gave a massive sigh of relief, and tears welled in his eyes. He turned to see Erica clapping and smiling, standing next to Greg and the rest of his crazy college crew.

"Thank you, Mr. Boyd," Deon said.

"Congratulations," the attorney replied. "Let's meet in one of the meeting rooms really quickly if that is okay with you."

"Yeah, sure," Deon replied.

Deon and Mr. Boyd walked to an empty room and had a seat. "Look," said Mr. Boyd. "Since this case was dismissed, I will prorate the charges for some of the fees. We don't normally do that, by the way. Keep in mind it can still take up to a year to get the charges permanently taken off of your record."

"So what do I do in in the meantime?" asked Deon.

"When I get a copy of the final disposition, I will give that to you. I would advise making copies just in case," said Mr. Boyd. "What are your plans?"

"I am going to see about getting a job back at the hospital," said Deon.

"Okay," said Mr. Boyd. "If you want to consider being a paralegal in our office that's a possibility as well."

"I appreciate that," Deon replied.

"In the meantime, I would advise you to find another means to make quick money, right?"

"Yes, absolutely," Deon agreed.

"You don't want to have to go through this kind of thing again," the attorney said with a smile. "Once again, a million thanks, Mr. Boyd," said Deon.

Deon met Greg and the crew outside the courtroom. "Hey, where are we going?" they asked.

Erica poked Deon in the side. "Hey, I got to get Eric and take him home," she said.

"Okay, well, let's get out of here!" said Deon. He asked Greg to drop him off with Erica, and he would find his way back to campus.

Deon and Erica walked and talked. "You still think about that small little country house?" he asked.

"Yeah, I always do," she said, laughing. "Don't forget the swing on the front porch!"

"If things work out," Deon said, "I'm going to see about getting my job back at the hospital."

"That would be nice," she said. Then she insisted, "Hold my hands. Let's do a prayer together."

Deon held her hands, and they both closed their eyes. She began, "Father God, please bestow your blessing on us, to always be humble in the Lord and give praise and thanks. Please help us work through our problems and be blessed with gainful opportunities to work and love each other and praise you, Almighty God. Thank you, God, for helping us both through the storms, and continue to be with us as we make our way in your name. These blessings we ask of you in your name, amen." She looked up at Deon and said, "Now watch how prayer works."

The next morning, Deon arrived at his desk at the community center.

"Deon, may I see you a moment?" called Sister Joseph Mary.

"Yes, sister, just a second."

Deon went into her office. "Mr. S. L. Wright is being transferred to an assisted living senior community on Westchester."

"Oh, those are nice," said Deon. "I'm happy for him."

"He wants to talk to you about renting that house," she went on. "He doesn't want much for rent—eight hundred dollars a month—and he wants to speak to you about buying it at some point."

Deon thought for a second.

"You need a place to live in," said Sister Joseph Mary. "You cannot continue to live in that room. The room is not up to code, and it is small and cramped."

"Yes, I know," Deon agreed, still thinking.

"The house does need some work," Sister Joseph Mary said.

"Just a little paint on the outside to spruce it up," said Deon. "As soon as I get a job, I will consider it."

After Deon got off from the community center, he walked around Upton. Most of the storefronts had been repaired and business was going on as usual. Deon felt like things were getting back to normal—whatever normal was.

Preacher, the Rasta man, was outside in his front yard. Deon walked over, trying to sneak up on Rasta playfully.

"Yah bredren yuh nuh dead yet?" laughed Preacher.

Deon laughed. "No, not dead yet," replied Deon.

The Rasta man looked at Deon. "Yah mi ave sinting tuh gi yuh."

Deon and the Rasta man went inside the house. The smell of Jamaican food was everywhere, making the house smell like a restaurant.

"Wid di grace ah Jah mi gi yuh dis," said Preacher. He handed Deon a very old styled diamond ring in a paper napkin.

"What is this for?" asked Deon.

"Eh will cum tuh yuh soon fi wah mek yuh need ih," said Preacher wisely.

Deon shrugged his shoulders. "Thanks, Rastafari," Deon said as he accepted the ring in the paper napkin.

"Nuh muh buds fi yuh fi now. Yuh will tek ah tess soon," Preacher said.

I'm going to take a test soon? Deon thought.

"Mi fell aff ah ladder once an hat fi mi bac mi did hav tuh gwaana rehab," Preacher said as he got up out of his seat. "Mia gud now."

Rasta man's clairvoyance was frightening, he thought. He's trying to tell me something.

Deon walked the quarter mile back to the center. I wonder if I should Have this ring appraised, he thought.

Deon looked up an appraiser on his phone to find one not too far away. "Are you closed?" he asked as he walked into the establishment. The sign said seven, and it was six fifty-five.

"No, we are open. Can I help you?" asked the man behind the counter.

Deon went into his pocket. "I was just given this and just want to know what it's worth," he said.

"Okay, do you have any paperwork on it?" the man asked.

"No, I'm sorry," said Deon.

He looked at the ring. "It's an old ring, old-style. What, did you get it from your great- grandmother?"

"No," said Deon. "I guess it may have been my friend's mom or something, I don't know."

The merchant looked at it with his eyeglass. "It's about a full caret. I'd says it may be worth five thousand dollars, maybe more."

"Wow," Deon said. "I wonder why he gave this to me?" Deon said to the merchant.

"Maybe he doesn't know how much the ring is worth, I don't know. Are you looking to sell it?" the man asked.

"I don't know yet," Deon replied. "But thanks. I will keep it."

"Okay," the merchant said. "Find a post office box or something to keep it safe. We have one here."

"Thanks, I appreciate it. I will just keep it," Deon said.

Deon went to his room and thought about looking for jobs with the hospital again. Maybe he could get his job back in security.

Deon downloaded an old résumé and started making edits. He then sent it to the hospital, hoping to maybe land his old job.

The next day, Deon went to the hospital and made his way to the security department. He happened to walk by Dr. Ford, who was the lead in physical therapy.

"Hey, don't I know you?" Dr. Ford asked. "Deon, right?"

"Yeah, that's me."

"So where are you going all dressed for an interview?" Dr. Ford asked.

"I just wanted to see about getting my job back in security," said Deon.

"Tell you what, come upstairs and talk to me for a minute," Dr. Ford insisted.

Deon went upstairs with Dr. Ford.

"Do you have any experience in direct patient care?" the doctor asked.

"I have experience in athletic training and rehabilitation at the Mid Union University," Deon answered.

"Are you still in the program at school?" asked Dr. Ford.

"I will start back up next semester," said Deon.

"We could use some help in our rehab department. Would you be interested?"

"Yes, I would," Deon replied.

"Okay, you can apply online, and I will have my receptionist call you."

"Thank you, Dr. Ford."

Deon went to see Mr. Wright

"Hey, Mr. Wright, how you are doing, and how to do you like it here in your new place?"

"Oh, it's okay, I guess," said Mr. Wright. "These old folks want to play bingo and play shuffleboard and horseshoes and checkers. I don't want to do none of that stuff."

"Oh, Mr. Wright, you got to lighten up," said Deon.

"They got some nice-looking nurses," said Mr. Wright. "You know what my first name initials stand for—S. L.? Super lover."

Deon burst out laughing.

"But that house," said Mr. Wright. "Look here, we have had this conversation before. I want someone living in there that can keep that property up. I know it's a tiny house, but it raised two. And although they have gone on to glory and I will too, I want that house to be taken care of while I'm still here and after I'm gone. How much can you afford for rent?"

"I don't know; what are you asking?" said Deon.

"How about eight hundred a month?"

"I will take some of that for an option to buy, or if you can come up with fifty thousand dollars, you can have the house."

"I can't come up with Fifty thousand," said Deon.

"I can't come up with twenty thousand," said Deon.

"Well, rent it for a while. See if you can get a bank to finance you later on. What do you think?"

"Well, Mr. Wright …"

"Ok, how about seven fifty?" That little money helps me with my social security and my small retirement. What do you say? You got to move out of that room you're in. It's not up to code and real small, you know?"

"I can't remember where I have heard that before," laughed Deon. "It seems like one blessing after another. Thank you, Mr. Wright." Deon remembered how Erica said that prayer works.

"So, I see you have worked something out with Mr. Wright," Sister Joseph Mary said as Deon sat at the community center desk.

"How did you find out?" he asked.

"I just talked to him last night. News travels fast," she said with a smile as she whisked into her office.

Jesus walked up. "You going to need any help with that front yard? It's a mess."

Deon laughed. Then he received an alert on his phone. "Check your email," it said.

Deon opened his email and saw a message to open a court document sent by Deon's attorney: the final disposition of state vs. Deon White. It read, "The court finds the defendant not guilty. The case qualifies for immediate expungement of a criminal record to take place no later than one calendar year from the final disposition." Deon looked at the file and wondered if he should print it out.

"Sister Joseph Mary!" Deon called out. "May I copy this final disposition for my records?"

"Sure," she replied, almost ordering Deon to do so.

Deon downloaded the copy and sent it to print. The text printed up nicely Deon found a discarded manila envelope and put the copy in it. He walked back to his desk.

"Did you get it?" Sister Joseph Mary asked from across the room.

"Yes, thank you," Deon replied with a huge smile. Again, the song "Never Would Have Made

It Without You" played in his head.

The phone rang, and Deon picked it up. "Yes?"

"Hi, this is Dr. Ford's office. Dr. Ford was wondering if he could see you this afternoon, say about four o'clock."

Deon looked up at the clock. "Yes, I can make it."

"Great, I will see you at four," said the receptionist.

Deon went to Sister Joseph Mary. "I have an interview at the hospital at four," he said.

"Okay," she said, "you go!"

Deon could not believe the good fortune that seemed to be happening. It just could not be a coincidence. He remembered what Preacher had said a few days before. *Erie*, he thought. *Maybe it was the prayers with Preacher and Erica that are coming true.*

Deon sat in the waiting room area. Dr. Ford came to the door. "Let me see you really quick in my office."

"Thank you," Deon said as he followed Dr. Ford.

When they were seated in his office, Dr. Ford said, "We did a background check and found this issue with an arrest of some sort. Can you tell me about that?"

"Yes, sir. I was arrested in a sweep and charged with being involved in something I was never involved in. I obtained an attorney, and I was found not guilty on all charges. I must have had intuition, because this was just emailed to me by my attorney, and I made a copy of it before you called me."

Dr. Ford looked at the final disposition and nodded. "Which explains why you had to stop working security, huh?"

"Yes, sir. I went through some challenging circumstances."

Dr. Ford said, "You listed as one of your references Officer Joe Brown, as I remember He was once hailed as going beyond the call of his duty."

"Yes, sir."

"He had some positive words to say about you," Dr. Ford said. "So what date can you start?"

Deon almost lost his breath. "Huh?"

"What date can you start?" the doctor said again.

"Uh, anytime, Dr. Ford," Deon said, finally getting the words out.

"Okay, today is Tuesday. Let's start you out Thursday. Is that good?"

"That would be perfect, sir," said Deon.

"Okay," said the doctor, "we have a contract with Mid Union for rehabilitative services along with their athletic training department. You will be assigned there with Dr. Allen. Do you know Dr. Allen?"

"Yes, sir, I do. He was my professor."

Dr. Ford smiled. "The pay isn't too great to start," he told Deon. "Just fifteen dollars an hour, and there is always overtime in outpatient care, which you can work for as well."

Deon was speechless. He held his chest.

"Are you okay? I don't want you to have a heart attack," joked Dr. Ford.

"No, I'm fine. Thank you so much, sir."

"Thank you," said Dr. Ford. "We will see you on Thursday."

They say prayer works, thank you God, Deon thought again.

It was a sunny and bright late fall day. The once barren yard was now covered with green grass. It had been almost a year since Deon started his job at the hospital, and Deon and Jesus had worked in that yard just about every weekend off. Now only one tree graced the front yard of the house, and a beautiful new off-white railing stood at the front porch. A small wooden swing sat on the front porch, and it rocked slowly in the wind.

Deon's dad and his brother Sean stood in the front yard looking at the house, "This is nice, Son," Deon's dad said. "I told you that you needed to stand on your own two feet. Well, you're doing it."

"Thanks, Dad," Deon said. "I'm glad you could make it."

"Your mother says she is coming."

"Oh, Lord," Deon replied.

"Speak of the devil," his dad said as Deon's mom drove up in a rental car.

"We would never miss your graduation for nothing, Son. I'm so proud of you."

Sister Joseph Mary and Jesus drove up in the community center van. They both got out and gave Deon a huge hug. "I had all the confidence in the world in you, and God has blessed you so much," Sister Joseph Mary said. "Don't forget to give thanks to our Lord."

"Yes, Sister, thank you so much."

Jesus shook Deon's hand. "I'm proud of you too, Deon," he said.

A small delicate soft hand touched Deon muscular arm. The third finger on her left hand had an antique ring on it, about a caret.

"And who is she?" asked Deon's mom.

"Mom, Dad, this is Erica."

"Oh, how nice," Deon's mother said.

"Nice to meet you, young lady," said Deon's dad.

Eric came up to them, wearing his Isaiah Islam football jersey. "Mom, Dad, this is Eric, Erica's son."

"Well, he's a little man, nice to see you!" Deon's mom said.

"Well, let's go in and get you guys situated," said Deon.

"Yeah, let's get something to eat!" said his Brother.

Everyone entered the house, with Deon's mom raving about what a cute house it was. Deon's family and friends went inside, and Deon and Erica stood together with the screened door partially opened. They looked at each other and smiled. She placed her left hand with the ring she was so proud to wear on his chest, covering his heart. Deon bent down to kiss her pretty soft lips. He took her hand and held the screen door open for her. It closed behind her, slowly closing shut.

Later Sister Joseph Mary smiled and said a prayer for both Erica and Deon as she and Jesus got in the van to return to the community center.

"It is lovely how everything turned out for Deon," Jesus said as they backed out of the driveway.

"Yes, I'm happy for them," replied Sister Joseph Mary.

They headed to the expressway ramp with smiles on their faces.

Driving down the expressway was a pickup truck. The driver noticed the sister and Jesus trying to merge into expressway traffic. He slowed down his vehicle to cut them off.

Sister Joseph Mary slowed and then sped up, looking for the courtesy to merge onto the expressway. That courtesy never came. She ran out of space and went head-on into the bridge abutment, scattering the car across the expressway. The red truck sped ahead with its Confederate flag in its back window. The driver looked in his rearview mirror. Niggers, he laughed as he continued driving down the expressway.

Jesus pulled himself from the wreckage and found Sister Joseph Mary lying in the emergency lane. He crawled to her and took her into his arms.

"Lord help us, are you ok Jesus?" she whispered. "Yes Sister Joseph Mary I think so." She looked into Jesus eyes, as she slowly raised her head, "The hate keeps going on and on" she said as her soft eyes faded to glory.

Printed by Libri Plureos GmbH in Hamburg, Germany